Hot Arabian Nights

Be seduced and swept away by these desert princes!

You won't want to miss this new,
thrillingly exotic quartet from Marguerite Kaye!

First, exiled Prince Azhar must decide whether to
claim his kingdom and beautiful unconventional
widow Julia Trevelyan!

Read
The Widow and the Sheikh
Already available!

When Sheikh Kadar rescues shipwrecked mail-order
bride Constance Montgomery, can a convenient
marriage help him maintain peace in his kingdom?

Find out in
Sheikh's Mail-Order Bride
Available now!

*And watch out for two more tantalising novels,
coming soon...*

To secure his kingdom's safety, Sheikh Rafiq must win
Arabia's most dangerous horse race. His secret weapon
is an English horse-whisperer...whom he does *not*
expect to be an irresistibly attractive woman!

Daredevil Christopher Fordyce has always craved
adventure. When his travels lead him to the kingdom of
Nessarah he makes his most exciting discovery yet—
a desert princess!

D0434065

Author Note

The notion of having an astronomer heroine first occurred to me when I was researching Julia, the botanist heroine of the first book in this series, and stumbled across Caroline Herschel, sister of William—who discovered Uranus—in Richard Holmes's brilliant book *The Age of Wonder*. I share my heroine's sense of awe when looking up at the sky on a clear night—although, unlike Constance, when I first started on this book I had no idea what I was actually looking at.

It struck me, as I read up on the history of astronomy, that although today we know exponentially more—not only about our own galaxy but about the billions of others in the far-flung reaches of the universe—that the feeling of our humbling insignificance in the grand scheme of things, and the excitement of knowing there must be as yet undiscovered wonders out there, would be very similar to what she would have felt two hundred years before. In this sense I felt a true affinity with my stargazing heroine.

Sadly, living in Argyll on the west coast of Scotland, I find clear nights are a rarity, but writing this book has ignited a new passion which finds me huddled up under blankets in the darkest spot of the garden with my guide to the night sky. I should say at this point that my enthusiasm still far exceeds my knowledge, so any errors I've made in Constance's celestial observations are entirely my own.

I hope you enjoy escaping to this romantic fantasy kingdom as much as I did when writing about it.

SHEIKH'S
MAIL-ORDER BRIDE

Marguerite Kaye

Published in Great Britain 2016
by Mills & Boon, an imprint of HarperCollins*Publishers*
1 London Bridge Street, London, SE1 9GF

© 2016 Marguerite Kaye

ISBN: 978-0-263-91714-7

Our policy is to use papers that are natural, renewable and recyclable products and made from wood grown in sustainable forests. The logging and manufacturing processes conform to the legal environmental regulations of the country of origin.

Printed and bound in Spain
by CPI, Barcelona

Marguerite Kaye writes hot historical romances from her home in cold and usually rainy Scotland, featuring Regency rakes, Highlanders and sheikhs. She has published almost thirty books and novellas. When she's not writing she enjoys walking, cycling (but only on the level), gardening (but only what she can eat) and cooking. She also likes to knit and occasionally drink martinis (though not at the same time). Find out more on her website: margueritekaye.com.

Visit the Author Profile page
at millsandboon.co.uk for more titles.

For my nana, Mary Macfarlane Binnie,
who bestowed her love of historical romance
on my mum, who in turn imparted it to me.
I hope you approve of my own modest efforts.

Chapter One

❦

Kingdom of Murimon, Arabia—May 1815

Daylight was just starting to fade as he neared his journey's end. He guided his deliberately modest caravan, consisting of the camel on which he sat and two pack mules, through the broad sweep of the valley floor where the largest of Murimon's oases fed the fields and orchards, sheltered from the fierce heat of the desert sun by the serried ranks of date palms laden with their ripening fruit. Towering above, the crags of the Murimon Mountains he had just traversed provided further shelter, the silver-grey rock streaked with ochre, gold and umber glinting in the sun's rays.

The small town which served the oasis was built into the foothills of the mountains, consisting of a steep jumble of houses and rooftops which clung precariously to the hillside, leaving every precious scrap of level land free for cultivation. The delicious aroma of roasted goat meat wafted on the faint breeze, along with the soft murmur of voices. There was precious little chance of him being recognised for who he was. His recently ended seven years of self-imposed exile and the kingdom's state of hibernation due to the current period of deep mourning saw to that. But he kept his gaze turned away all the same, leading his camel and his little train of pack mules past the town towards the final mountain pass he must negotiate, *keffiyeh* pulled over his face leaving only his eyes uncovered.

His brother would not have countenanced travelling in such a low-key manner. Butrus would have ridden in regal splendour at the head of a caravan of magnificent proportions designed to proclaim his majesty, to encourage his people to pay homage to their ruler, to marvel at and to revere him, to bask in the opulent glare of his princely person. But Butrus was dead. He, Kadar, was Prince of Murimon now. Ostentation sat uneasily with him, though he was beginning to realise that his personal views quite often differed from those of his subjects, and their expectations of him.

Three short months Kadar had reigned, and

the full gamut and weight of responsibility he had been forced to assume were becoming clearer. Responsibilities that would never have been his, had fate not twisted and turned so cruelly. He had returned from his exile to attend his brother's wedding as an honoured guest. Instead, he had attended his funeral. Kadar's domain was no longer the palace library he had more or less inhabited while growing up here, but this entire nation. People and not books were his subjects. Instead of studying and interpreting the complex legal systems, both ancient and modern, of other lands, for other rulers, he must apply the laws of this land himself, sitting in judgement on a royal throne rather than interpreting dusty tomes in a seat of learning.

Emerging from the narrow pass onto the plateau, Kadar brought his camel to a halt. Below him lay the palace, the wide courtyard already lit by the lanterns hanging in the distinctive rows of palm trees which stood guard with military precision at the entrance to the palace itself. The serpentine road which wound down the cliffs to the port was also lit, lamps winking in the fast-fading light, like stars greeting the dusk. And below that, the two enveloping arms of the harbour, the dark mass of ships and the vast sweep of the Arabian Sea.

The sun was setting on the horizon, a golden orb casting streaks of vermilion, scarlet, orange and dusky pink into the sky. The rhythmic swish of the waves on the shore was like a whispered lullaby. It was the sea he had missed most in his years abroad. No other sea was so brightly blue, scenting the air with that unique combination of salt and heat. Kadar took several deep breaths. The relatively short journey to a neighbouring kingdom he had just completed, his first official state visit, had changed him irrevocably, forcing him to accept that his wishes, his desires, were no longer relevant. Or rather the outcome of this visit had done so. He was a prince first now, a man second. His unwanted inheritance must take priority over all else. Accepting custody of the kingdom he had always loved, he could reconcile himself to that. But as to the stranger he had inherited as a bride…

No! Every instinct rebelled. The echoes of the past, the dark, painful memories which he had travelled half the world to escape, still had the power to wrench at his heart. He could not endure it. Yet he must, and he could.

He must not draw comparisons between the past and the present. He must not dwell on the similarities, must focus on the differences. For a start, this particular woman had made her indifference to him very clear, a sentiment he reciprocated entirely, despite her beauty. It ought to make it easier. No need for pretence. No requirement for false declarations of emotions he was incapable of feeling. Not now. Not ever again.

It ought to make it easier, and yet still he struggled to reconcile himself to this passionless contract. He must steel himself. He must remember that this wedding was what his people demanded, his country required. To honour his brother's memory by fulfilling his brother's vision of a new royal dynasty and a suitable heir. And more importantly for Kadar, a large dowry, money with which he could transform Murimon, bring it into the nineteenth century, implement his own golden vision for his people's future.

Yes, he could do that. It was a huge personal sacrifice, but it was one worth making.

Arabian Sea—three weeks earlier

The storm had been gathering ominously on the horizon for some time. Lady Constance Montgomery, standing in what had become her habitual position on the deck of the East Indiaman sailing ship *Kent*, watched as the grey clouds mustered, rolling onto the distant stage one after the other as if in response to some invisible cue.

They had been at sea for nine weeks. Captain Cobb reckoned it would be another three before they reached their destination, Bombay. Only three more weeks before Constance would meet, for the first time, the prominent East India merchant who was to be her husband. No matter how hard she tried, she was still unable to prevent that sickening little lurch in her stomach every time she was reminded of this call of duty that took her halfway around the world.

She had resisted this marriage which was convenient for all but herself. She had reasoned. She had come up with any number of alternatives. She had even, to her shame, resorted to tears. But when all her stratagems failed, when it became clear that her fate was sealed, she had resigned herself to it. Boarding the *Kent* at Plymouth, she had felt as if she was jumping off a cliff rather than stepping onto a ship, her eyes screwed shut to avoid the ground rushing up to meet her. The ground, in the form of this arranged match, was not rushing, but it was inching inexorably closer as the East Indiaman sailed across the ocean on fickle winds, edging ever nearer to Bombay. Constance had begun to dread their arrival. This marriage—or any marriage for that matter—ran counter to all her inclinations.

Oh, dear! She had promised herself not to

pick over it all again. The deed was done, the deal had been made—for a business transaction by another name this marriage most certainly was. The exorbitant sum of money Papa required to save the estates had been despatched by Mr Gilmour Edgbaston. The goods, in the form of Constance, were in transit in the opposite direction. 'And there's no point in railing against your fate,' the most expensive piece of cargo on the ship told herself firmly. 'The only thing to be done is to make the best of it.'

An excellent resolution and one, she had persuaded herself before she sailed, which was quite achievable. But before she had sailed, she had been bolstered by Mama's happy smiles and confident assertions that Constance was doing the right thing. Now, very far from home indeed, with far too much time to consider the reality of the situation, she was not at all sure that Mama's simple philosophy that money was the root of all evils and the source of all happiness had any foundation at all. Not that she had ever believed it. She'd simply had no option but to pretend to do so, because Papa had given Mama no choice, and so Mama had been forced to demand this ultimate sacrifice of her daughter.

It hurt. It hurt a great deal more than Constance had ever permitted Mama to see. A great deal more than she cared to admit even to herself too, so she endeavoured not to think about it and she succeeded, mostly. Save that here she was again, dwelling on it most pointlessly. 'When my time would be a great deal more productively spent dwelling on how I can make sure my marriage does not become a prison cell in which I must serve a life sentence,' she told herself sternly.

Her heart sank. She didn't want to think about it. She didn't want to force herself to feel positive about something so very negative. She had three more weeks at sea. Three last weeks of freedom, and three more weeks to make the most of the spectacular stargazing opportunities the long sea journey had granted her as they travelled under unfamiliar skies, crossing the equator into the southern hemisphere before crossing back into the northern hemisphere again on this final part of the journey.

Mind you, it was doubtful whether she'd see anything of value through her telescope tonight, Constance thought. The clouds had merged into one roiling mass now, an angry pewter colour, dense iron grey at the centre. Around her on the deck the crew were struggling with the rigging. The calm deep blue of the Arabian Sea, with its crystal-tipped waves, like the clouds, seemed to be forming into one foaming mass, a more sinister sea which moved in one great rolling motion, sending the *Kent* high above the horizon before plunging low, into the depths of the swell.

Constance retreated into the lea of the main mast in the middle of the ship, but spray soaked her face and travelling gown. Above her, terrifyingly high on the crow's nest, a sailor signalled frantically to the crew.

'Best get down below decks, your ladyship,' one of the ship's officers told her. 'We're going to head in towards the shelter of the coast, but I'm not sure we'll be able to outrun the storm. It's going to get a tad rough.'

'A tad?' Staggering as the *Kent* crested the swell like a rearing stallion, Constance laughed. 'That sounds to me rather an understatement.'

'Aye. So you'd best get below sharpish. If you thought the Bay of Biscay was rough, I assure you it was nothing to what's heading our way. Now if you'll excuse me.'

The ship listed again. Above her, the mast creaked alarmingly. Barefooted Jack Tars clung tenaciously to the sodden decks, going about the business of steering the huge three-master towards safer waters. Several of the soldiers of the Thirty-First Regiment of Foot, en route to a posting in India, were helping out, looking decidedly unsteady in comparison to the sailors, but Constance was the only civilian left on deck. The wives and children of the soldiers and the twenty other private passengers including Mrs Peacock, the returning merchant's wife whom Papa had paid to act as companion and protect his daughter's valuable reputation during the voyage, were all safe and dry below.

She really ought to join them. It was becoming treacherous on deck, but it was also incredibly invigorating. Here was a breath of true freedom. Constance found a more secure spot under the main mast, out of the way of the crew and mostly out of sight too. Though her stomach lurched with every climb and dip, she had discovered very early on in the voyage that she was an excellent sailor, and felt not remotely ill. Spray, heavy with salt, burned her skin. Her hair escaped from its rather haphazard coiffure, whipping her cheeks, blowing wildly about her face. The wind was up now, roaring and whistling through the rigging, making the sails crack. The ship too was protesting at the tempest, the timbers emitting an oddly human groan as they strained against the nails and caulking which bound them together.

The spray had become a thick mist through which Constance could make out only the very hazy outlines of scurrying sailors. The ship listed violently to port, throwing her from her hiding place, sending her sliding out of control across the deck, saved only when her flailing hands caught at a rope. The swell was transformed into terrifyingly high walls of water which broke over the decks. Clutching desperately at her rope, she was dimly aware of other bodies slipping and sliding around her. The ship listed again, this time to starboard. Men cried out, their voices sharp with fear. Below decks, women were screaming.

This time when the *Kent* tilted on her side, perilously close to the water, Constance didn't think she could possibly be righted. By some miracle, the vessel came round, but a blistering sound preceded the sheering of the mizzenmast from the decking.

Chaos ensued. Screaming. Tearing canvas. Crashing timber. The hoarse, desperate cries of sailors trying to save their ship and their passengers and themselves. The thud and scramble of feet on decks. And above all the roaring and crashing of the sea as it fought for supremacy.

It was no easy battle. The *Kent* was built to ride such storms, and her captain was a man experienced in doing so. Staggering like a drunken sot, the ship careered towards the calmer waters of the Arabian coast. Women and children, soldiers and sailors, spilled out onto the top deck, scrambling up from below to cling to the remnants of the fallen mast, to the rigging, to the torn sails, to each other.

Constance, flung against the foremast, her skirts tangled in rope, saw it all through a sheen of spray, frozen with fear and at the same time fiercely determined to live. It was invigorating, this determination—proof that her spirit was neither tamed nor broken.

She would not allow herself to perish. On she clung, and on the ship tossed and dived, corkscrewing and listing, so that even Constance's strong stomach protested, until finally land came into sight and with it the promise of safety, the force of the storm either spent or left behind them.

She was loosening her painful grip on the rope when the main mast suddenly went, taking the foremast with it. The *Kent* rolled onto her starboard side, hurling Constance overboard, throwing her high into the air before she plunged headlong into the Arabian Sea.

Kingdom of Murimon, Arabia

She had been marooned here in this remote Arabian fishing village for about three weeks when the authorities finally came for her. Constance watched from the shore as the large dhow moored at the mouth of the inlet which served as a harbour, dwarfing the little fishing boats which had returned with the day's catch. The slim hull was glossily varnished and trimmed with gold, with an enclosed cabin built to the aft, the top deck of which formed another deck covered with a large awning. The lateen sail was scarlet.

The villagers crowded around her. They too knew that the arrival of this ship signalled her imminent departure. She didn't want to leave, though she knew she must. It was impossible for her to remain here, becalmed for ever. The sea had temporarily washed all her responsibilities away, but the future she dreaded still loomed somewhere on the horizon. This sleek ship would be the first step of the journey she must resume.

Bashir, the village elder in whose home she had been cared for, made a formal greeting to the official-looking man who stepped from the boat almost before it was tied up. A tall angular man with piercing nut-brown eyes set beneath luxuriantly bushy brows, his beard was trimmed to a sharp point. His bony fingers were impeccably manicured. His pinched face and pained expression were at odds with his expensive-looking robes. Screwing up his face, he produced a piece of parchment and unrolled it with a flourish. 'Lady Constance Montgomery?'

Her name sounded odd when spoken with his accent, but it was definitely her name. With a sinking heart, Constance made an awkward curtsy. The wound on her head began to throb. One of the women had removed the tiny stitches only that morning. The skin felt tight, but the stabbing pain behind her eyes had long since faded, and the resultant headaches were all but gone.

'Welcome to the kingdom of Murimon. You will come with me.'

It was a command, not a request. Constance had time only to make swift and rather tearful farewells while the official took Bashir aside. A few minutes later, she clasped the elder's hands, expressing her abject thanks as best she could, before being ushered aboard the dhow.

She spent the journey huddled in the cabin, unexpectedly overcome with fear as the ship set sail. It was ridiculous of her, for the sea was flat calm, the skies above perfectly clear, the wind a gentle zephyr, but as she placed her bare feet on the deck and felt the gentle sway of the boat, a cold, clammy sweat broke out on her skin. Her ears were filled once more with the roar of the waves, the crack of the masts, and the screams of the *Kent's* passengers. Thankfully, the official who escorted her seemed content to leave her alone, though whether for reasons of propriety or simply because he was offended by her presence here, she had no idea.

The sun was going down when they arrived at the port. Constance staggered from the dhow and into a covered chair, caring nothing save that they were on dry land. The chairmen moved off swiftly. As she closed her eyes in an effort to compose herself, she was aware that they were climbing but of little else. Set down in a huge enclosed courtyard, she blinked in the glow of what seemed like a thousand candles, but the zealous official was already waving her on urgently, giving her no choice but to follow.

She padded in the wake of the man along the smooth, polished marble floors of endless corridors. She couldn't begin to imagine how she must look, with her skin burning from the day's sun, her wound like a brand on her forehead, her feet bare, and the rough brown tunic she wore big enough to encompass at least two of her.

As they came to a massive double door presided over by a hulking guard with a huge sabre, the reality of her situation dawned abruptly on her. She was in a foreign country, quite alone, and completely at the mercy of whoever was on the other side of this door. Captain Cobb? She presumed there must be other survivors of the shipwreck. It was too awful to contemplate that six hundred souls had perished and that miraculously she had not. An official equerry? A prison guard? A harem eunuch? The colour drained from her cheeks.

Constance shook out the copious folds of her borrowed tunic over her bare toes, and pushed her hair back from her face. Her heart was racing. Her legs were shaking. The butterflies in her stomach fluttered wildly as the doors were flung open.

Chapter Two

Constance found herself in a huge room with a domed ceiling illuminated by three massive, glittering chandeliers lit with hundreds of candles so bright they dazzled her, making bright spots dance in front of her eyes. In the doorway beside her, two identical statues stood sentinel, some type of mythical sabre-toothed felines who looked as if they were about to pounce and devour her. She shivered.

A man stood at the far end of the salon gazing out of a row of tall windows into the darkness beyond. He was dressed from head to toe in white silk robes, his cloak woven with golden threads. Diamonds glittered in the band which held his headdress in place. He was both tall and lean, yet she had the distinct impression of a latent strength in the broad set of his shoulders.

'Lady Constance Montgomery,' the official

announced in his thick accent, giving her a little push. 'His Most Royal Highness, Prince Kadar of Murimon.'

The heavy wooden doors closed behind her with a resounding thud, the Prince turned around, and Constance's heart skipped a beat, her mouth went dry, and the muscles in her belly clenched in a visceral surge of desire that took her entirely by surprise.

He was young, no more than thirty. His brow was high, his face long, his nose strong. Austere features, not handsome in the conventional sense, actually slightly forbidding, framed as they were by his headdress. Definitely not a man who needed his regal robes to underline his natural air of authority. It was evident in his demeanour, in that haughty expression, and in those remarkable eyes, which were almond-shaped and wide-set, a curious colour which was neither grey nor green. Like all the men in this land, he wore a beard, but his was trimmed very close, not much more than a dark shadow, drawing attention to the contrasting smoothness of his cheekbones, the disturbingly sensual curve of his mouth. Beneath her rustic tunic, Constance felt her skin flush as heat suffused her. Those lips were sinful.

'Lady Constance.'

With a start, she dropped into a low, sweeping curtsy. She had been staring at the Prince like a ravening wolf. Her eyes lowered, she had the sense of a lithe grace as he crossed the room towards her, his feet clad in black slippers embroidered with gold, his robes fluttering around the long length of his legs. Dear heavens, she should not be looking at his legs. She raised her eyes. Slim hips. She oughtn't to look at those either. A belt slung around his narrow waist, chased with gold and at the centre, an enormous jewel glowed red and luminous, like a diamond lit by fire.

'Please, rise.'

His voice was husky. It made the hairs on the back of her neck stand on end. *For goodness' sake, Constance, pull yourself together!* The hand he extended was slim, the long fingers artistic, the nails neatly trimmed. His skin was cool to the touch. Mortified, she realised her own palms were clammy, her skin most likely ruined beyond recognition by a combination of salt and sun. Which all paled into insignificance when compared to her windswept hair, which most likely looked as if it had birds nesting in it, her sack-like gown and her grubby bare feet. She felt like Cendrillon in Monsieur Perrault's story. It was a shame this prince had no slippers to offer her. She curled her toes further under her tunic.

'Your Highness, it is an honour,' Constance said.

'In the circumstances, I am not sure that "welcome" is the most appropriate epithet to use to describe your somewhat unconventional arrival in Murimon, but I hope you will allow me to welcome you to my kingdom nonetheless.'

Surprise made her forget protocol. 'Oh, you speak English beautifully.'

'Thank you. My childhood tutor would be most gratified to hear that.'

Colour flooded her cheeks, for his words were lightly ironic. 'I did not mean to imply astonishment that you can speak my language, only delight. It is a pleasure, Your Highness, to make your acquaintance.'

'I fear that sentiment may alter when you hear what I have to say. Please, won't you sit down?'

The chamber was even bigger than she had realised when she first entered it. Now that her eyes had grown accustomed to the blaze of light cast by the extraordinary chandeliers, Constance could see it was almost the same proportions as the tea room in the Bath Assembly Halls, with the same style of double-columned balcony on the side opposite the windows. But there the similarities ended. Every available wall surface in this salon was tiled, row after row of rich gold and earth colours, separated by elaborately carved rococo dados. On the furthest wall was something which looked rather like a four-poster bed, and which Constance assumed must be the royal throne. Though the floor immediately in front of it was covered in thick silk rugs, there was, however, not a single other seat, cushion or chair to be found.

Prince Kadar seemed to realise this at the same time as Constance did. 'I'm sorry,' he said ruefully, 'the Royal Saloon is designed to intimidate visitors, not offer them comfort. I had forgotten.'

'Forgotten?'

'I have used this room but once before. When I took my vows.'

'Your vows,' Constance repeated, wondering if she was being obtuse. 'Ah, I see now. This room is used for royal weddings?'

'I am not married.' A flicker of something—pain? Sorrow? Regret?—passed over the Prince's countenance, but it was gone so quickly Constance might well have imagined it. 'The solemn vows I took when I assumed the crown,' he said.

'Oh, you mean your coronation.'

Another shake of the head. 'No, that ceremony was postponed until after the period of national mourning for my elder brother, who died suddenly three months ago.'

'I am *so* sorry, how dreadful. My most sincere condolences.'

She had reached out to touch him in an automatic gesture of sympathy. The Prince was staring at her grubby, tanned hand with its ragged nails, which contrasted starkly with the pristine sleeve of his tunic, as if fascinated. Or more likely repelled. Or simply appalled at her lack of deference. Constance snatched her hand away. 'Were you close, you and your brother?'

He took so long to answer she wondered if he had heard her question. Or perhaps posing it had been another breach of protocol. When he finally spoke, his tone was flat. 'I have been living abroad for the last seven years.'

Which was no answer, but his frosty expression made it clear the subject was closed. When he turned his back, Constance began to panic. She had offended him. The audience was over before it had begun, and she knew not a single fact more than when she had arrived. 'Please, Your Highness, if you could…'

He held his hand out to silence her. 'One moment.' The throne or divan or whatever it was, was covered in scarlet cushions tasselled with gold. Prince Kadar began to strew them on the floor. 'There,' he said, when the throne lay bare and the floor contained two heaps of cushions, 'now we may both be seated in comfort.'

He sank down with a fluidity she could not dream of imitating, crossing his legs with enviable ease, indicating that she sit opposite him. Considerably impeded by her voluminous tunic, Constance did as he bid her. The Prince tugged off his headdress, casting it carelessly, with its diamond-encrusted band, onto the stripped throne. His hair was black, silky, dishevelled, curling down over the collar of his tunic at the back, the contrast with his austere countenance adding another dimension to his allure. He really was a very, very attractive man.

'You were saying?'

Constance started. 'What?' She blushed. 'I mean, I beg your pardon.' She pushed her wild tangle of hair away from her face. 'I mean, yes, I was. I was wondering—that is—the other passengers on the *Kent*, the crew, Captain Cobb.'

'Of course.'

Prince Kadar rested his chin on his steepled fingers. His eyes really were an extraordinary colour, like stone speckled with lichen. What was he thinking? She shifted uncomfortably on the cushions. She wished he would say something. 'Your Highness? I cannot be the only survivor, surely?'

'No. No, of course not.' Another pause. 'You are anxious. Forgive me, the situation is somewhat awkward, I was trying to think how best to explain it.'

'I much prefer the unvarnished truth. I find it is less painful in the long run.'

This remark earned her another of those looks. Assessing, that was the word she had been searching for. 'You speak as one who has experience of—er—painful truths?'

'That's not what I said.'

'It is what you implied.'

'Goodness,' Constance retorted, 'am I on trial?'

Prince Kadar flinched. Then he smiled ruefully. 'I beg your pardon, of course not. I find you—interesting.'

Which was no compliment, she was sure, but she was blushing all the same. 'Well,' Constance said, flustered, 'I find you interesting too.' *Could she find anything more fatuous to say!* 'I mean, I have never met a prince before.' *Or inane!* 'You were right.' Deflated, she smiled at him awkwardly. 'I have had a great deal of experience in painful truths of late, but if you are thinking that I am likely to dissolve into hysterics at whatever it is you have to tell me, then let me reassure you, I am not the hysterical type.'

'After what you have been through, I am surprised that you have any equanimity at all,' the Prince replied. 'Your composure is admirable.'

'Oh, it's not. Trust me, beneath this stylish piece of clothing, which is the only one I possess, I am shaking like a jelly.'

The faintest trace of colour stained his cheeks in response to this remark. His gaze was fixed on the gaping neck of her tunic. She had embarrassed him. And now she had embarrassed herself again. Constance bit back her apology, realizing just in time that it would only make matters worse, deciding to take a leaf out of the Prince's book, and hold her tongue. And stop fidgeting. And stop staring.

'The sinking of the *Kent*,' Prince Kadar pronounced finally, as if he were reading from Shakespeare. 'First of all, I must apologise. I was out of the country on state business when the ship went down, and since my return I have been required to devote my time to dealing with the consequences of the shipwreck. I am afraid the message sent to the palace informing us of your survival was overlooked until yesterday. Be assured that I acted upon it immediately.'

'The man you sent was certainly efficient,'

Constance replied, 'though I confess I found the sea journey somewhat more of an ordeal than I anticipated. I fear I can no longer claim to be such an excellent sailor as I once was.'

'I am sorry. It did not occur to me that another sea voyage so soon after your ordeal would be a fraught experience for you. I thought only to have you brought here by the fastest route possible.'

'Please, think nothing of it.' Constance repressed a shudder. 'My only regret is that my expression of thanks to Bashir, the village elder whose family cared for me, were woefully inadequate.'

'You need not fret about that. I instructed my Chief Adviser to ensure that the village was rewarded for the care which they took of you. I am sure that Abdul-Majid said and did everything that was appropriate. He is a most—a most conscientious servant of the crown.'

Though not a servant close to Prince Kadar's heart, if she did not mistake that tiny little moue of distaste. 'A Chief Adviser,' Constance said, 'implies that you have many others.'

'A great many, all most anxious to air their opinions, none of which, I am fairly certain, coincide with mine.'

The words were spoken with some feeling.

The Prince looked as if he would prefer them unsaid. Tempted as she was—very tempted—to pursue the matter, Constance decided not to risk a further retreat into that haughty shell of his. Her fingers strayed to her wound, which was beginning to throb.

'Does it pain you? Will I call a physician? Has the journey exhausted you? Would you prefer to postpone this discussion until you are rested?'

'No.' She smiled reassuringly, for the Prince looked genuinely concerned. 'No and no.' Constance sat up, wrapping her arms around her knees as butterflies started up in her stomach again. 'Please continue.'

'Very well,' he said brusquely. 'First of all, I should inform you most regretfully that there were fatalities. Twenty-seven—twenty-six, now that we know you are not one of them, a small percentage from a ship's complement of six hundred. The captain managed to steer close enough to our waters for our fishing dhows to rescue the vast majority of people on board, and to recover the bodies of all those unfortunate souls who perished. You are the only one who seems to have been swept so far from our main port. The piece of broken mast you were found clinging to in all likelihood saved your life.'

'Is Captain Cobb among the survivors?'

'Yes, it is from him that we gained some basic knowledge of you. Your name, your place of embarkation, your destination, and your companion for the journey. I am afraid, Lady Constance, that she was one of the souls who perished. Please accept my condolences for your loss.'

'Oh, dear. Excuse me.' Constance dabbed at her eyes with the sleeve of her tunic. 'Mrs Peacock was returning to India to rejoin her husband after an extended visit with her family in England. Poor woman.'

'We had assumed she was a relative.'

'No, I met her only the day before we boarded, but I am truly sorry to hear that she has perished. My father paid her to play companion to me. We shared a cabin. It would not have been proper for me to have travelled alone.'

'Your father is in England, then, and not in Bombay?'

'Both my parents are in England. Why do you ask?'

Prince Kadar looked grave. 'A full report of the fate of the *Kent,* its cargo, its passengers and crew, and the numerous steps my kingdom has taken to provide assistance, has already been sent to your Consul General in Cairo. I am not sure how long it will be before that report arrives in England, but I fear it will be before we can have an addendum sent.'

'Addendum?'

'Lady Constance, in my report you are listed as missing, presumed dead. Yours was the only body from the ship's complement unaccounted for. As time passed it became ever more certain that you had perished, unfortunately.'

Constance stared at him in dismay. 'You mean my mother will be informed that I have drowned?'

'I am afraid so. And so too will whoever was to receive you in Bombay when Captain Cobb arrives to break the news.'

'Captain Cobb? Arriving in Bombay? But...' Her head was beginning to reel. 'I'm sorry, I don't understand.'

'We were most fortuitously able to provide the captain with a replacement ship. He was most anxious to reach his destination, and since all hope of finding you alive had been abandoned, there was no reason for them to delay their journey further. They set sail almost a week ago.'

'A week! A whole week! Then there is no chance of my joining them?'

'No chance whatsoever,' the Prince replied with an air of finality. 'May I ask, Lady Constance, why you were aboard the *Kent*? These

East India ships have a very high attrition rate. Your parents must have been aware of the risks when they made arrangements for you to sail east.'

'They were assured that I was in safe hands, since Captain Cobb enjoys an excellent reputation as one of the finest captains in the entire fleet and—and it seems it was deserved, for to only lose twenty-six lives from six hundred, when it could have been so much worse, is admirable seamanship.'

'Assured by whom?'

'The man who arranged my journey, who as a major shareholder is therefore extremely well versed in such matters.'

'Ah, you mean this man is a merchant of the East India Company?'

'Yes. Mr Gilmour Edgbaston.'

'A relative?'

'Not as such. Mr Edgbaston and I are— We are— The fact of the matter is that I was on my way to India to marry Mr Edgbaston,' Constance said faintly. 'And now when Captain Cobb arrives he will have the sad task of informing my future husband that his bride has drowned at sea.' She swallowed a bubble of hysterical laughter. 'You can have no idea, Your Highness, how convenient that would be if it were true.'

* * *

Having absolutely no idea at all what to make of this last remark, Kadar studied the English-woman in some consternation. When he had first spotted it on the list of those who had perished, Lady Constance Montgomery's name had con-jured up an image of a very proper middle-aged matron. He could not have been more wrong. The rough peasant's tunic she wore was far too big for her slim figure. Her hair, a deep glossy brown, tumbled down over her shoulders in wild waves. There was a roundness to her cheeks, a fullness to her lips quite at odds with the rather fierce brows. Her brown eyes were wide-spaced, fringed with thick lashes. Her gaze was direct and intelligent, a striking contrast to the vul-nerability of her softer features and one which Kadar found unexpectedly—and most inappro-priately—beguiling.

'You cannot mean that you wish yourself dead,' he said, wondering if the raw pink scar on her forehead had deranged her mind.

She shook her head slowly. 'No, no, of course I don't mean that literally only—oh, I don't sup-pose you will understand. Being a prince, I ex-pect you are accustomed to arranging your life exactly as you wish it, but...'

'You are mistaken,' Kadar answered with

some feeling. 'I had a great deal more freedom when I was not a prince.'

'Oh?'

Her gaze was curious. He was oddly tempted to explain himself, which was of course ridiculous. Instead, he found himself contemplating Lady Constance's feet. They looked vulnerable, her dainty little toes peeping out from her tunic. But he should not be looking at her toes, dainty or otherwise. 'You were telling me why you wished yourself dead.'

'I was telling you that I don't truly wish that. Only that I wish— Oh, it sounds silly now. I wish I could have remained undiscovered. Missing presumed free, so to speak.' She gave a wry little shrug. 'My marriage was arranged by my parents. I've never met Mr Edgbaston, and know very little about him at all, save his name, age and circumstances. When I left England, I thought I had resigned myself to making the best of the situation but I've had the whole sea voyage to—to reconsider.'

'And while you were—what did you call it?— undiscovered you could pretend that it would never happen, is that it?'

Lady Constance nodded. 'As I said, it was silly of me, but...'

'But understandable,' Kadar said, with feeling. 'Bad enough that you are being forced into a marriage to a man you have never met, but to have to travel halfway across the world, to leave behind all your friends, all your family, your most intimate acquaintance a woman you met for the first time on the day you boarded the ship, it is outrageous.'

'When you put it like that, I rather think I would be better off dead.'

'I apologise, I did not mean to upset you. It is merely that I—' Kadar broke off, shaking his head. 'My words were quite out of turn,' he said stiffly. 'I have no right at all to comment on your personal situation.'

None! And no right to express his own feelings on the matter. He was a prince. How many times must he remind himself of that fact? It did not matter what brought Lady Constance Montgomery here. He had more than enough troubles of his own without becoming embroiled in what amounted to a family matter, no matter how much sympathy he felt for this woman with her clear gaze and her wry smile, the wild curl of her hair trailing down her back over that peasant's tunic, and her bare little toes. Now was not the time to be distracted by any of these completely irrelevant attributes, nor to delve further into the precise nature of her betrothal. The vast majority of marriages in the higher echelons of society were arranged, in both England and in Arabia. What he needed to do was to concentrate on resolving her sudden and frankly inconvenient reappearance.

'The question now is,' Kadar said, 'to decide what is to be done for the best.'

'There really is nothing to discuss,' she replied flatly. 'I too spoke out of turn. I have had my little idyll, and I rather enjoyed it, with no one knowing who I was or what I was or even knowing where I was. But it is over now. I am back from the dead, and must find a way of resuming my journey to India.'

Must? He did not like the implications of that word, but it was not his place to consider them. She was no child; she looked to be at least twenty-four or five, and she clearly knew her own mind. 'I am afraid you don't quite grasp the implications of what I have told you, Lady Constance,' Kadar said. 'When Captain Cobb reaches Bombay, this man to whom you are betrothed will be informed of your death. The missive which I have sent to the Consul General in Cairo will at some point in the near future result in your parents also being informed of your demise. I am very sorry to be so blunt, but you did say…'

'I did, I said I wanted the unvarnished truth.' Lady Constance winced. 'I did not expect it to be quite so brutal, but in essence it changes nothing, save that it makes it even more important that I complete my journey as soon as possible. I do not wish Mr Edgbaston to acquire another bride to take my place.'

Kadar nodded slowly. 'Very well, then I will have the matter investigated, but I should warn you that as things stand, the next ship heading east to Bombay is not expected in our port for at least two months.'

'Two months!' Lady Constance blanched. 'Which means I would not arrive in Bombay for another three months. And in the meantime, Mr Edgbaston will continue under the illusion that I am dead.'

'The alternative is to return to your family in England. Under the circumstances, the traumatic ordeal you have endured, no reasonable person could condemn you for wishing to do so.'

'Unfortunately, my father is not a reasonable person, and would be more than likely to condemn me,' she retorted. Her cheeks flamed. 'I beg your pardon, I should not have said—but there can be no question of my going back to England. I should not have given voice to my doubts. I should not even have allowed them into my head.

I beg you to ignore them. I am honour-bound to marry Mr Edgbaston, Your Highness. My father received, in advance, a rather substantial dowry in return for my—my promise to wed, you see.' She summoned up a smile. 'In effect, I am bought and paid for.'

'You are not a piece of cargo, Lady Constance.'

'Oh, but that is exactly what I am, Your Highness.' Her fingers strayed to her wound. 'Damaged goods at that, currently lost in transit.'

There was just a trace of bitterness in her tone. She obviously knew perfectly well that she was being used and abused, but was determined not to be diminished by the fact, or to show her hurt. Was this how his affianced bride felt? No, he must not allow his mind to travel down that path. The contract had been agreed. As it had been for Lady Constance and her East India merchant.

Kadar smiled faintly as the legal implications of this struck him. 'You know, as things stand at present, your situation is a rather interesting conundrum. Since in your own words you have been—er—bought and paid for, from your father's point of view, the contract has been fulfilled.'

'Which is why I cannot return to England, and am duty-bound to marry Mr Edgbaston.'

Which meant, presumably, that her father had

already spent his ill-gotten gains. 'On the contrary,' Kadar said through slightly gritted teeth. 'Mr Edgbaston cannot marry a woman who has drowned. According to the English law of contract and the customs and conventions which govern international trade, loss which results from *force majeure*, in other words the storm which sank the *Kent*, frees both parties from either liability or obligation.'

Her smile was slow to come as she began to comprehend the meaning of his words, but it was worth waiting for. Her big brown eyes gleamed with humour. Her lips had a wicked curve to them. It lit up her face, that smile, quite transforming her hitherto serious expression, revealing a very different woman. Carefree. Captivating. Yes, that was the word. Under other circumstances, untrammelled by the burden she carried, she would be quite captivating. Kadar was certain, though he had absolutely no grounds to be so, that the faceless merchant she was to marry would not see this side of her. He wanted to set her free, which was impossible. He also wanted her. Which was unusual. And equally impossible.

'So, provided I remain technically dead, the contract is void?'

Had he been staring at her? Kadar gave himself a little shake. 'Precisely. At this moment in time your life is quite literally shipwrecked, cast adrift from both the past and the future. You can make of yourself anything you will.'

'I could be reborn.' Lady Constance sighed. Her smile faded. 'It is an attractive conceit, but without the means to survive, I'm afraid I must remain in my current incarnation.' She smothered a yawn. 'I am so sorry, it has been a very long day.'

The journey she had just made under Abdul-Majid's escort, the trauma she had so recently endured, was clearly taking its toll. Her skin was pale, the raw pink wound on her forehead angry in contrast. 'You have been through a difficult ordeal,' Kadar said. 'We must not act precipitously. I will consider your situation carefully overnight. We will discuss it further tomorrow, when you are rested. In the meantime, you will be my honoured guest here at the palace.'

'I don't want to inconvenience you any further than I already have.'

'Your company has been a very pleasant distraction, I assure you.'

He had spoken without thinking, but it was the truth. Her fingers had strayed again to her scar. Now he acted without thinking, reaching over to catch her hand. 'You should think of it as a badge of honour,' Kadar said. 'Proof of your will to survive. You are a remarkable woman.'

A faint flush coloured her cheeks. Her tongue flicked over her bottom lip. 'Am I?'

He pushed her hair back from her forehead, his fingers feathering over the thin line of her wound. He felt her shiver at his touch, and realised, to his embarrassment that he was becoming aroused. 'Remarkable.'

'You have been much more understanding than I deserve.'

'You deserve a great deal more than you expect.' The neck of her tunic gaped, giving him an inadvertent glimpse of the generous swell of her breast, stirring his blood. Kadar turned his eyes resolutely away. 'Now, if you will excuse me, I will have a suite of rooms prepared for you.'

Chapter Three

As Kadar reined his horse in from a final breakneck gallop along the scimitar-like crescent of beach, the sun was well on the rise. The pure-bred Arabian stallion, flanks heaving and glistening with sweat, cooled his fetlocks in the shallow waters of the sea as Kadar watched the sky turn from pale grey, to pale pink, and then to gold, the colours reflected in the turquoise hue of the sea like a vast glittering mirror. He felt invigorated. His skin tingled with dried salt and sweat, his thigh muscles felt pleasantly tired, and his mind was as sharp as the air here on this, his favourite part of the coast.

His early morning ride was one of the very few things Kadar had not sacrificed since Butrus's death had led to him assume power. This precious hour was often the only one he was granted in the space of a whole day to be alone, to gather his thoughts and to brace himself for the challenges of the day to come. But today, as he stared out at the sea, watching a little line of fishing dhows in the distance emerging from the port like ducklings paddling upriver, he was not thinking about his duties, he was thinking about Lady Constance Montgomery.

Almost from the moment she walked into the Royal Saloon, clad in that peasant tunic, with her wild hair, and those big hazelnut-brown eyes, he had been drawn to her. When he returned to the Royal Saloon last night he had found her asleep on the cushions, curled up like a little mouse, her hands tucked under her cheek. Her hair tumbled in waves over her shoulder. The softness of her flesh when he lifted her made his groin ache with desire. Her body was so pliant. The curve of her breast, the roundness of her rear, that sweetly female scent of her as he carried her to her quarters and laid her down on the bed. What man would not be aroused?

He did desire her, there was no point in denying it. It had been a long time since he'd felt that immediate tug of attraction, that frisson of awareness that was entirely physical, a primitive recognition that this particular woman, her particular body, was exactly suited to his.

Perhaps that was why he felt it so strongly?

There had been women, over the years. His heart was closed and sealed, but his body was virile, his appetites healthy. He was careful in his choices. He had learned to recognise the women whose passions burned, like his, with a cool flame. But there had been no woman in his bed since he had departed the university at Athens en route to Murimon to attend Butrus's wedding. And there had been no woman with the visceral allure of Lady Constance for a very long time.

Kadar closed his eyes, permitting himself a rare moment of indulgence to imagine how it would be to make love to her. He remembered that wicked smile, imagined those lips on his, teasing kisses, her hair a cloud of curls on her bare shoulders, and those generous breasts he had glimpsed, heavy in his hand. Pale-pink nipples? Dark pink? Or that shade of pink that was tinged with brown? Hard nipples. When he ran his thumbs over them, she would shiver, arch her back, thrusting her breasts higher. The curls which covered her sex would be the same burnished chestnut colour as her hair, perhaps a shade darker. She would sit astride him. She would slide onto him, slick and hot. When she rode him, her breasts would quiver, bounce. When he came...

Kadar swore long and viciously. He was fully

aroused, painfully aroused, which was no state to be in while sitting on a hard leather saddle on a highly strung horse. He dismounted, leading the beast onto the dry sand. Now he was to be married, his desire must be reserved for his wife. He tried to conjure up her face, her body, but all he could recall were her eyes above the veil she wore, cool, distant, indifferent. He swore again as the blood ebbed from his manhood. It was to be hoped that this was not an ill omen.

Constance clambered back to consciousness, resisting the impulse to snuggle back under the thick blanket of drowsiness which enveloped her. Awareness came slowly. First of the bed she lay in, of the softness of the mattress, the pillows like clouds of feathers, the light, sensual flutter of the cool cotton sheets on her limbs. She was wearing something silky that caressed her skin, quite unlike the rough material of the tunic Bashir's daughter had given her. She stretched luxuriously, from her toes all the way up to her fingertips, rolling her shoulders, arching her back. She felt as if she had been asleep for a very long time.

Opening her eyes, she gazed up at the ceiling. It was domed, painted a dazzling pristine white. The room was suffused with sunlight. The window through which it streamed was set high in the wall opposite, covered by some sort of carved wooden grille. Beautiful colours adorned that wall and all the others. Tiles. Red and yellow and blue and green, in an unfamiliar pattern that repeated every fourth row. There was a small table set beside her bed. On it sat a silver pitcher frosted with condensation. She was very, very thirsty. She poured herself a glass from the jug and took a tentative sip. Sharp lemon, sweet sugar flavours burst onto her tongue. It was refreshing and delicious. She drained the glass and poured another.

The nightgown she wore was cream, embroidered with tiny white flowers. She had never owned anything so pretty. How long had she been sleeping? Who had put her to bed? The whisper of women's voices, the gentle hands massaging something soothing into her forehead, she had thought that a dream. The fog in her head began to slowly clear. She recalled the journey from Bashir's village. The boat. She shuddered. Don't think of the boat. And then the sedan chair. And then…

Prince Kadar.

Constance gave a little shiver, then frowned at her reaction. She was twenty-five years old and not immune to the appeal of a handsome

man, but this was different, no passing fancy
but a shocking pang of—of base desire. She had
never felt such a very primal attraction before.
She wasn't at all sure that she liked it.

She smiled. No, that was a lie. She did like it,
very much. She liked this tingling feeling she
felt, and she liked the fluttering low in her belly,
and she liked the little shiver—there it was again,
that delicious little shiver, of feeling something
she was pretty sure no lady should, and of wanting to do something no lady should either. That
a man like Prince Kadar would ever—that she
would ever—no, no, no, she never would. But
goodness, the sheer impossibility of it was part
of the allure.

She stretched again, enjoying the caress
of silk and sheets of the softest cotton on her
skin. Sinful, sinful, sinful. And decadent. Sin-
fully decadent. Decadently sinful. Constance
laughed. It was not like her to be so frivolous.
Then again, it was hardly commonplace for her
to be lying in a bed in a suite in a royal palace,
the guest of an Arabian prince. It was fantastical, a dream. Or the continuation of a dream,
for nothing had seemed real to her since she had
awoken in Bashir's cottage. It was as if time was
suspended, and her life too.

How was it that Prince Kadar had described

it last night? 'Cast adrift,' that was it. Cast adrift from both the past and the future. She liked the idea of that, it was an alluring conceit. The Prince had a way with words. And his command of English was extremely impressive. He had told her he had lived abroad, but he had not told her where. Or why. Seven years, he had said. Through choice? What had he been doing, wherever it was he had been? And why had he come back to Arabia? She didn't even know how his brother had met his fate—an accident, an illness? Constance frowned. Now she came to think it over, he had given away remarkably little, while she—she had revealed far too much.

She pulled the sheet over her head. Far, far too much. She had aired thoughts she shouldn't ever have. So she would not permit herself to have them now. Instead, she would think of the Prince. Never mind all the things she didn't know about him, what did she know? There had been moments when he let his guard down, but they had been very rare. Prince Kadar considered his words very carefully. He was one of those men who made good use of silences too. Deliberately, she was sure of it. He'd be the type of man to whom secrets would be blurted out, crimes confessed.

I am not married. One very interesting piece of information he had let slip. There had been something in his expression when he said those words, but she couldn't articulate what it was. Why on earth was a man so—so fascinating and so tempting as Prince Kadar not married? It could certainly not be for lack of opportunity. Even without an Arabian kingdom and all its trappings, even if Prince Kadar were not a prince but a footman, or a groom, she could not imagine he would lack opportunity. Mind you, she couldn't imagine him taking orders either. So perhaps not a footman. Or a groom. Or any sort of servant.

Oh, for goodness' sake! To return to the point. Why wasn't he married, when surely he could have his choice of any woman? Save women like her, of course, who would never choose to marry. Constance groaned, casting off the sheet. Except that was precisely what she was going to do just as soon as she could board a ship heading east. Provided she could force herself to actually board the ship. Which she would have to do, no matter how terrifying the idea was, because Mr Edgbaston had paid for her in good faith, and much as she'd like him to continue to believe her lost at sea, she was not lost at sea.

Her mood spoilt, her sense of impending

doom returned, Constance dangled her legs over the edge of the high divan bed. She felt decidedly shaky. The floor was marble, cool on the soles of her feet. Pulling on a robe which had been helpfully draped at the bottom of the bed, she made her way carefully to the double doors set in the far wall. They were wooden, ornately carved, similar to the grille covering the window above. Pulling them wide, she found herself in a sitting room with a view out to a courtyard. Dropping onto a huge cushion beside the tall window, she leaned her cheek against the glass. What if she really could decide not to return from the dead? Who would miss her, truly? Mama…

A lump rose in her throat. Tears burned in her eyes. She had come all this way at Mama's behest, even though she was pretty sure—no, she was absolutely certain—that what Mama wanted was not in her best interests. What would Mama want her to do now? The answer to that had not changed. She certainly would not want her to return to England. Constance sighed, her breath misting the glass. It was rather dispiriting to discover that whether one was dead or alive didn't much matter to anyone. Save herself, of course.

A gentle rap on the door preceded the entrance of a small procession of servants, which diverted her from her melancholy introspection. One after another, they clasped their hands and bowed slightly before her in formal greeting. One maid set out breakfast. Two others began to lay out a selection of clothes in the most delightfully cool materials, and yet another maid presented her with a note, written in English. Prince Kadar requested her presence.

Constance gazed around her at the flurry of activity, which included two more maids setting out a huge bath in the bedchamber. Honestly, she had no cause at all to be downhearted. She had days, perhaps even weeks of respite ahead of her here as a guest in this fabulous royal palace. Days in which to enjoy being becalmed, cast adrift, shipwrecked. She was going to savour every one of them.

Constance learned that it took an inordinately long time to prepare one for an audience with a prince. First she was bathed in water delicately perfumed with rose petals. Her freshly washed hair was tamed into something resembling submission thanks to some scented oil. The clothes, which she had eventually allowed the collection of maids to select for her, were also unlike anything she had ever worn. Loose pantaloons, gathered tightly at her ankles and cinched at her waist, made from a creamy gossamer-fine fabric that clung revealingly to her legs. A thin-strapped camisole was her only undergarment. Over this, a simple tunic in cream muslin which stopped at her thighs, and on top of that, a sort of sleeveless half-dress in apricot silk which fastened with tiny pearl buttons, leaving the slip beneath, and the bottom of those shocking pantaloons, exposed. Soft kid slippers adorned her feet.

Studying her reflection, quite unrecognizable to herself, Constance thought she resembled something between a milkmaid and a concubine. Not that she'd ever actually seen, far less met, a concubine. It felt decidedly odd, being fully dressed without being laced into a corset. Though the overdress was buttoned tightly at her waist, the neckline skimmed the top of her breasts, which were confined only by the thin muslin of the tunic—or rather cradled rather than confined. Staring critically at the swell of her bosom, she supposed she was at least more decently covered than if she had been wearing a ball gown in the latest fashion.

And the posse who had created this vision seemed to be happy with the effect. She was, finally, fit to be seen by the Prince. Smiling and miming her thanks, Constance trailed in the wake of another servant through a warren of corridors before being ushered up a narrow flight of spiral stairs. She paused for a moment at the top, her eyes dazzled by the brightness of the sun. Blinking, shielding her eyes while she became accustomed to the glare, she found herself on a large rooftop terrace.

The floor was laid out in mosaic, white with swirling patters of green and yellow and red, like the floor of a Roman villa. A parapet of red stone bounded the terrace, and tall terracotta pots filled with exotic ferns stood sentry at each corner. In the centre a large angular object shrouded in canvas took up much of the available space, and over in one corner an awning had been set up, under which a desk strewn with papers, scrolls and stacks of leather-bound books had been placed. Seated behind it was Prince Kadar.

'Lady Constance.'

His hair was damp, slicked back over his head, though it was already beginning to curl rebelliously. He wore a long tunic in broad grey-and-white stripes, grey trousers, black slippers. She still couldn't decide whether his eyes were grey or green, but she had been right about his mouth. Sensual. There was no other word for it. Except perhaps sinful. And if she didn't want to appear like a blushing idiot, she had better stop thinking about it.

'Good morning.' The Prince bowed over her hand, in the European style. 'I trust you are feeling better? You look quite—quite transformed.'

'I have certainly never worn exotic garments such as these,' Constance replied, flustered by her thoughts, and by his touch, and by that gleam in his eyes when he looked at her, which she must have imagined.

'I regret our markets were unable to provide the kind of clothing you are accustomed to—or so I was informed by the female who selected these. The wife of one of my Council members.'

'Please thank her. And please believe me when I tell you that I like these clothes much better. They are infinitely more suitable to this climate. In my own clothes, I would be far too hot. All those petticoats and...' *stays* was not a word one said to a gentleman, never mind a prince '...and things,' Constance finished lately. 'What I mean is, thank you, Your Highness, for being so thoughtful. I am afraid that I have no means to pay you back for these, but...'

'Do not, I pray, insult me.'

His manner changed so abruptly that Constance flinched, only then realizing how informal he had been moments before. She bit her lip. She dropped into something that could be construed as a curtsy. 'I assure you, no insult was intended.'

Silence. A nod. More silence. Constance stared down at her feet. 'I expect you've brought me up here to tell me I'm to be packed off on a ship at first light,' she said resignedly.

Prince Kadar pushed his fingers through his hair. 'It is, unfortunately, uncommon for trading vessels from the west to call in at our port. Most sail straight for India once they have navigated the Cape of Good Hope. I have confirmed that the next ship is not expected until August.'

'August! But this is only May.'

'Unfortunately we have no other ship here at Murimon which is fit for the voyage. Apparently my brother commissioned a schooner to be built. A three-master. Ocean going.' Prince Kadar shook his head. 'Why Butrus imagined he needed such a thing, I have no idea, but it is beside the point. It is not completed, and will not be until July at the earliest.'

'So I am effectively stranded here for two months,' Constance said.

'Possibly three.'

'I'm terribly sorry.'

Prince Kadar gave her one of those assessing looks. 'For what?'

'I shall be inconveniencing you. Three months is a long time for an uninvited guest to stay.'

The Prince smiled. 'But I did invite you, last night, to stay for as long as you wish.'

'Yes, but…'

'Lady Constance, I repeat, your presence here is most welcome.'

Goodness, but when he smiled she quite lost track of her thoughts. It was like the dazzle of a faraway star captured in the lens of her telescope, temporarily blinding her to everything else. 'Thank you,' Constance said, blinking. 'If there is anything I can do while I am here to work my passage, so to speak, then I would be delighted to help. I'm afraid I'm not a very good needlewoman, but I'm very good with accounts. Though I can't imagine why you would need a bookkeeper when you most likely have a treasurer.'

'And an assistant treasurer and any number of scribes,' the Prince said. 'There are any number of needlewomen here at the palace too, I expect. Your time will be your own.'

'I'm not sure I'll know what to do with it. I like to be busy.'

'Then you must see some of our country, explore its delights. Which brings me to the reason I asked you up here, to my private terrace.

Come.' Prince Kadar ushered her over to the waist-high parapet. 'There, take a look at Murimon.'

The view which confronted her was quite stunning. Sea and sky met on the horizon, both brilliant azure blue, the sky streaked with wispy white cloud, the sea sparkling with little white-crested waves. A line of fishing boats was strung out in the distance, too far away for her to make out more than the distinctive shallow hulls and single lateen sails. The wide sweep of the coastline to her left consisted of a number of little bays and fishing villages similar to Bashir's village, with white strips of sand, the houses huddled together on the narrow shoreline. Behind the nearer villages, narrow strips of green cultivated land could be made out. On the right, the terrain was more mountainous, rolling red-and-ochre hills guarding much steeper, jagged peaks. Here, there were few vestiges of green, and even fewer villages.

The port of Murimon sat proudly in the centre, directly below the palace. The harbour was formed by two long curves of rock embracing the sea. At the end of each arm stood a lighthouse. On the furthest-away point, buildings covered every inch of available space, some three or four storeys high, some squat and low. Presumably wharves, their huge doorways opened directly onto the jetties which sat at right angles to the shoreline. The nearer harbour wall was higher and rockier, housing a small defensive fortress. The port was nothing like the size of Plymouth, where she had embarked on the *Kent*, but it looked to have a similar sense of bustle. Ships of all shapes and sizes sat at anchor in the middle of the bay or were moored to the jetty. Dhows, much bigger than the fishing boats of Bashir's village, darted in and out between the statelier vessels.

The town attached to the port lay spread out below them. Constance leaned over the parapet to get a closer look. The path she must have followed in her chair last night zigzagged up the hillside below, past houses, tall and narrow, and tinkling fountains set in small squares.

She leaned over further. The roof terrace seemed to be at the highest point of the palace, in the very centre of the building. There looked to be three or even four storeys below the huge central edifice on which they were perched, with two low terraced wings on either side. A vast piazza, tiled with marble and bordered by two straight sentry-like lines of palm trees, formed the entrance to the palace itself, with a sweeping staircase on either side of an arched portal meeting on the first floor. It was exotic and absurdly impractical and utterly foreign and completely overwhelming.

'Well, what do you think of my humble domain?'

Constance turned too suddenly, snatching at the edge of the parapet as the heat and the glare of the sea and the sky and the sun all combined to make her dizzy.

A strong arm caught her as she staggered. 'Careful. I would hate to have to report your untimely death for a second time.'

She laughed weakly. Her cheek rested against the Prince's shoulder. She closed her eyes to combat the dizziness and breathed in the clean scent of cotton dried in the sunshine, warm skin and soap, and the slight tang of salt from the sea. Her senses swam. She put her hand onto his chest to right herself. Hard muscle over bone. Which she had no right to be touching.

'Thank you, I'm perfectly fine now.' Constance turned back to the view, shading her eyes. 'Your humble domain is absolutely spectacular. I've never seen anything remotely like it. How far from the harbour was the *Kent* when she went down?'

'You see that dhow out there?' He stood directly behind her, his arm pointing over her shoulder at a distant boat. 'She lies not far from there. Almost all of her passengers and crew were rescued by the boats which were harboured at the port. A few of those who perished were found in the next bay, over there. The bay where you were washed up is beyond that outcrop, as you can see, a fair distance away. The piece of broken mast you clung to must have drifted with the tide and carried you there before depositing you on the beach.'

The sea looked so calm, she could hardly credit that it could have been so violent. 'I don't remember anything,' Constance said with a shudder, 'save being thrown overboard. Absolutely nothing after that.'

'It is as well.' Kadar stepped back. 'I think you have more than enough terrible memories of the storm to keep you awake at night.'

'Not last night,' Constance said. 'I slept like the dead, rather appropriately.'

Prince Kadar set his hands on her shoulders and turned her to face him. 'But on previous nights, you have had nightmares, yes?'

His touch unsettled her. 'Sometimes,' Constance said, slipping from his grasp. 'It was one of the reasons I spent so many hours stargazing. It was a distraction from the prospect of torrid dreams.'

'Stargazing!'

'The study of the cosmos, the stars and the planets,' Constance elaborated.

'You are an astronomer?'

'You seem astonished. Is it because I have a passion for studying the night sky, or is because I am a woman with a passion for stargazing?' Constance turned away, absurdly disappointed. 'My father too, finds it inexplicable. He can see no practical purpose to it, and if there is no prospect of him profiting from something he is utterly uninterested.'

'I don't think it's inexplicable, and I most certainly do not think the fact that you are a woman should disbar you from scientific study. Quite the contrary. It is to your credit and to be commended.'

'Oh.' She turned back to face him, her cheeks hot once again. 'I'm terribly sorry. You sounded so— And then I assumed— And I ought not to have— Only my father— And I should not have spoken to you as I did, but I keep forgetting that you are a prince. I mean I don't forget, exactly, especially not when you give me that *assessing* look and I wish that I was thinking something a little more interesting for you to assess, but I fear that you would think my mind rather boring if you could read it, which you can't, obviously, though truly you do give one the impression that you can, and—and—oh, dear, that is another thing you do. Those silences. They make me want to fill them, and I start babbling and here I am, doing it again.'

Her face, she was sure, was bright scarlet. 'You're probably now wishing there was a ship for Bombay due tomorrow after all,' Constance said, once again failing to keep to her resolve to stop talking.

'Actually, quite the reverse. I was thinking that I have the perfect solution to occupy you for the three months you will be here.'

'Ah, you have a vacancy for a court jester?'

Smiling faintly, the Prince took her hand, leading her over to the covered object which stood in the middle of the terrace. 'Lady Constance,' he said, tugging at the knot which held the tarpaulin in place, 'I have no need of a court jester, but I do have a vacancy for a court astronomer.'

Kadar pulled the tarpaulin away, and Lady Constance's mouth fell open. 'A telescope! And such a telescope!' She ran her hands along the polished wooden barrel. She touched the little stool which was contained in the instrument's mounting box. She stroked her fingers along the system of pulleys and the brass handle which allowed the unwieldy tube of the telescope to pivot and rotate on its axis. She peered into the eyepiece. Finally, she ran her hands once more along the barrel. 'I have never seen anything so beautiful,' she said, her voice hushed with awe. 'How did you come by such a sophisticated instrument?'

She was staring at it as if it were made of gold. 'I share your passion for studying the stars. You have no idea how rare it is to meet a fellow astronomer. This particular instrument is a seven-foot reflector,' Kadar said. 'It was built in Mr Herschel's workshop. I purchased it five years ago, when I spent some time at Oxford. It has travelled with me ever since.'

'This actually comes from William Herschel's own workshop?' Her big brown eyes glowed. Her smile was soft, almost tender, as her fingers strayed compulsively to the telescope again. Captivating, he had thought she could be last night, and she was. There was a sensuality in the way she touched the instrument, mingling reverence and passion. And he was once again becoming aroused!

'I met the great man himself,' Kadar said, dragging his eyes away. 'Mr Herschel, I mean. I went to see the forty-foot reflector that he had constructed in Slough. A most impractical instrument, I thought, far too cumbersome to be of much use. Mr Herschel himself admitted as much. He, however, was fascinating. The telescope with which he discovered the new planet is very similar to this one.'

'*Georgium Sidus*, he named it, in honour of the King,' Lady Constance said. 'I like Uranus much better though, after Urania, the goddess of astronomy. Is it wrong for a court astronomer to confess that she prefers mythology to science as an explanation for the construction of the constellations?'

'You are a romantic, then?' Kadar asked, in some surprise.

'Who can deny the romance of the stars? Aside from my father, that is,' Lady Constance added wryly. The mention of her parent seemed to visibly deflate her. 'How long will it take, do you think, for a letter to reach England? I must write to Mama.'

'Weeks, perhaps a month or so. The securest and quickest route is to send it by way of the Red Sea to Cairo, where it can be handed over to your Consul General. I will ensure it is given priority.'

'Thank you, once again I am indebted to you. You know, this morning I thought about what you said last night. The fact that I am legally dead, the notion that I could choose to remain so. It was only for a few brief moments, but I did think about it, though I know it would be very wrong of me. It was rather a sobering experience, for the sad fact is that the only person who will be truly mourning me will be Mama, and in a way, she has already mourned my passing. When I sailed, though we neither of us could admit it, it was pretty certain that I'd never see her again.' She blinked furiously. 'Oh, for goodness' sake, please ignore me. It is not like me to be so morbid. Nor to feel sorry for myself.'

Kadar thought the feeling justified, but could see no point in saying so. 'Come into the shade of the awning, and let me pour you a cool drink.'

'I've embarrassed you again.'

'No.'

'You must think me a very volatile creature, one minute letting my tongue run away with me, the next falling into a swoon over a telescope, and the next bubbling like a—a stream.'

'I think you are a very brave creature, and a very honourable one.'

'You do?'

'Constance—Lady Constance—I never say what I do not mean.'

'Constance. I like the way you say my name. You make it sound quite exotic, and quite unlike me.'

'At this moment you look quite exotic but I believe you are very loyal, as your name implies.'

She rolled her eyes. 'Reliable. Dutiful. Why not say dull?'

'Because that would not be true. Come out of the sun.' He motioned her to a bundle of cushions, pouring them both a glass of lemon sherbet before sitting opposite her.

She took a long drink. 'Thank you. And my apologies again. I assure you I am usually perfectly even tempered. Perhaps I have had too much sun. I have certainly taken up too much of your time, Your Highness. I can see that you are very busy,' she said, waving at his paper-strewn desk.

'Lady Constance…'

'Please do just call me Constance. It sounds so much nicer.'

'Constance. Then you must call me Kadar.'

'Oh, no, that would be quite wrong.'

'While we are alone, then. When I am not the Prince, and you are not the Court Astronomer.'

'I did not take your suggestion seriously. I assumed it was said in jest.'

'I think it's an excellent idea.' Kadar topped her glass of sherbet up. 'It solves several problems. First and most important, as Court Astronomer, you will have a legitimate role in the palace, so there can be no suggestion of your presence here being open to conjecture. A few months ago, another Englishwoman, a botanist, caused a great deal of speculation when she visited the court in the kingdom of Qaryma. I wish to avoid that.'

'A female botanist? That sounds interesting. Is this kingdom far away? Do you think I would be able to meet her?'

'I heard that she has since returned to England,' Kadar said, wondering fleetingly how his childhood friend, now crowned King of Qaryma, felt about his botanist leaving. Azhar had been most defensive when challenged about her position at court. All the more reason to make sure that he had no need to defend Constance.

'To return to your own position. You told me yourself that you prefer to have an occupation. By coincidence, we have no accurate star maps of this region. It was my ambition to remedy that, but I now realise that, as Prince, I will not have the time to devote to it. Anything you can do to update the charts I have would be most welcome.'

He was pleased to see the sparkle return to her eyes. 'You really mean it?'

'I told you, I never say what I do not mean.'

'Oh, my goodness, I could kiss you!' Con-

stance's cheeks flamed. 'Not that I meant—
That is I would not dare— I mean, it would be
highly inappropriate, given that I hardly know
you. And even if I did know you, I am not in
the habit of bestowing kisses on any man—and
even if I was, well, I ought not to kiss you now
that I am betrothed. So there's no need to look
as if you…'

'As if I want you to kiss me,' Kadar said.

'What?'

'I don't know what my expression was, but
what I was thinking was that I would, not-
withstanding all the perfectly valid reasons
you have given why you shouldn't, like you
to kiss me. And would very much like to kiss
you back.'

Constance looked every bit as surprised as
he by this admission. He should not have said
it, but he had, and it was true. He wanted to do
a great deal more than kiss her, and he hadn't
been able to stop thinking about just what that
entailed, in all its delicious detail, since her arrival last night. But if she was going to be here
at the palace for the next three months, he'd have
to find a way of ensuring that he did not kiss
her, so Kadar said the one thing he was certain
would make it impossible for either of them to
act on their impulses.

'But I can't kiss you. It would be, in your own words, highly inappropriate since I too am betrothed.'

Chapter Four

Two nights later, Constance stood next to the low parapet on the roof terrace, watching the sun sinking over the port of Murimon, evoking the completion of the daily journey of the mythical Greek Titan Helios and his sun chariot, returning to the east in preparation for the morning. The spectacle of night falling over the Arabian Sea filled her with awe. The colours of the last rays streaking the sky, reflected in the sea, were so blazingly vibrant they deserved new names. Existing colours could not do them full justice. The night fell so quickly too, dusk was over in a heartbeat. One minute the sky was blue. Then multi-hued. And then indigo. The stars did not emerge hesitantly like a gaggle of shy debutantes as they did at home, they exploded into the sky, huge discs of silver and gold, not cautiously twinkling, but with all the confidence and bravado of the most celebrated of courtesans.

She left the parapet to make her way over to the heap of cushions she had set out by the telescope. Lying back, she gazed up at the sky, accustoming her eyes to the dark. Above her, the nightly parade of stars had begun in earnest. The moon was on the wane, a mere sliver of a crescent. The moon god Anningan had been so busy chasing his love, the sun, that he had not eaten. In a day or so, he would disappear from the sky for three days while he came down to earth to hunt. When he returned he would grow fatter, waxing from a crescent to his full, buttery pomp. And then once again, he'd become distracted by his lady love, and forget to eat. This tale was Constance's favourite of the many depictions of the moon's phases, though she pitied poor Anningan, tied to the flighty sun, forced to do her bidding, without a will of his own. He might as well be a wife.

She wriggled more deeply into the mound of cushions and reminded herself that it was destructive to think such negative thoughts. Her mother had given her a list of positives, a litany she had recited over and over to her daughter, as if repetition would give them veracity. They were all variations on the same theme. Constance's marriage would be carefree because Constance's husband was rich. Constance would be happy because her husband was happy, because how could a rich man not be happy, when he wanted for nothing. At a stroke, Constance could both secure her own future, and rescue Mama's.

Her mother's logic was fatally flawed, but she could not be persuaded that replenishing Papa's coffers would secure nothing, save a hiatus while he invested it recklessly with his usual flair for picking those schemes most unlikely to succeed. As for Constance's future—that logic had more holes than a sieve. Mr Edgbaston's money was his own to do with as he wished, as was his wife. Having paid such a large sum for her, rather than increase her value to him, wasn't it likely that he'd expect a great deal in return, whatever the *devil* that turned out to be!

Far from attaining any sort of independence, as Mama had repeatedly claimed she would, for she knew her daughter almost as well as her daughter knew her, Constance would be entirely beholden. Papa had dismissed her pleas to include any personal allowance in the betrothal contract or even any widow's jointure, as a matter of detail, not wishing to risk asking for anything that might endanger the deal. Constance was effectively penniless. Worse in fact, because now that her trousseau was at the bottom of the sea, she was going to be starting out married life in debt to her husband for the very clothes on her back.

Just thinking about it made her anxious. What if she didn't please this stranger she was to marry? What if he disliked her? What if she disliked him? The very idea of pretending made her skin crawl. The fact that she would have to, that she would be expected to, that she would have no choice—that was the worst, the very worst part of it. She was twenty-five years old. She knew her own mind. She didn't want to get married. She never had. It was quite simple. She didn't want to do it. She really didn't want to do it.

But she had to, so there was no point in working herself up into a state. It had to be done. Though not quite yet, thank goodness. There would be no ship for months. Two months, perhaps three. Plenty of time for her to come up with a strategy to make the best of a bad lot. More than enough time. In fact, so much time she would be best putting it out of her mind entirely and turn her thoughts to more immediate concerns.

Such as the fascinating and enigmatic Prince of Murimon and the revelation that he wanted to kiss her. That he, Kadar, was engaged to be married. Constance could still not decide what to make of either fact. Or which was the most interesting to learn.

She knew absolutely nothing more than these stark facts, and since he had communicated with her only through brief dispatches since, she had had no opportunity to press him further. Mind you, she doubted very much that tactic would be successful. If he didn't want to talk about it, he would give her one of his looks. She had labelled them in her head. Number one, the Haughty Prince. Number two, the Mind Reader. Number three, the Sphinx. And then her two favourites. Number four, the Bone-Melter. And Number five, the Blood-Heater.

Kadar wanted to kiss her. Kadar would not kiss her because he was promised to another. And so was she. Was it sophistry to argue that such a kiss was permissible *because* it could mean nothing? Probably. Wouldn't she make a better wife if she knew how to kiss? Perhaps, though she couldn't pretend that she would be kissing Kadar for any other reason than that she wanted to kiss him. Which she did, despite knowing it was wrong of her, she really did. And he wanted to kiss her. If only he did not, it would be easier. She should be hoping that he had changed his mind. She would be fibbing if she told herself she hoped any such thing.

The sky above her was inky black, giving the brightest stars a bluish hue. With the moon so emaciated, and now that her vision was adjusted, she could see hundreds of distant pinpricks of light in addition to the main constellations. Libra, Scorpio and Sagittarius were all clearly defined tonight. As ever, looking up at all this celestial beauty, Constance was filled with a sense of wonder. She was one tiny being, on one tiny planet in a nebulae spinning at unimaginable speed through a vast universe filled with a myriad of other nebulae. All of this had existed for countless thousands of years, and would endure for thousands more to come.

In comparison, her lifetime was the mere blink of an eye. Her three months here in Arabia was too tiny a period to even register. Constance began to set up the telescope, making the necessary adjustments, deciding tonight to point it due south. She had better not waste a single moment. With a growing sense of excitement mingled with anticipation, she looked through the eyepiece and was instantly transported to the spellbinding creation that surrounded this little world.

The invitation to accompany Kadar on his early morning ride had been in her suite when she returned from her stargazing. The outfit which she wore for the occasion was perfectly suited for the purpose, consisting of a soft white sleeveless tunic under a long dark-red cotton coat with matching trousers. Her boots came up over her knees, the brown kid soft on her skin, the long pointed toes decorated with red stitching.

He had been waiting for her in the stables, had chosen for her mount the most beautiful Arabian mare she had ever seen. She rode astride like a man, there being no side-saddle available. It was a perfect morning, and she could not have asked for a more even-tempered equine companion. Above them, in the celestial blue of the early morning sky streaked with wispy cloud, the sun was pale gold, the air tangy with salt. As they reached the furthest edge of the long beach Constance reined in her mount. Kadar was already there, waiting. The sea was like liquid turquoise, breaking white onto the hard-packed golden sands, foaming around the legs of the steaming horses and pooling around an outcrop of rock. The shoreline was a cliff formed of the same ochre rock, the first trees which she had seen in the kingdom growing in neat rows further inland.

'Olive trees,' Kadar said, in answer to her unspoken question. 'They screen some of our precious crop-growing land from the salt and the winds coming in off the sea.'

'It is so beautiful,' Constance said. 'And this horse, she is so perfectly behaved. Whoever trained her is most skilled.'

'She was bred in Bharym, as was my stallion. Rafiq, the prince of that country has the best stables in Arabia. I am fortunate enough to be one of the few men to whom he will sell his prized bloodstock.'

'Does he sell only to his friends?'

'He sells only to those he deems worthy to own and enjoy his precious horseflesh,' Kadar said, with a faint smile.

'Ah.' Constance laughed. 'I can see why he deems you worthy. You ride as if you were born in the saddle. I am extremely privileged to ride this beautiful creature.'

Kadar smiled. 'Rafiq would approve of your horsemanship. My instincts told me you would know how to handle her. I was right.'

'Thank you.'

'The tide is far enough out this morning for us to venture around the headland,' Kadar said, 'unless you have had enough?'

'I don't think I could ever have a surfeit of this,' Constance replied. Sea, sky, sands, horse and man, any of it, she thought, following in his wake. Kadar's riding dress was similar to hers, consisting of plain cotton trousers and a tunic of blue-and-grey stripes. He sported long riding boots of black-kid leather. He sat perfectly upright in the saddle, holding the highly strung stallion with the careless-seeming ease of a naturally gifted horseman. His head was bare, his black silky hair dishevelled by the wind. Sweat made his thin tunic cling to his back, revealing the rippling muscles of his shoulders. For such a lean man, he was very powerfully built. He and the stallion were a perfect match.

The sea was receding further as they followed the headland, where the olive trees gave way to scrub on the cliff top, and the regular rush of the waves onto the sand quieted to a sigh. The mountains which Constance had spotted from the rooftop terrace yesterday came into view on the horizon now, and the cliff tops became more rugged in appearance. They turned sharply around the headland, and she gasped with delight at the perfect crescent of sand completely enclosed by the steep cliffs, a natural harbour formed by the outcrop they had just traversed, and an almost identical one on the other side of the bay.

'What do you think of my special retreat?'

'I am lost for words. Your country is so very,

very beautiful. The light is magical. The blue sky, the azure sea, it is like living in a perfect picture. Everything here is so vivid, the colours so vibrant. So different from the muffled shades of grey so typical of England. It does something to the soul. Lifts the spirits.' She laughed, embarrassed. 'I don't know what it does save that it makes me feel as if I am full of bubbles. I expect you think that is fanciful.'

'I think that you reflect the scenery here,' Kadar replied. 'Bright. Vivid. Alive.'

'Oh.' Her cheeks heated. 'Thank you,' Constance said, both flustered and ridiculously pleased.

He helped her down from the saddle, his hands light on her waist. She watched him as he hobbled the horses, seating herself in the shade of the cliffs which ringed the bay. Her boots were extremely comfortable, but her feet were hot inside them. She pulled them off, wriggling her toes into the deliciously cool damp sand, leaning back on her hands to enjoy the breeze on her face. When she opened her eyes, Kadar was standing over her, looking down at her bare toes. 'I was hot,' she said, embarrassed, for she would never have dreamed of removing her shoes in company at home.

'Yes,' he said, giving her his Sphynx look, and

dropping onto the sand beside her, prepared to follow her lead.

His boots were much longer than hers. His calves rippled as he removed them. His skin was the colour of the golden sands darkened by the sea. His feet had a very high arch, like her own.

'Tell me how your stargazing is coming along.'

A subject even more distracting than Kadar's feet! 'I thought you'd never ask,' Constance said, smiling. 'You're probably going to regret doing so.'

It was easy to be transported to the heavens, especially in the company of a man who shared her passion, and could plug several gaps in her knowledge. Finally, she forced herself to stop talking not because she had run out of words but because her mouth had run dry. 'I did warn you,' she said.

Kadar was leaning back on his elbows. His hair was tousled by the wind. And he was smiling that special bone-melting smile. 'I could not ask for a more diligent or enthusiastic court astronomer.'

'You could, I suspect, easily obtain a far more learned one.'

'Who would number the stars and plot their positions with mathematical precision. I much prefer your way of mapping the heavens. A night sky teeming with legends and mythological creatures. A romantic cosmos full of passion and wonder. I am very happy with my choice of court astronomer, thank you very much.'

He smiled again. Their gazes locked. He reached over to tuck her hair behind her ear. His fingers brushed the line of her scar. Her heart began to hammer. His fingers fluttered down her cheek, her neck, to rest at the pulse at the base of her throat. She surrendered to the urge to lean just a fraction closer, and he did the same. Shoulders touching. Legs. His breath on her cheek. She lifted her hand to his face, mirroring his touch, flattening her palm over the smoothness of his cheek, the roughness of his chin.

He dipped his head towards her. His lips were soft. His kiss was gentle. He tasted salty. She felt as if she was melting. Her fingers curled into the silky softness of his hair. She parted her lips for him, returning the pressure tentatively. Then he sighed. Lifted his head. Their hands dropped. Their bodies separated.

What had happened? Was that a kiss or wasn't it? How had it happened, when they had both been so clear that it could not? Constance stared out to sea, completely at a loss. 'I don't understand it. I knew that I shouldn't, my mind knew it was wrong, but my body wanted...'

Kadar muttered something under his breath in his own language. She risked a fleeting glance. 'Your habit of speaking your thoughts quite unedited is sometimes dangerously enlightening.'

'What do you mean?'

He ran his fingers through his hair. 'Constance, it took considerable willpower to break that kiss. Telling me that your body wanted—' He broke off, shaking his head. 'I don't want to think about what your body wanted, or my body will—will wish to do something it must not.'

'Oh.' Her inclination was, shockingly, to wish that Kadar had not exerted his considerable willpower, but had instead continued to kiss her. That kiss, which was only really the beginning of a kiss, had been so deliciously arousing that it was very hard indeed to think of anything at this moment save what might have been. Save what still might be, if she put that considerable willpower of his further to the test, and reached over and touched her lips to his again, and—and then she would discover what it was that his body wanted to do to hers.

Kadar was pensively picking up handfuls of sand and letting it trickle slowly through his fingers so that it formed a mound, like the contents of an hourglass. He didn't look like a man struggling to regain his self-control. 'My lack of experience has disappointed you,' Constance said, because of course that's what it was. 'It's fine, you don't have to pretend that you enjoyed my inexpert kissing.'

He studied her face, a faint frown drawing his brows together. 'Constance, I never pretend. I enjoyed kissing you more than I ought, if the truth be told. When I first set eyes on you I had a feeling that our lovemaking would be memorable, our bodies and desires perfectly matched. What just happened proved that I was right. We would be wise to heed the warning contained in that knowledge.'

'You mean it would be more difficult to stop the next time?'

Kadar winced. 'I mean we would be wise not to contemplate a next time.'

Resisting the temptation to kiss him again was one thing, but to deny herself the pleasure of imagining it—no, she wasn't sure she could do that, so Constance remained silent.

Kadar measured out another handful of sand. 'My coronation takes place in two weeks.'

She accepted the change of subject gratefully. 'You will be King of Murimon.'

'Prince of Murimon. We do not adopt the title of King here. The ruler is Prince, and his heir has the title of Crown Prince. You will of course attend the ceremony in your official capacity. You will require robes. We've never had a court astronomer before, so you can have them designed to your own specifications.'

'That sounds wonderful, but rather wasteful, since the position is temporary.'

'Temporary, but nonetheless legitimate. I have already announced your appointment to my council. I do not wish your reputation to be compromised by speculation, nor do I wish to dishonour my future bride. The marriage will be onerous enough for both parties. I do not wish to start the journey on a note of resentment.'

'Onerous? Don't you wish to be married, Kadar?'

'No more than you do.' Another measure of sand trickled down. 'But like you, my personal preferences are of little consequence. My fate, like yours, has been defined for me, my bride chosen for me. Duty, honour, obligation are my motivation, though we differ in one fundamental way, you and I. The beneficiary of your marriage is your father. The beneficiary of mine will be my kingdom.'

Constance stared at him open-mouthed. So much, contained in those few clipped words uttered in that expressionless tone. 'Your bride— did you say she was chosen for you?'

'Actually, that's not strictly accurate. She was in fact chosen for my brother,' Kadar said drily. 'I inherited her, along with his kingdom.'

'No, no, you can't possibly be serious.' But one look at Kadar's expression told her he was perfectly serious. 'Goodness,' Constance said, 'that is very—odd to say the least. Don't you object to having a hand-me-down bride?'

'There you go again with your unedited, albeit truthful observations. As I said, my personal preferences...'

'...are of no consequence. But you are a prince!'

Another of those harsh little laughs. 'Exactly, and as a prince I must put my kingdom first, my own desires—last. My people were anticipating a royal wedding, the dawning of a new era. The date was set for a mere two weeks after my brother was tragically killed.'

'What happened to him?'

'A riding accident.'

There was the tiniest flicker, not quite a blink, of his right eye. She had noticed it before, when he mentioned his brother. She had asked if they were close, and he had not answered. She decided to try a more roundabout approach. 'Was he much older than you?'

'Two years.'

'I don't have any brothers or sisters,' Constance said. 'I've always wished—'

'We were not particularly close,' Kadar interrupted, 'if that is what you want to know. It was one of the first things you asked me about Butrus the night you arrived.'

'You didn't answer me.'

'Until I returned for his wedding, I had not seen him for seven years. We are very—unalike. Butrus found my love of scholarly pursuits simply incomprehensible. As did our father, who was for ever grateful that I was the second son and not the first born. I was temperamentally, intellectually and in many ways ethically unsuited to life in the palace, while Butrus...' Kadar shrugged. 'Oh, Butrus was cast in our father's image. The only thing we had in common latterly was a love of horses. Unfortunately, he had a rather higher opinion of his ability to ride than was warranted. Even more unfortunately, he was not a man who learned from experience. I found it easier, in the end, simply to refuse to race him.'

'It was not—dear heavens—it was not in a race with you that he died, was it?'

'No.' That tiny flicker of the eye again. Kadar stared out at the sea. Constance waited, holding her breath to prevent herself from speaking, and her patience was eventually rewarded. 'He had a new horse. A wedding present, ironically. A wilful brute of an animal which most certainly did not come from the stables at Bharym, though that is what Butrus had been told. I advised him at once that he should not attempt to master it. Perhaps if I had held my tongue, he would not have felt the need to prove himself to me. It threw him. He hit his head on a boulder, he was dead before I reached him.'

'Kadar, I am so sorry. How very, very terrible for you.'

Constance reached for his hand, pressing it between her own. He went quite still, allowing her to hold him for a few moments, before freeing himself. 'Terrible for the people of Murimon. Butrus was a very popular prince. His betrothal was very favourably received by the people.'

Constance frowned. 'How long was your brother Prince of Murimon?'

'Seven years, why do you ask?'

'You say he was popular, and you say that your people expect a prince to be married, yet your brother waited seven years to take a bride.'

Kadar seemed to—to freeze, there was no other word for it. What on earth had she said? When he spoke, his tone was icy enough to make Constance shiver. 'Butrus was married on the day of his coronation. The Princess Tahira would have been his second wife.'

'Second!' Was that it, was he affronted because she had mentioned the forbidden subject of polygamy?

'My brother was a widower,' Kadar said, obviously still capable of reading her thoughts despite his frozen state. 'His first wife died just over a year ago.'

Mortified, Constance dug her toes deeper into the sand. 'I'm so sorry. How dreadful. Was she very young? Were there no children?'

'She was three years younger than me. No, there were no children.'

What was she missing? Constance wondered, for Kadar had curled his fists into the sand. Her brow cleared. It was obvious! 'If there had been a child, you would not now be Prince,' she said gently.

His eyes were bleak. 'She died trying to give him an heir. Who knows what difference it would have made if she had? But it was not to be.'

Poor woman, Constance thought, her heart touched by this tragedy. And poor Kadar, the only one in this sad little story left alive, to bear the consequences. 'Your brother left no heir, but he did bequeath you a bride. Is that why you feel obliged to honour the betrothal?'

He did not answer for a long moment, but she was becoming more accustomed to his silences. 'It has been made very clear to me that it is what the kingdom needs and wants, but I am taking a bride because I consider it the right thing to do for Murimon, not to court popularity by giving the people the spectacle of a royal wedding. I will not be the kind of ruler my brother was.'

Had he answered her question? She couldn't help but feel there was more to this story than Kadar had admitted, but it was a very sad story, and she was happy to move on from it. 'What kind of ruler was he?' Constance asked.

She was pleased to see Kadar's expression lightening a little. 'Butrus was like your Prince Regent before he ate too much and spent too much,' he replied with a trace of a smile. 'You know, the epitome of what people expected of their Prince, charming and hospitable, ebullient, gregarious, and always more than happy to put on a display of pomp and ceremony.'

'And the other side of that coin?'

Kadar's smile broadened. 'You're quite right. He was thoughtless, quite selfish. It came of growing up knowing that the crown would be his. He had an air about him, of...'

'Entitlement! My father is just such a one, though he had but two subjects to command.'

Kadar raised his brows, but Constance shook her head impatiently. 'We were talking of your brother.'

'I need not say any more. It sounds as if you have his measure perfectly.'

'Well, I hope you'll make a very different prince.'

Kadar laughed. 'Then that makes two of us.'

'Only two?'

His laughter died. Constance was treated to his Sphynx look. 'People do not know me as they did Butrus, and my father before him.'

'But you said you had only been abroad for seven years, and you are—thirty?'

'I am twenty-nine. My inclinations have always been scholarly. Butrus and my father thought I preferred books to people. It was not true, but sadly there were very few people who shared my interests here in Murimon. We are a seafaring kingdom, and have not a tradition of learning.'

'You must have been very lonely,' Constance said. 'Though I have often dreamed of being locked away in a huge library for ever, I think I would very quickly become one of those people who mutter to themselves under their breath all the time. "Now, Constance, where did you put that book?" "Oh, Constance, surely we read that tome just the other day." "For goodness' sake, Constance, you've got crumbs in Dr Johnson's dictionary, and you've forgotten to feed the cat." Though I suppose if I had a cat in the library with me, I could talk to it instead. Dr Johnson had a cat, you know. Its name was Hodge. It is mentioned in Mr Boswell's *Life*.'

'I know. I'm familiar with the work.'

She made a face. 'I've done it again, haven't I? What did you call it, let you have my thoughts unedited. You're looking at me as if— Actually, I'm not sure I can tell what you're thinking.'

'I was thinking that I have never met anyone like you. You like to read, then?'

'Anything. Everything. We did have a huge library once, at Montgomery House, but Papa sold all the books. Some of them were very valuable. So now the library is home to a collection of cobwebs.'

'Meticulously catalogued by you, no doubt. Montgomery House is your family home?'

'In Surrey. It's been in the family for hundreds of years, and will hopefully remain so for hundreds more, if my father makes good on his promise.' Which would, Constance knew, be a small miracle. He had indeed promised, but Papa seemed to think promises made to a wife and daughter were not like real promises. Kadar was giving her look Number Two. The Mind Reader. She didn't want him to ask her about this depressing subject, and besides, she was far more interested in him. 'Do you have a library?'

He hesitated, but then to her relief, he nodded. 'A very substantial one. I have a weakness for books, and have had ample opportunity to collect many rare editions in the course of my travels. The bulk of them have not yet even been unpacked.'

'Did they travel far, then?'

'Is that your way of asking me where I have been since leaving Murimon?'

'Yes,' Constance agreed, grinning back and pushing her hair away from her face.

'I made my home in Naples, though I have spent time in England…'

'Oxford, you said.'

'Yes, but most of my time was spent in London. Madrid, Lisbon and Paris I have also spent a great deal of time in. I have visited most of the great cities of Europe.'

'Visiting libraries?' Constance hazarded.

'Mostly consulting with governments,' Kadar said, smiling faintly. 'I am one of the very few men who understand both the ancient and modern traditions and customs of Arabia and the east, and those which govern the west.'

'I'm afraid I don't quite understand. Are you a lawyer?'

Kadar shook his head. 'No, but I advise those who make the laws. Governments. Diplomats. Large trading companies like the East India. When they want to expand their trade or their influence from west to east, then they ask me how to do so without getting into a war or, as they tend to put it, a little local difficulty.'

'Goodness,' Constance said, eyeing him with renewed respect. 'That explains a lot. The first time I saw you, in the Royal Saloon, I thought that you had an air about you, you know, that you were the kind of person who was used to having everyone listen to them, hang on their every word. I thought it was because you were a prince, but then you said you hadn't been a prince for very long, and I wondered—but now I know. And I've done it again, haven't I?'

'It is fascinating.'

'That is a polite way of saying baffling. Or perhaps simply terrifying.'

'I believe I told you I always choose my words carefully?'

Constance laughed. 'I must try to take a leaf from your book.'

'No, don't.' Kadar smiled. 'I like you just as you are.'

That smile. It made her catch her breath. It made her hot. It really did feel as if her bones might be melting. Constance dragged her eyes away. 'It sounds like fascinating work.'

The smile disappeared from his face. 'It was, but that is in the past now. Murimon requires all of my time and energy. I have plans, ambitious plans to change it from a simple seafaring kingdom to a seat of learning. I want to bring the world to our kingdom, and to bring our kingdom into the world of the nineteenth century.'

'That sounds very ambitious. What do your people think of these proposed changes?'

'I haven't shared my ideas with anyone yet. I want to—to perfect my vision first before ushering in a new era.'

Constance frowned. 'A new era. You used that phrase in relation to your brother's marriage. It implies that he too had change in mind.'

'The year of mourning for his wife had elapsed. A new princess and an heir were his only priorities.'

'Did you know her well, Kadar—his first wife?'

'Why do you ask that?'

Constance flinched, for the words emerged like the crack of a whip. 'You said that you left seven years ago, and your brother was married on his coronation day seven years ago, so you must have been acquainted with her. I simply wondered what she was like.'

'Yes. I knew her.' Kadar picked up his boots and began to pull them on. 'If we don't leave soon, the tide will cut us off.'

The morning was more advanced than he realised. As they rode back, Kadar had to repress the urge to let loose his tight hold on the reins, to fly cross the sands in a wild gallop that would take all his strength to control. And would stop him from thinking. But Constance was tired, so he held to a trot. She sat straight in the saddle, but he could see it was an effort. He had to remind himself that she was still recovering from her ordeal. She seemed so full of energy, so full of life, it was easy to forget.

He had talked too much. He had talked of things that he never talked of, and as a result his head was full of other things that he never thought of. If he was not careful, those memories would stir up all that suffering he had worked so hard to eliminate. He would not allow that. Never again would he be a hostage to his emotions. Never again would he expose himself to such heartache. Seven years since it happened.

Not once in seven years had he allowed anyone to breach his defences.

Until now. What was it that made Constance different? It was not his desire for her. He did not confide in her as a preliminary to any sort of lovemaking, for that was not possible. Why then? Because she had a way of seeing past his carefully considered words, his cautiously constructed sentences, to the feelings he hadn't even known lay behind them. She had a way of looking at him as if she could read his innermost emotions, and it threw him off-kilter.

It was all of that, but it was something else too. It was her. Constance. Kadar glanced over at her, and was forced to smile. Her hair was a delightful tangle of curls, streaked copper and burnished red by the heat of the sun, which had turned her face, her hands, her feet a lovely golden colour. The clothes suited her too, flowing loosely around her, giving him tantalizing glimpses of the curves beneath. She was so *unlike* the Lady Constance Montgomery he had first imagined. He found the way she launched into speech, strewing the contents of her mind before him like rose petals, utterly captivating—that word again—and completely disconcerting. He had never known anyone so candid, and yet

he got the impression that she was far more accustomed to keeping those thoughts to herself.

He liked her. Odd thing to say, but he did. He
liked talking to her, and he liked making her
laugh, and he found her interesting. So wildly
romantic when it came to her precious stars, and
yet so prosaic when it came to her marriage.

Just like him.

He had not always been so. There had been
a time when his passion had been earthbound.
His stomach lurched. There were some things
that even Constance would never be able to get
him to talk about.

Chapter Five

His chief adviser was, to Kadar's irritation, waiting for him at the stables, pacing the straw-strewn
cobblestones. His intimidating presence was pre-
venting the various grooms and stable hands
from getting on with their duties, for Abdul-
Majid was a traditionalist, a man who believed
that all subordinates must bow solemnly and
maintain their deferential stance while in his presence. Despite the Chief Adviser's unquestionable
loyalty and his many years of diligent service
to the kingdom, every time Kadar looked at the
man, his hackles rose. Abdul-Majid had been
unable to disguise his satisfaction when Kadar
announced his intention to depart Murimon
seven years ago. The man was no fool. Abdul-
Majid knew, without a shadow of a doubt, exactly why Kadar had felt compelled to leave.

And had been mightily relieved when he had done so.

'Good morning, Chief Adviser. Your eagerness to get on with business does you credit.' Kadar dismounted, wincing inwardly at the faint trace of animosity in his tone.

If Abdul-Majid noticed it, he gave no indication. 'I thought perhaps you had forgotten our meeting, Highness,' he replied, making the low bow he insisted upon, no matter how many times Kadar had asked him to forgo such formality.

'You are already acquainted with Lady Constance,' Kadar said in English, 'but I do not believe you have met my newly-appointed court astronomer.'

Abdul-Majid looked around him with a puzzled look.

'They are one and the same,' Kadar said. 'An inspired choice if I may say so.'

'As Prince, it is your prerogative to say anything you wish, sire.' Another formal bow was made. 'The Court Astronomer is a most welcome addition to the court,' Abdul-Majid said stiffly.

Constance made a curtsy. 'Thank you, it is an honour and a privilege. I did not realise you spoke English, sir.' She waited, but Abdul-Majid made no reply, and Constance, sensing her presence was unwelcome, bid them both good morning.

'It is a pity that no ship can be found to remove the Englishwoman from our shores with alacrity,' Abdul-Majid said, folding his hands into the voluminous sleeves of his tunic. 'Your bride must be the foremost woman in the palace. She will not like to have her nose put out of joint by a foreign woman who makes horoscopes and pretty patterns of the night sky.'

'Lady Constance will be making detailed and accurate star charts, and she will be gone long before my wedding.'

'How so, when there is no ship bound for India for at least two months?'

'We have a coronation to organise first, Abdul-Majid. Let us wait until that is over before we start discussing wedding plans.'

'Highness, that is precisely what I wish to discuss with you.'

'Then we will discuss the matter in private,' Kadar snapped, summoning his groom. 'Let us leave these good fellows to tend to the horses while we engage in horse-trading of a different kind.' He wanted to bathe and to change out of his riding clothes, but the thought of Abdul-Majid waiting and anxiously pacing made him determined to conclude their business sooner rather than later, and so he led the way straight to his private dining salon.

The room had been favoured for confidential meetings by many princes of Murimon, since it contained no windows, being lit through the glass of a domed cupola. All four walls were covered from floor to ceiling in heavily glazed tiles whose garish colours and macabre design Kadar had always found unconducive to digestion, but which meant the walls themselves were too thick for conversation to penetrate any of the neighbouring chambers.

An elaborate breakfast was set out on the long marble table, where a small mountain of carved fruit formed the centre piece, surrounded by a selection of sweet and savoury pastries, three sherbets, a stack of freshly baked flatbreads, cheeses, honey, olives and a large dish of tomatoes sprinkled with mint. There was enough food on the groaning table to feed twenty men, far less two, but his predecessors' insistence on abundance in all things was clearly deeply ingrained in palace life. The only thing which prevented Kadar from putting a stop to this wasteful excess was the knowledge that the copious leftovers were taken home by his kitchen staff to feed their families.

Abdul-Majid made an elaborate show of dismissing the servants and securing the doors. Kadar washed his hands, then helped himself to his favourite dish of *hunayua*, a porridge made of ground dates, butter and semolina flavoured with cardamom, while his adviser took a frugal plate of flatbread and tomatoes.

'As I mentioned, Highness, the mourning period for your much-lamented brother is now officially over.'

'I am aware. You wish to discuss the formalities of my coronation. Proceed.' Kadar finished his porridge and ate a slice of partridge which had been marinated in pomegranate molasses before being grilled on an open fire. It was delicious and he ate with relish, ravenous after his morning exercise, listening with half an ear as his adviser outlined the interminable protocols, rituals and formalities which had to be observed.

'I might add, Highness,' his adviser concluded, 'that this woman—your new court astronomer— her presence here is… The timing is most unfortunate and will need to be handled sensitively lest we upset the court's traditionalist sensibilities.'

Did he mean the court or was he actually referring to his own ingrained conservatism? Was he making some subtle comment on the events of the past? Or were the memories that Constance had stirred up skewing Kadar's own perspective? Which brought him back to the point of the discussion. 'You will treat our court astronomer with all the deference and respect you would give were she a man. I require you to set an example to the council, the court and the people. Do I make myself clear?'

'Highness. Very clear.'

'Was there anything else relating to the coronation you wish to discuss?'

'Only one, Sire. Your council wish me to propose that we combine the coronation ceremony with your wedding.'

'Categorically no!' The forceful negative was uttered instinctively before Kadar could even consider the question.

'Highness, the people have been most eager to welcome a new royal princess to Murimon, and with it the promise of a new chapter in the history of this most august royal family.' Abdul-Majid continued nervously. 'The council believe that by combining the two ceremonies as your most revered brother did, the reminder of the past, the continuity...'

'Out of the question!' Kadar eyed the man across the table incredulously. 'You cannot seriously imagine that I would wish to be reminded of that day, any more than you?'

Abdul-Majid blanched. 'The eventual outcome was not what any of us hoped for,' he said, 'but now is not a time to dwell on the past, Highness.'

But the past was all Kadar could dwell on when dealing with this man who had placed power and politics above the happiness of his own flesh and blood. Had the *outcome*, as he referred to it, been different, then they would not be sitting here now. But they were, and Abdul-Majid was right about one thing. It was time to move on.

'What you suggest is impossible,' Kadar said in more measured tones, 'and it is not what I agreed with the Princess of Nessarah's father. The marriage will take place after the coronation.' A good deal after, if he had his way. 'I require time to grow accustomed to my new role as prince. Time for the people to grow accustomed to me.' *Time to reconcile myself to this marriage.* 'Time to consider my plans for Murimon.'

'Plans, Highness?'

'The time has come for Murimon to enter the modern world. Though I hesitate to sound critical of my brother, he was hardly the most forward-thinking of rulers.'

Kadar managed a very small smile, but Abdul-Majid simply tugged at his beard. The man would resist the turning of the tide, if he could. With a sigh of exasperation aimed mostly at himself, Kadar got to his feet. His hair was full of salt and his clothes smelt of horse and Abdul-Majid looked as sick as one. 'The Nessarah dowry is a very substantial sum of money. We must invest it wisely. When they are complete I will reveal my plans to the council. I will expect your full support when I do so.'

Without waiting for another beard-tugging reply, Kadar left in search of his bath.

Bathed and changed into a beautiful silk robe with a wide skirt, tied at the waist with a broad sash rather like a dressing gown, Constance gazed out of the window at the fountain playing in her courtyard, trying to compose a letter to her mother in her head.

Dearest Mama,
No doubt you will be greatly surprised to receive this letter in my hand, given that you will most likely have heard by now of my demise.

No, that wouldn't do at all. Would her mother see the letter bearing her daughter's distinctive hand and think it had been sent *before* her supposed death? What if she was then too upset even to break the seal? The letter could lie unopened for weeks or months, and Mama would not know the glad tidings it contained. Perhaps she should ask Kadar to write a covering note explaining the situation, something which Mama would read first. Or perhaps she should ask the Consul General in Egypt to write first on her behalf, have her re-birth announced through the same official channels as her death, leaving Constance to tell her mother all about Murimon.

Dearest Mama,
Now that you are aware that I survived
the shipwreck, I want to reassure you that
I am in good health and am being very
well cared for in the palace of an Arabian
prince.

Absolutely not! Mama would imagine her daughter forming one of a small army of concubines. That wasn't right. A bevy of concubines? A cavalcade of concubines? No, no, it was a harem, of course. Constance chuckled. She could not imagine that Kadar would have a harem. It was very, very easy to imagine that Kadar would know what to do in a harem, though.

Unlike her! Today was the first time she had been kissed properly. The memory of it made her shiver. Such a brief touch of his lips to hers, did it count as a real kiss? It had certainly been enough to make her want more. She closed her eyes, trying to imagine what more might be like. The pressure of his lips firmer, more insistent. The touch of his tongue? Another delightful shiver. And those long fingers of his running down her back or—yes—cupping her breast. Without any stays, with only this fine layer of silk between them, her nipples would harden at his touch. The tingle would spread, making her hot, her body ache for more. He would trail his fingers down her stomach, releasing more tingles, butterflies, heat. And then further down…

Constance's eyes flew open. It was broad daylight. What on earth was she thinking! She leaned against the glass windowpane to cool her burning cheeks, and it immediately steamed up. Retying the sash of her robe, she took herself out to the courtyard and splashed water from the fountain over her face. It dripped down from her hair, onto her chest. She half-expected it to sizzle.

'I suppose that is one way of indulging this— this lust without compromising my reputation,' she muttered, sitting down on the edge of the fountain. 'My thoughts, impure or otherwise, are my own for the time being, as is my body.'

For the time being. Another shiver ran down

her spine, but it was not in the least pleasurable. She didn't want to give her body to this faceless man she was to marry.

'Oh, let's face it, Constance, you don't want to marry him at all.'

She kicked off her kid slippers and dipped her toes into the fountain. The courtyard was shaded from the direct heat of the afternoon sun though it was still very warm, a lovely salty heat that made her skin tingle. She closed her eyes, lifting her face to the sky. Scarlet and gold points of light danced behind her lids.

Dearest Mama,
I am in a seaside desert kingdom in a fantastical palace, the guest of the most devastatingly attractive and quite fascinating man who rather astonishingly seems to find me attractive too and, even more astonishingly, seems to be interested in what I have to say.

I am very well, Mama, and finally able to think clearly. Though it pains me to say this, I believe you blackmailed me into this marriage. I do not mean that you lied, precisely, when you said you thought I would be happy, but you chose not to listen to me. I have told you countless times that I have no wish to be married. I do not wish to be the property of another man—not even a rich man.

Because here is the nub of the problem, Mama. Mr Edgbaston's money is his, not mine. Just as the money he gave Papa is his, not yours. I doubt he will have used it to pay the mortgage or even many of the bills. My sacrifice will change nothing for you, and I fear it will make me very unhappy.

Despite what you said to me, I believe we could have managed. We would not have starved. I am even willing to wager that Papa would have found a way to prevent you from having to go a-begging to your family. He does not love you but he needs you, because you are the only one, save himself, who believes in his pipe dreams.

Here I am, paying for those dreams, and it occurs to me that if I marry Mr Edgbaston I will be expected to go on paying—or to persuade my husband to go on paying.

I don't want to do it. I don't want to marry Mr Edgbaston. I don't want to marry any man.

In this beautiful Arabian kingdom I am free. I know it is an illusion, but it has given me a taste of what might be. What could be if I set my mind to it. I thought I had no resources to fall back on, but I underestimated myself. I have no idea what that means—before you ask.

I would love to remain here as court astronomer—yes, I omitted to tell you that astonishing fact—but I know I can't. One thing I do have is time. I will apply my mind not, as you suggested, to how best to make myself into an amenable wife, but how to avoid being any sort of wife. How to be free.

Constance heaved a deep, heartfelt sigh. It was the truth, but she could not possibly commit it to paper. She felt considerably better for having thought it, however. She lifted her feet from the fountain, setting them down on the tiles. Within seconds they were already drying in the heat. Mama would not want to know her daughter's real thoughts. If Mama had been interested in the truth, she would not have waved Constance off on the boat. All that Mama would want to know was that her daughter was safely married. Constance would ask Kadar to write his addendum to the Consul General. She would save her own missive until she was married to Mr Edgbaston and could truthfully tell her mother what she wanted to hear.

It was very late. Kadar pushed aside his papers, rubbing his neck and shoulders, stiff from poring over documents. Soon, he would reveal his plans to his council and to his people. Abdul-Majid had been strangely hesitant, and though Kadar knew it would be beneficial to have the chief adviser on his side, he was reluctant to share these most precious and private aspirations before he was fully prepared.

These last few days, the past had been creeping up on him at odd moments. The constant talk of his impending coronation could not but remind him of the day that Butrus took the throne. Abdul-Majid's outrageous suggestion of combining wedding and coronation—Kadar shuddered. A different bride, but in a horrible twist of fate, once more his brother's choice.

Though this time there was no question of love. He dropped his head onto his hands. Was his chief adviser twisting the knife? But why would he do that? Perhaps it was as simple as he claimed, that re-enacting the past was the best way to reassure his people and make them warm to him.

Kadar rubbed his brow, looking down at the

scatter of papers and notebooks. His plans. If Butrus was still alive, they would be happier, his people, but they would not be prosperous. This kingdom would slide into a slow decline.

'No,' Kadar said aloud. 'The time has come for change.'

And long past time for him to set this complex task aside and seek the solace of his bed, but he knew there was no prospect of sleep. The miniature gold clock on his desk informed him that it was past two in the morning. Kadar turned the clockwork key of his orrery and watched the planets start their mechanical orbit. Three days had passed since he and Constance had ridden out. It was now a full week since she had arrived at the palace. He had been deliberately avoiding her. He knew that all eyes in the palace were trained on him. He knew that too much time spent with her, even as his court astronomer, would be noted and discussed and analysed. He had avoided the court when he was growing up here, but he knew all too well how it operated.

Was Abdul-Majid the only one who knew the real reason for his departure? Butrus, he was absolutely certain, had been ignorant. The orrery slowed, planet by planet, until Jupiter ground to a halt with a jerky click. *Georgium Sidus* was not represented on this model, which had been made before Herschel discovered the new planet. Uranus, as Constance preferred to call it. After the goddess of astronomy.

The gold clock struck three. His goddess of astronomy in residence would have finished surveying the stars for the night, leaving the telescope free. At this moment, Kadar could think of nothing more pleasurable than to spend the remainder of night under the stars with her. To enjoy the charms and allure of a heavenly body that was certainly not celestial in nature. He allowed himself to dwell on this very pleasurable image for a few moments.

Pleasurable though also very frustrating. Some night air and a little stargazing would put him to rights. Kadar got to his feet wearily, and headed for the solitude of his roof terrace.

Constance had come up to the terrace at nightfall, and had spent several long hours painstakingly mapping a small region of the southern sky. When her eyes became too tired to observe any more, she had lain down on the stack of cushions by the telescope, meaning only to do so for a moment before retiring to her bedchamber. She awoke with a start just in time to see Kadar turning away.

Sitting up hastily, adjusting the gaping neck

of her dressing gown, under which she had donned only a flimsy cotton shift, Constance called his name. 'Were you wishing to use the telescope?'

He stopped some feet away. 'I thought you would be in bed.'

'I meant to be. I fell asleep. If you wish to be alone…'

'No.' He took a couple of hesitant steps towards her. 'I'm glad to find you here.'

'And I am glad of the company since I spend the greater part of my day alone.'

'Are you lonely? Would you like me to arrange for you to have some female companionship? A wife of one of the council members, perhaps? I'm afraid that none of them will be able to speak English, but…'

'I'm not lonely,' Constance said, meaning it. 'I have your beautiful mare to ride along the beach during the day, and your wonderful telescope to transport me to the stars at night.'

'You have not yet resorted to talking to yourself then?'

She chuckled. 'No, but I have got into the habit of talking to the telescope. "We're going to see if we can find Perseus tonight." That kind of thing.'

'And did you? See Perseus tonight, that is?'

'No, he is a fickle hero and prefers the winter sky.'

'I have always thought him a rather cowardly hero,' Kadar said, sinking onto the cushions beside her. 'He is said to have slain Medusa in her sleep.'

'And then he cut off her head and used it to turn Cetus to stone, when he probably had a perfectly good sword he could have used. You are quite right. Not a noble hero at all.'

She sensed, rather than saw his smile. 'Algol, the star which forms Medusa's head in Perseus, is known in our language as the head of the demon, sometimes the ghoul. What were you looking at tonight, if not our Greek coward?'

'Scorpius and Sagittarius.' It was very dark up here on the terrace. She could see only shadows of Kadar's face. The gleam of his teeth, the glint of his eyes. His hair looked more tousled than usual. She could feel the heat of his body, shoulder to arm, thigh to foot, beside her on the cushions. He was wearing his preferred informal robes, a tunic and trousers, in some soft cotton material. 'You're up very late. Could you not sleep?'

'I was working.'

'On your plans for the kingdom?'

'Yes. They are almost ready to be revealed to my council. Would you like to see them?'

'You know I would.'

'Soon, then. But first, I must show you my library. I should have done so before now.'

She had tried very hard not to miss him these last three days, but she had failed miserably. His presence filled the palace. When she was alone here on the roof terrace, or when she mounted her horse at the stables, she had the sense that she had only just missed encountering him. It felt as if he had recently vacated every room she entered. The reality of him, the flesh and blood of him sitting beside her on the cushions was so much more than her imagination had been able to conjure. Her skin felt as if it was straining, reaching towards him. 'The telescope is still aligned,' Constance said a little desperately, trying to distract herself, 'if you would like to make some observations of your own?'

'I'd much prefer you to show me what you've been looking at.'

This was one of the many things she had allowed herself to imagine. Constance wasn't sure she'd be able to cope with the reality. 'You'll have to lie back.'

'I'll get some more cushions.'

A very sensible thing to do. She should have

thought of it, she chided herself as Kadar collected several from under the awning, setting them out about a foot from hers, before lying down next to her. She followed his lead, awkwardly arranging the full skirts of her robe around her. She had kicked off her slippers, as usual. It didn't matter, he couldn't see her bare feet in this light.

'I'll give you a moment for your eyes to adjust to the darkness,' she said, when what she actually wanted was a moment to adjust to the intimacy of having Kadar lying full length beside her. The night air was soft, heavy with diffused heat. The ferns in their terracotta pots gave off an odd scent, not mint or pine or coconut, but a mixture of all three, with something else she could not define mingling in there too. Kadar's soap smelled of coconut. His clothes smelled of lemon. And none of this was helping!

The stars, Constance reminded herself. 'Are your eyes accustomed?' She risked a glance at Kadar, and found his eyes on her. 'You're supposed to be looking at heavenly bodies.'

'I am,' he said softly. Then he gave himself a little shake and broke eye contact. 'I'm ready.'

'Scorpius and Sagittarius,' Constance said firmly. 'Scorpius first. You can see his claw pointing north there, and then the curve of his sting there. And there,' she said, pointing, 'there is Antares. Tonight, through the telescope, it was a very vivid red, a beating heart right at the centre of the scorpion.'

'Antares—Equal to Mars,' Kadar said, 'from the Greek, they say, but I prefer to think that it is named after Antar, the Arab warrior.'

'Another warrior. The stars are a bloodthirsty lot, but so very beautiful,' Constance said with a happy sigh. 'Look at the Milky Way tonight, it is quite viscous, like a huge ribbon of spilt cream sprinkled with diamonds stretching right across Scorpius and Sagittarius.' She paused for a moment to drink in the sheer beauty. 'It never fails to astonish me. Here we are, thinking that our lives are so very important, that all our cares and worries are the only cares and worries that matter, and then you look at all this, and nothing matters.'

She waved her arm in the direction of the Milky Way. 'I mean look at it, Kadar, just look. Sagittarius is positively teeming with clusters of stars we don't even have a number for, never mind a name. Those patches you can see, like mist—no, not mist, shimmering silver clouds, those are new stars forming.'

Constance rolled onto her side, anxious to see whether he shared her sense of wonder. 'Think of it,' she said fervently. 'Brand new stars forming right up there, an unimaginable distance away, and yet it is happening right before our very eyes. Is it not magical?'

'Magical,' Kadar said, turning towards her. 'And for all we know,' he said, leaning closer, 'there could be still more magic happening up there. Things we can't guess at. Who knows, there may even be other people on other stars looking up at us.'

'Do you think so? What would they see?'

'A court astronomer who can turn science into magic. Her hair,' Kadar said, pushing it gently from her face, 'is as wild and untrammelled as her soul, when she forgets herself. When she smiles, it is like lifting the veil which covers her true self.'

He smoothed his hand down her hair, her shoulder, her arm, under the wide sleeve of her robe. Skin on skin. A soft, rhythmic stroking up and down that tingled along her whole body, making her shimmer like the Milky Way high above them. 'If they looked very closely they would see that she has a way, this court astronomer,' Kadar continued softly, 'of making a prince forget his regal duties, and remember only that he is a man.'

Somehow they were close enough for her

knees to brush his legs, for her feet to brush his ankles. 'She does not mean to,' Constance said, surrendering to the need to touch him, her fingers tangling in his silky hair. 'Though it is the same for her. Every day she tells herself, this court astronomer, that he is forbidden, this prince.'

'And every day, so too does the prince. She is forbidden, he tells himself. But it only makes him want her more. Though he will never...'

'And she will never...' Constance whispered.

'Never,' Kadar said softly, as his lips claimed hers.

Kissing Constance was like kissing the stars. Dazzling, fiery, she blinded him to everything but his desire. Her lips were so soft, she tasted so sweet, he could swear her scent was distilled essence of moonlight. He had dreamt of this kiss, he had wanted this kiss, longed for this kiss, since that first gentle touch of her lips on the beach three days ago. Her mouth opening to his, her kiss both tentative and bold, a combination that made his pulses race and his blood heat. He rolled her onto her back, running his fingers through her hair. How could curls be so silky? He kissed her eyelids, the line of her jaw, her throat, but the allure of her mouth could not be resisted. Her hands were in his hair, on his neck, on his shoulders. Her breath was coming in soft little gasps. When his lips claimed hers again, it was she who deepened the kiss, her tongue touching his, making his heart skip a beat, his pulse roar.

She lay on the cushions, her hair spread out like a wild halo. Her breasts rose and fell, rose and fell, beneath the filmy silk of her robe. He kissed her again, and she moaned, and his already stiff member throbbed. Her hands fluttered over his shoulders, his chest. He kissed her throat, and then the hollow at the base. And then her mouth again, because he could not get enough of her mouth.

He ran his hand down her side to the dip of her waist, the flare of her hip. 'Captivating Constance,' he whispered, kissing the tender skin just behind her ear.

'Captivated,' she said, rubbing her cheek against the stubble of his beard. 'Captivated Constance,' she said, 'quite utterly captivated.'

Their kisses became passionate. He stopped thinking, desire taking hold of him, breaking the iron bands of control which had been squeezing the life out of his body for days, weeks, months. It was such a relief, such a wild relief, just to be two bodies, to revel in the melding of flesh, to allow the simmering need which had been there since Constance first walked into the Royal Saloon to boil over, to envelop them both. He inhaled her kisses, he devoured her kisses, falling half on top of her, his leg between hers, groaning as she arched closer.

Her robe had come undone. She was covered only by a filmy night garment, revealing the sweet swell of her breasts, the peaks of her nipples. Breast warm and heavy in his hand, nipple a hard bud, and Constance, eyes wide, suddenly still as he touched her. He lowered his head to take her nipple in his mouth through the sheer fabric. She sighed, a sound of pure pleasure that made his groin tighten. He sucked. She whimpered. And then she sighed. A very different sound. Her hand on his shoulder. A tiny shake of the head, and Kadar finally came to his senses.

He sat up, thankful that his tunic more or less covered his modesty. Constance lay perfectly still, gazing up not at him, but at the stars. 'Will they be shocked by our wanton behaviour, those people looking up at us?' Before he could answer, she sat up, pushing her hair over her shoulder. 'No,' she said firmly. '"Look at that sky," they will say. "Look at those stars. Is it any wonder that such a thing happened?" I don't think they will be at all surprised. It was bound to happen.

It may even be a good thing that it did, because now we will stop wondering.'

Kadar, shifting on the ground in an unsuccessful attempt to get comfortable, was forced to laugh. 'Very true. I can now stop asking myself whether your kisses can possibly be as delightful and arousing as I have imagined them. The problem is I will now move on to asking myself whether making love to you would be as delightful and arousing as I am very sure it would prove to be. I would imagine,' he added hurriedly.

'Oh.'

'I'm sorry. I should not have...'

'No. Now I know what it's like for you, to be on the listening end of my raw thoughts. I'm just surprised that you—you normally weigh every word before you utter a sentence.'

'I'm not exactly thinking straight, Constance.' Kadar groaned. 'I wasn't thinking at all.'

'Nor was I, and it was rather refreshing. I'm tired of thinking. It changes nothing. Must we really spend the rest of the night berating ourselves for one lapse in judgement, one moment of weakness?' she asked wistfully.

She was right. One moment of weakness, that was all it was. Kadar helped her to her feet, smoothing down her hair. 'One kiss, which only the stars witnessed. I think we can forgive ourselves that.'

'Provided our friends up there don't tell,' Constance said. 'You don't really think we've made it worse, do you? You were teasing, weren't you, when you said that now you would think…'

'I was teasing,' he lied. 'It was—it was cathartic.'

'Cathartic,' Constance repeated, with a faint smile. 'I earnestly hope you're right.'

Chapter Six

Constance would never have found the entrance to the souk by herself. It was tucked away at the end of one of the narrow streets which zigzagged down to the port, an innocuous-looking arch hewn into the rock face. Yasamin, the wife of one of Kadar's advisers, the same woman who had selected Constance's clothes, urged her forward with another shy smile. She had smiled coyly when Constance had somewhat ineptly gesticulated her thanks for the outfits, and now Constance was beginning to regret that she had not made more of an effort to learn the language. She resolved to bring the matter up with Kadar when she saw him later, in the library. Perhaps there was a book there she could borrow to help her learn, though if it was written in Arabic, she couldn't imagine it would be of much use.

Come, Yasamin indicated, and Constance followed, stepping into a world she could not have imagined would exist beyond that simple stone arch. The souk was hewn into the mountain. A cavernous warren which was obviously formed from natural caves, it was lit by a series of oil lamps hanging from the simple vaulted ceiling which cast dancing shadows on the walls. Underfoot, the cobblestones formed a slightly convex but straight road, with individual shops cut into the rock on either side.

The air was cool but quite dry. The musty smell of the rock was overlaid with that difficult-to-capture smell of new fabric, oily wool and leather which momentarily took Constance straight back to London, to the linen drapers at Bedford House. There were linens for sale here too, from the plain to the exotic, set out in alluring heaps of scarlet and emerald, emblazoned with beading or bright embroidery. Heavy damasks were draped in the opening of one shop. Yet another was a mercer, displaying cards of thread in a rainbow of colours, wheels of satin and velvet ribbons, buttons of horn and of wood and of brass and silver. One shop was devoted to needles and hooks and some very complicated fastenings, while still another specialised in every conceivable kind of basket, from raffia bowls to cane linen chests and a huge lidded container, rather like a Roman amphora, that looked as if it just might house a genie.

Yasamin was very patient and more than happy to allow Constance to drink her fill at every little shop, encouraging her to touch, to marvel, clearly delighted by Constance's miming of her pleasure. Finally though, at the furthest end of the souk, they came to the silk merchants, and to business. There were several shops, but Constance was drawn to the smallest, where a very old man sat with a flexibility which belied his years, cross-legged on a silk rug in front of his wares. The little cave was lined with wooden shelves. The silks were organised in columns of colours, the deepest shades on the bottom shelves, rising to the lightest at the very top. Mahogany became garnet, segued to vermilion, became scarlet then cherry then rose. There were forest-greens and moss-greens and emerald-greens, sage and mint and pistachio-green. There were more shades of blue than Constance could describe. There were gold and yellow silks, pink and orange silks, there were silks the shades of desert sands and silks the hues of every sky she had ever seen. There were sea-coloured silks and storm-coloured silks, there was chiffon and crepe and georgette and gauze, and silks to which Constance could put no name at all.

Dragging her eyes away from this galaxy of the fabric world, Constance made her formal greeting, aware of Yasamin's dismay, waving her at the other vendors, obviously eager that she make a more informed choice, but Constance had taken an immediate and probably irrational liking to this shop and this wizened tailor. He reminded her of her maternal grandfather, not so much in his appearance but in his expression, his kind eyes and gentle smile.

She touched Yasamin's arm, trying to reassure her, and the old man, getting lithely to his feet, did the same. Yasamin put her hand to her heart, then touched the old man's chest, and Constance finally realised that she had picked the shop belonging to Yasamin's grandfather—or another close relative, at any rate. 'It's fine,' she said, hoping her expression would convey a little of her meaning, 'I will tell Prince Kadar this was my choice, I will tell him that you showed no bias.' The old man smiled and nodded and more arms were patted. Then a woman appeared from behind a curtain bearing a salver with glasses of mint tea, and the greetings and the patting and nodding and smiling began again. By the time she sank onto the carpet to take her tea, Constance's smile was somewhat fixed.

She had allowed her imagination to run wild

in her design for the court astronomer's coronation robes, carried away with the notion of imbu-
ing the outfit with some of the magic of the stars.
Though she had brought a drawing depicting this,
she had also brought something more prosaic,
and it was this which she handed over. Though
Yasamin and her grandmother seemed to approve
however, the old man did not, and pointed at the
other scroll.

Expecting gales of laughter to greet her design,
Constance was astonished when the man clapped
his hands and leapt to his feet. With an energy
which was quite exhausting, he began to pull bolt
after bolt of silk from the shelves, throwing them
at his wife and his granddaughter with orders to
lay them out on the carpet, then snatching them
up again and setting them out in a different way.
Several times he stopped to puzzle over Constance's design, took some bales away, replaced
them with others. She stood, quite bewildered,
watching this flurry of activity, but when it was
done, she was utterly entranced by the result.

Behind the curtain, Yasamin and her grandmother took over the business of measuring.
Then there was another glass of mint tea, another round of exaggerated gestures of thanks,
and it was over. The court astronomer's coronation robes were duly commissioned.

* * *

The business of the day had left her little time to dwell on what had happened out on the terrace under the stars last night. Now, in the full heat of the day when everyone but the most foolhardy retired out of the sun, Constance sat in the shade watching the tinkling fountain, and examined her conscience.

Last night, she had lain awake for a long time, trying to summon up the guilt she ought to be feeling, but she had failed signally. It was not the fact that her intended husband would never know that she had kissed Kadar, it was that she simply couldn't bring herself to believe that she intended to take the man as a husband. Though her marriage was, in a manner of speaking, looming closer with every passing day, paradoxically, every day that passed made it seem like a more and more remote event.

Kadar was unique. The time she was spending here in his kingdom with him was a unique experience, but it had a defined ending, whether she sailed for India, England or some other land where she could melt anonymously into the background. Kadar was no threat to her freedom. Quite the contrary in fact, for it was his appointing her court astronomer which had given her a taste of what true freedom could be like.

So it was partly due to him that she was edging ever more closely towards a decision not to go through with this marriage.

Definitely nothing to do with his kisses. No, she didn't feel guilty about those kisses. Though there could be no question of her enjoying any more of them. Kadar must reserve his kisses for the wife he did not want but was determined to take. Duty and honour were his motives for marrying the woman his brother had chosen. Though he hadn't said it outright, he required an heir, the future prince which his poor dead sister-in-law had been unable to provide.

Constance pursed her lips, frowning deeply over the memory of that conversation. There had been something odd about it. Kadar had been— Yes, she remembered now. She had thought him turned to ice. Was it his brother's lack of an heir, the missing piece in the family tree which had changed Kadar's life for ever? That certainly made most sense, but it did not explain Kadar's reaction when she had asked him, quite naturally, if he had known his brother's wife.

'Oh, for goodness' sake, Constance, it is probably quite simply a case that they disliked each other.' Yes, she thought, nodding slowly to herself. That would explain it. Given how *unalike* he and Prince Butrus had been, to use Kadar's own word, it was very unlikely that their taste in women would coincide. Which also explained Kadar's animosity to the Princess Tahira. He really did seem very set against her. Given this much clearer picture, it made it even odder that he was also very set upon making her his wife.

It was late afternoon when Kadar had a servant bring Constance to his library. She was dressed in pantaloons and a tunic in matching mint green sprigged with darker green-and-lemon flowers, with a dark green half dress over the top and a pair of silk slippers on her feet. Her hair, burnished by the sun, had streaks of colour in it that made her think of autumn leaves. Her skin, which Mama would say was tanned beyond repair, Constance thought rather glowed with health. She still thought she looked like a cross between a concubine and a milkmaid, but it was a combination she rather liked.

The room to which the servant delivered her was not in the main body of the palace, but in one of the terraced wings. The usual tiled-and-marbled corridor led to the usual style of arched wooden door in line with the rest of the palace, but the room revealed when this was flung open was wholly different. Kadar's library was completely lined with glass-fronted bookcases on all save one wall, where a set of tall windows looked out onto the great piazza with its sentry guard of palm trees which formed the main entrance to the palace. In front of this, there was a small reading table and two comfortable-looking and rather battered wing-back chairs. Another set of low bookcases set back-to-back sat in the middle of the room, the surfaces stacked with books. There were several crates placed seemingly randomly, some opened and spilling books, others still sealed.

Kadar was sitting behind an enormous mahogany desk at the far end of the room, but he dropped his pen and got to his feet when she was announced. His tunic and trousers were charcoal-grey silk, the edges worked with elaborate black embroidery. He looked very much the Prince today. Haughty. Remote. His mouth set, his eyes dark, the faint trace of a frown making him even more forbidding.

'I'm afraid state business took up a great deal more of my time than I anticipated,' he said by way of greeting.

'If you're too busy then I can see your library another time, Kadar,' Constance said, dropping into a half curtsy. It was a struggle not to call him Your Highness.

'No.' He smoothed his hand over his face, as if he were trying to erase his cares, and managed a faint smile. 'My business did not only concern Murimon. I had a visit from a man who served with Napoleon in Egypt. He had sailed all the way down the Red Sea in search of me. Flattering, but frustrating for us both, since the problem he has is complex, and while extremely interesting, unfortunately I don't have the time to advise him.'

'You miss your old life, don't you?'

Kadar shrugged. 'It is easier when I am not confronted with it. It is looking likely, incidentally, that Napoleon and your Duke of Wellington will do battle very soon. It is to be hoped that the outcome is definitive. Europe will benefit from an extended peace.'

'And your visitor today, is he in the vanguard of wishing to be one of those beneficiaries?' Constance hazarded.

She was rewarded with a proper smile and a look of approval. 'You are both perceptive and correct. But enough of my travails. Please, sit down,' Kadar said, ushering her to one of the wing chairs at the window. 'Tell me, did you enjoy your visit to the souk?'

'Oh, it was wonderful. I ordered my robes from Yasamin's grandfather. I think she was worried that the other shop owners would accuse her of exploiting her connections, for I did not even look at their shops, but I just— You will think this silly, but her grandfather reminded me of my own grandfather. My mother's father that is, who first taught me to look through a telescope when I was a little girl.' She smiled wistfully. 'It was he who told me the story of Anningan, the moon god. I miss him.'

'He died?'

'About eight years ago, but I had not seen him for some time. My mother is from a very wealthy family. When she married Papa she brought with her a substantial dowry. When I was little, we were, as far as I can remember, comfortably off. But her dowry ran out, and then our visits to Grandfather's became fraught because Papa expected him—or rather expected Mama to ask him, and it became all about the money, and eventually my grandfather told Papa that he was no longer welcome, and Mama—' Constance broke off with a sigh. 'Mama chose Papa, as she always does,' she concluded wearily, 'and this is very old history.'

'Then tell me about the souk, if that is what you would prefer.'

She smiled gratefully at him, launching into an enthusiastic description of her day, recounting every detail of her visit. Kadar's questions and smiles were somewhat mechanical, his mind clearly still dwelling on his own day. It hadn't occurred to her until now just how radical a change this must be for him. 'You know,' Constance said, interrupting herself, 'you are very much to be admired.'

'Because I have not once interrupted your extremely colourful story?'

'Do you mean boring? I was only trying to distract you.'

'You think I need distracting?'

A faint lift of his brow, but it was clearly a warning. Should she swallow her words? But if she did, then who else would say them? They deserved to be said. 'It struck me only just now,' Constance said, 'that you have given up a great deal to be here. People think that being a prince is an honour, which it is of course, but that doesn't necessarily mean it's an honour you would have chosen.'

She waited, but Kadar said nothing. 'They don't appreciate you as they ought. I mean, they don't appreciate that you've been forced to give up the life you really love, to surrender a position that was highly influential, not so say extremely powerful, even if it was played out very much behind the scenes, so to speak. And now you are forced to take centre stage, and not just to wield power of a very different nature, but to be seen to do so, which is something that doesn't come naturally to you, because you're not your brother. And the thing is, Kadar—the thing is—well, as I said, I think you are very, very much to be admired, and instead of feeling so—so *crushed* by not being able to help this man who called, you should be feeling proud of the fact that you've put honour and duty before what you really want and—and there,' she concluded, crossing her arms, 'that is all I wanted to say.'

Still he said nothing, though there was that tiny flicker in his right eye which she'd noticed when he talked of his brother. Was he angry? Had she been outrageously presumptuous? 'I've said too much. Should I leave?'

He shook his head. 'Constance.' Kadar got to his feet and took her hand between his. 'I am not often at a loss for words. It is most reassuring to know that I am…that my struggle to come to terms with the changes in my life is not without justification. Thank you for recognizing that.'

He kissed her palm. His mouth lingered for a few seconds, his lips warm on her skin. It was a mere nothing of a kiss, yet it snatched her breath away. Their eyes held for a moment. And then he released her and sat back down again, and Constance, foolishly clasping her hand to her breast, was once more at a loss as to what was going on behind that enigmatic expression of his.

'Your library is quite wonderful,' she said, desperate to prevent the silence from becoming strained. 'Not at all what I expected and so very different to every other room and salon in this palace.'

'The furniture as well as the books are mine. I had them shipped from Naples. As you can see, I have not yet finished unpacking them.'

'Is there a catalogue? I could help...'

'Naturally, there is a catalogue. I have many thousands of books.'

'I can see that.' Constance got to her feet and began to prowl around the room. She peered through the glass cabinets at the stacked shelves of books, folio, octavo and quarto, most bound, some in their raw state. Kadar's interests seemed to be as diverse as the languages in which he was clearly fluent, though there were a preponderance of legal tomes, including Napoleon's *Code Civil* in French and Justinian's *Corpus Juris Civilis*. On the next shelf, which contained maps, she found Saxton's *Atlas of England and Wales* and Seller's *Atlas Maritimus*, and exclaimed in surprise. 'Oh, these are exactly like the editions which my father owned. The Saxton is very old and rare, I think.'

Kadar joined her, taking the fragile book from the shelf and setting it down with care on one of the reading tables. 'Sixteenth century.'

Constance turned the pages reverently, breathing in that familiar smell of very old parchment and worn leather binding. 'Yes, it looks like the same edition.'

'I believe you said your father sold his copy?'

'Did I?'

'"We did have a huge library once, at Montgomery House, but Papa sold all the books. Some of them were very valuable. So now the library is home to a collection of cobwebs." Which I teased you about by suggesting you had meticulously catalogued them.'

'Good grief, do you remember everything in such detail?' Constance asked, awed.

Kadar shrugged.

'And books too, do you memorise those when you read them?'

'Not everything. Certain things stick in my mind. You haven't answered my question.'

'You answered it for me.'

'Constance, it is not like you to be obtuse.'

She flushed, still slowly turning the pages of the atlas. 'My father is one of those men who believe that the latest hare-brained scheme in which he invests will finally be the one which makes his fortune. Sadly, his eternal optimism has yet to be rewarded.'

'That is why you are en route to India? To provide your father with more funds, to permit him to continue this—this financial mania of his?'

Constance closed the atlas carefully. 'I've never considered it a mania, but Mama has always said he can't help himself.' Her lip curled slightly. 'He certainly seems incapable of listening to reason when he is in the grip of it.' She picked up the atlas, slotting it back into its place on the shelf, and then began to walk along the length of the bookcases, gazing sightlessly at the volumes. 'Whatever one calls it, the result is that he has sold everything of value that can be sold, he's deep in debt and the estates which have been in the Montgomery family for generations have been mortgaged to the hilt. Frankly, I believe a spell in a debtor's prison might be the only thing to bring him to his senses, but his title protects him from that fate which is probably just as well, because Mama would see it as her duty to go with him. Mama thinks—'

Constance broke off to clear her throat. 'My mother is convinced that the funds which my—my betrothal has provided will be the saving of him. Enough to pay off the mortgage on the estate and all his debts and provide them with a comfortable income. But comfortable has never been sufficient for my father. I don't really think he's particularly interested in being rich either. It's not the money, it is the pursuit of it which excites him.'

'And will continue to excite him while he has money to fuel his mania,' Kadar said.

'Yes,' Constance said in a small voice, 'that is exactly what I fear. I knew—I knew in my heart, Kadar—that it was a mistake, but Mama begged me and begged me. And she was so— I think she truly did believe that he would turn over a new leaf as he promised. As he has promised so many times. He doesn't care who has to suffer and my mother makes it easy for my father to ignore *her* suffering. But this time there was nothing left, you see.'

'Except you.'

'Except me.'

'So that is why you agreed to this marriage. Not for your father, but for your mother?'

Constance risked a glance at him, but Kadar's expression gave nothing away. 'Yes.' She wandered over to the window to gaze out at the rows of palm trees, noticing with vague surprise the posse of guards climbing the slim trunks with practised ease to set the lanterns in their fronds.

'You must not think Mama wholly lacking in feelings for me though, it is just that she cares first and foremost and quite foolishly for my father. She really thinks that money will make him happy and that in turn will make her happy, and if one accepts that logic then one can see that she would also believe that a rich husband would make me happy too. It is nonsense of course, but when one is faced with a distraught mother and a father reminding his daughter that he has supported her for twenty-five years and that the time has come for her to—' She broke off, embarrassed by the sudden well of emotion. ''Well, there you have it.'

'Indeed,' Kadar said drily.

'You think I should have resisted.' Constance leaned her forehead against the glass pane. 'I tried. Perhaps not hard enough. I don't know. I didn't see the matter quite so clearly until after I sailed, and by then it was too late.'

'Constance…'

'I've never wanted a husband, Kadar, and do you know what the worst aspect is?' she demanded.

He shook his head.

'Acquiring a rich husband is the worst possible thing I could do, because my father has no doubt already spent my dowry. All my marriage will do is provide him with access to a further source of funds. My husband will become his banker. And where does that leave me, Kadar? I'll tell you where it leaves me—it leaves me in a prison of my own making.' Her voice quivered. She took a deep breath, refusing to give way to tears. 'There, now you know the sordid story of my betrothal, and no doubt find the whole situation as distasteful as I do.'

'It seems to me that of the three people involved, you are the only one who has behaved with integrity.'

Constance sniffed. 'Thank you, but if I had been true to myself, I would have refused. A wife has no freedom save what her husband grants her. Her body, her mind, even her children, belong to him. My mother told me that if I was an *amenable* wife, then I would never want for anything.' She laughed bitterly. 'You could not find a more amenable wife than Mama. She is the kind of wife whom people—my father included, naturally—commend for her unstinting loyalty, her unfailing affection, her many sacrifices and her determination to make light of them. I don't want to have to be that amenable.'

'You have never considered the possibility that after you are married, you may come to care for this man to whom you are betrothed?'

'How is it possible to feel affection for someone to whom one is utterly beholden? And even if one did—though I can't believe it possible—do you think a husband acquired in such a way would believe it anything other than cupboard love? Or were you thinking of true love, Kadar? Now that really would make matters worse, for it would make one not a prisoner but a slave. I would not be so foolish.'

'Have you ever been so foolish, Constance?'

'Oh, yes. I swooned over one of our grooms when I was sixteen,' she answered lightly. 'Then there was the Russian acrobat in a travelling troupe—I went to see his performance every single night. And there is a blacksmith in the village at home whose physique makes every female who sets eyes on him working the forge go quite weak at the knees.'

'You have a penchant for ineligible men,' Kadar said drily. 'That is one way of ensuring that you remain unmarried, I suppose.'

He was, embarrassingly, quite right. At least she was still running true to form. 'And you?' she said. 'Do you have a penchant for unattainable women?'

She meant it flippantly, To tease him, to deflect him from seeing any deeper into her mind, but her words made him flinch. 'Once,' Kadar replied. 'Which was more than enough. I will never make that mistake again.'

He had no idea what had prompted him to make such an admission. Constance was struck dumb. Outside, the sun had fallen, leaving the room mercifully gloomy, the light dim. Too dim, thankfully, for him to see her face. What a pitiable creature he had been back then. His toes curled inside his slippers as he remembered that doe-eyed youth, so certain that love could conquer all. How naïve he had been, how utterly lacking in worldliness. Butrus had been for ever teasing him about it, putting it down to his bookishness. Kadar shuddered. Thank the stars his brother had never guessed.

'I'm so sorry. I was merely funning, I did not mean—did not think for a moment...'

Constance's hand on his arm made him jump. He brushed her away, unable to bear her being close enough to read his thoughts. 'I am in no need of your sympathy. I do not know how we came to be discussing such a thing.' Too late, he realised it was he who had introduced the subject. 'It is quite irrelevant to either of our cases,' he continued hastily, before Constance could point this out.

He waited but she did not, as she usually did,

fill the silence. Did she sense how angry he
was that she had unwittingly opened up that old
wound? Coming home had brought it all back,
that was all. The memories—he had to find a
way of ridding himself of those memories. 'It's
late,' Kadar said gruffly. 'It must be past time
for your evening meal.'

'I'm not hungry.'

Was her voice teary? He had selfishly been
thinking only of himself, forgetting those painful
truths she had spilled out earlier. She had every
right to tears. He could be furious on her behalf,
if it would do any good. If he had any right to be
furious. Which he did not. 'You cannot stargaze
on an empty stomach. Let me have something
brought here. We can eat together.'

'It wouldn't be proper,' Constance said. 'Besides, you've probably got a thousand things to
do. I should go.'

She turned away. She was right, they should
not eat together. His meal would be set out in
great state as usual in the Royal Dining Salon,
and he did have a thousand things to do, but he
didn't want to let her go like this. 'Constance,'
he said, 'please stay. I'm trying to apologise.'

'What for?'

Kadar rolled his eyes. 'Forcing you to talk
about your father,' he equivocated. 'I gave rein

to my curiosity, even though it was clearly a painful subject.'

'You didn't,' she said, 'or at least, hardly at all. I blurted it all out, pretty much unprompted. It was embarrassing. It is I who should be apologising.'

She wasn't crying, but her voice had that brittle tone that made it clear how much of an effort she was making not to. 'Don't,' Kadar said, pulling her into his arms. 'You have nothing to be sorry for. You are the only one who has understood that the kingdom I have inherited comes at a cost to me. To those I can no longer serve, it seems I have been seduced by power, and as to those I now serve—I don't think any of them ever could understand the appeal of the life I forged for myself.'

'Have you ever tried to explain the appeal to anyone?'

Once, there had been someone. Had she really understood? He had thought so, but then he had thought them twin souls. Were his feelings so much stronger than hers? She had denied it. But she had not done as he had begged her. Kadar squeezed his eyes tight shut, as if the action would banish the memory. The past was dead, and so too was the life he had forged from its ashes. 'It is done,' he said, 'gone. What would be the point in explaining?'

Silence. Constance's face was pressed against his chest. Her hair tickled his chin, her body was warm against his, but he had no idea what she was thinking. Now he had a taste of his own medicine, for it made him uncomfortable, her silence. 'It was a long time ago, and no longer painful,' Kadar said. No lie, because it ought not to be painful, had not been painful until…

'But it must be painful,' Constance exclaimed. 'If you truly loved her, this woman. What was her name?'

'Zeinab.' It was the first time he'd said it aloud in years. It sounded so strange coming from his lips. Just thinking of her name, all those years ago, could conjure her up, but now he still couldn't recall her face. 'As I said, it was a long time ago.'

'Did she love you?' Constance persisted. 'Why wouldn't she marry you?'

'She *could* not,' he said stiffly.

'Oh.' He could see her struggling to suppress the obvious question, and felt unaccountably relieved when she succeeded, though the one she asked was not particularly welcome either. 'This woman is the reason you have never married, then?'

'It is a foolish man who does not learn from his mistakes. Now we will close the subject, if you please.'

'Of course.' Constance freed herself from his embrace. 'I think I'll go and do some work now, if you will excuse me.'

He didn't want her to go, which is why he stopped himself from asking her to stay. Nighttime was dangerous territory. Daylight was safer. 'Tomorrow, if you like, I will show you my plans for Murimon. Not the paper version, but the real locations. We can head out at dawn. Until then, Constance.'

She hesitated, then nodded. 'Until then, Kadar. Goodnight.'

After she had gone Kadar had some food brought to the library, but ate only a little fruit. Opening the window, he stepped out onto the small terrace above the piazza, drinking in the soft, warm night air. Constance had unsettled him. She was the only person who seemed to care anything for his thoughts and his feelings, the only person who saw the man and not the Prince, but her understanding, while it touched him, also disturbed him, stirring up feelings he was working hard to repress. Because they belonged to the man, and not the Prince.

What was the point in regretting what he had willingly given up? What was the point in hankering after a life that was no longer his? As much point as remembering a love that never was! He gave an exclamation of disgust. That again.

It was all this talk of marriage. It was Constance's talk of amenable wives. Her description of her mother. *The kind of wife whom people commend for her unstinting loyalty, her unfailing affection, her many sacrifices and her determination to make light of them.* Yes, he had known another woman determined to become such an amenable wife, and he was certain that her attempts to do so would have stripped her of everything that was beautiful and unique about her. Thank the stars he had not been here to witness it.

Constance had said she didn't want to be that amenable, but she knew, as he knew too, that she would have no choice. Did his Nessarah bride feel as Constance did? Kadar groaned, dropping onto the stone wall which separated his library terrace from the main piazza. He had tried to think of his marriage in the abstract, a contract which would give him the funding he needed to make Murimon into the kingdom it deserved to be, and provide his people with the dynastic stability they desired. The reality was that he found the thought of carrying out his role in providing that dynastic stability utterly distasteful. This betrothal was a purely commercial contract between a prince and a princess, between the kingdoms of Murimon and Nessarah, but the marriage would be made and endured by two people, a man and a woman. A man and a woman who felt absolutely nothing for each other. A woman who, as Constance had so rightly pointed out, had no choice. And a man determined to feel nothing. Ever again.

Kadar stifled a yawn, glancing up at the central edifice of the palace. Was Constance up there, looking at the stars? He wished he could be with her, but he did not trust himself. Last night he had been unable to resist temptation, having found her there so unexpectedly. But tonight, if he went up to that roof terrace, he would be deliberately courting it. He wanted her. She wanted him. It would be so easy to give in, to tell himself that it didn't matter, that the promise to marry was not his promise, that he could not be untrue to a woman he had not chosen until the day when he made his own personal vow. Their wedding day.

Once again, Kadar shuddered at the thought. It disturbed him that his blood heated when he thought of Constance, and yet it seemed to freeze in his veins when he tried to imagine making love to the woman who was to be his wife. Who might, at this very moment, be having the exact same thoughts about him. And as for Constance…

Kadar cursed under his breath. This was pointless. He had no right at all to interfere in her marriage, even if the thought of her enduring—no, he could not think about that. Would not. He found the very notion unbearable. Which was worrying in its own right.

Chapter Seven

Constance had decided to dress formally for this morning's outing. Acutely aware that her presence by Kadar's side would be noted, discussed, and much speculated upon by all they encountered, she was determined to do him credit as his court astronomer, and equally determined *not* to be perceived in any other, more compromising role. Her tunic was fashioned from straw-coloured cotton with a high, rounded neck. Her matching wide pantaloons were tucked into her long brown-leather riding boots, and her hair was carefully braided and tucked under a *keffiyeh* of the same cotton, held in place with a silk scarf of darker gold. It was her coat which lent this simple and demure outfit the gravitas commensurate with her office. Dark blue silk patterned with golden leaves, it fitted tightly to her waist, and was fastened with a long row of pearl buttons. Heavy gold brocade bordered the hem, the edges of the long sleeves at their widest point, the edges of the deep side pockets, and the slits formed in the side of the full skirt. It was a truly beautiful garment, surprisingly light, rich and yet austere, lending her just the touch of authority she was hoping for. One final adjustment of the headband which she was unaccustomed to wearing, and Constance was ready.

Kadar was waiting for her in the stables. He too was formally dressed. His tunic and trousers were fashioned from white silk, his cloak and headdress a deep, dark regal red. Standing as yet unnoticed in the doorway to the courtyard, Constance was reminded of her first sight of him in the Royal Saloon—was it really less than two weeks before? Latent strength had been her first impression then as now, in the set of his shoulders, in the straightness of his back, the long length of those muscled legs so clearly outlined beneath the thin silk trousers tucked into his long boots. Then he had turned, just as he did now, and her heart had skipped a beat just as it did now, and the heat of desire had taken her by surprise, just as it did now, her body responding on some visceral level to that combination of ascetic good looks, forbidding authority and the latent sensuality she now knew lay just beneath the surface. Fire, barely contained by a cool, impenetrable façade. That was what was so very appealing, Constance decided, the knowledge that there was a vulnerable man beneath that princely veneer he showed to the world. Kadar was a challenge. She would have to work very hard to remember that he was not *her* challenge, she told herself sternly. The task of bringing that restrained passion to life belonged to another woman.

In keeping with this resolution and her formal role, Constance made a low bow as Kadar approached. 'Highness, I bid you good morning.'

'Court Astronomer,' he replied, his mouth softening into a fleeting smile. 'I commend you upon your appearance.'

She blushed, and then blushed deeper for having blushed. 'I am aware— That is I thought that since we were— That because your people...'

'Constance, you have judged the occasion perfectly.'

'Oh. Thank you. I thought— Thank you. Are you sure you don't want to change your mind about this?'

'Very sure. Shall we?'

The groom appeared in response to his summons, but the animals which the man led out from the stables were not horses. 'Camels.' Constance turned to Kadar in dismay. 'Those are camels.'

'Here? In the desert? Who would have thought it possible?'

She could tell from his tone that he was teasing her, but she did not turn to see the quirk of his mouth which accompanied his remark, her eyes being fixed on the beast which now stood in front of her. It was huge, its legs with their prominent knock knees and horned toes level with the height of her shoulders. Its head, on the end of a very long neck, looked like the product of a mule and a sheep, with a revoltingly bristled muzzle, and lips which quivered over very large yellow teeth. The camel was eyeing her now with what she was certain was contempt, as if defying her to mount the ornate leather saddle with all its tasselled trappings which clung precariously to its humped back.

'It doesn't like me,' Constance said. On cue, her camel let out a sneering bray, making her jump and cough, as a gust of pungent camel breath assailed her. 'It's never going to let me on its back.'

Kadar took the reins from the groom, forcing the camel to its knees. 'It is a ship of the desert, Constance, not the ocean,' he said, smiling at her encouragingly. 'The only waves we traverse will be made of sand, not water. There is nothing to be afraid of. He is actually much more placid than that mare you've been riding, and much simpler to control, once you know the knack. Come, let me help you up and I'll show you the ropes, if you'll excuse the use of yet another naval analogy.'

She approached the animal cautiously. Though it was emitting a strange groaning noise, it seemed just as Kadar said, to be placid enough. She put a foot in the stirrup and scrambled without grace but competently enough into the saddle. Kadar handed her the long reins, instructing her on the basic techniques, and Constance settled herself.

'Ready?'

She nodded, thinking that she was, and then the camel stood up, leaving the ground very, very far beneath her. Her head swam. She gripped the reins. The camel executed several prancing backward steps. She was aware of Kadar signalling urgently to her, aware that she was slipping sideways, and just in time she remembered his instructions, righted herself, and took control. To her astonishment, the camel came to a halt and stopped braying. A few turns around the courtyard, and she was not quite at ease, but confident enough to control him. 'What do you think?' she asked, smiling smugly down at Kadar. 'Is this ship ready to set sail?'

She was rewarded with one of his smiles and his bone-melting look as he mounted his own camel, his red cloak flying out behind him. 'Into the desert, into the sunset and beyond,' he said.

'That is a most delightful idea,' Constance said wistfully.

Kadar's smile faded. 'A stupid saying. A traditional send-off, it means nothing more than safe journey. Let us go.'

They made their way directly uphill from the palace where the rough terrain of crumbling rock and narrow, zig-zagging paths clearly precluded the use of horses. With Kadar in the lead, her camel following nonchalantly behind, Constance very quickly became accustomed to the undulating sway of the saddle which was indeed rather like the swaying deck of a ship, and began to enjoy the scenery.

It was still very early, the sun only just appearing, a pale gold in the celestial blue of the sky, turning the scattering of wispy clouds assembled on the horizon a luminous pink. Ahead, Kadar informed her, were the Murimon Mountains. Looming crags of glittering grey streaked with darker-brown rocks shimmered in a bluish haze, a forbidding and seemingly impossible barrier until they rounded a sharp bend and the entrance to the mountain pass was revealed.

On they travelled at a steady pace, leaving the familiar coastline behind, until the trail began to widen, and the oasis was revealed. Coming to a halt at the head of the valley, Constance gasped in astonishment, gazing around her at the scene, which looked as if a stage backdrop had been rolled down before her eyes, so astounding was the transformation. The valley floor was perfectly flat, a huge oval space bordered by palms. At the centre, the oasis itself, and radiating out from it, neatly partitioned fields and orchards, like a huge web made entirely of shades of green. She could hear the gentle gurgle of the water as it flowed through the irrigation pipes. The air was heady with the scent of lush green and ripening fruit.

'It's like a—a mirage,' Constance said, turning to Kadar. 'I would never have believed that all this could exist, tucked away behind those mountains.'

'This is our largest oasis—it is rather unimaginatively known as the Great Oasis. And this is our biggest settlement apart from the port. It is here I plan to build the first of our schools.'

She had been so enthralled by the oasis, Constance had barely noticed the town which clung to the very edge of the seaward side of the valley, the houses rising in terraces up the foothills of the mountain, most constructed in red stone, but some more substantial ones built of the grey granite-like rock, and some painted sparkling white. 'There doesn't seem to be much spare land on which to build, unless you intend to use some of the fields,' she said.

'No, our fertile land is too precious for that. I plan to cut into the rock on the other side of the valley over there,' Kadar said, 'to build on terraces, in the same way as the town itself is constructed. Come, let us ride over, I'll show you.'

She followed him on her camel to the far side, round the perimeter of the fields, where the workers stopped to stare at them as they passed, though Kadar seemed not to notice this. 'That sounds like a very large project,' Constance said dubiously, when Kadar had finished explaining further. 'Surely there can't be sufficient children here to justify such a grand building?'

'I'm not talking about a simple village school,' he replied. 'Though I plan to build such schools in every village for children and their parents to attend. I want every one of our people to have the opportunity to learn to read and to write. But this school will be much more than that. It will be a—a gateway of learning, at the gateway to our port. Here, we will educate the scholars of the future. Here, we will plant the seeds that will make Murimon flourish.'

'The seat of learning you talked about,' Constance said, recalling their conversation on the beach a few days ago.

He beamed. 'Precisely. A destination for scholars from around the world to rival the universities of Constantinople, Cairo and even Bologna.'

She listened as Kadar warmed to his theme, talking with an enthusiasm which was at the same time infectious and concerning, for Constance couldn't help thinking that he had not considered the practicalities. 'And this is how you plan to bring the world to Murimon, this is what you meant when you said you wished to bring Murimon into the nineteenth century?' she asked, trying to keep her scepticism from her voice.

And apparently failing. 'It is a start,' Kadar said, his smile fading at her tone. 'I am perfectly aware that it will take time, and that there are many other issues to be addressed. There is the small matter of the port, for example. We must enlarge it significantly if we are to encourage trade, and we must also review our trade laws, our import and export regulations, if we are to promote Murimon over other ports in the region.'

'On that subject, at least, you are certainly extremely well placed to advise. Not,' Constance added hastily when Kadar's eyebrows snapped together in a frown, 'that you are not— That is, I did not mean— It is a great deal to take in,' she finished lamely.

'I know that my ideas are radical. I know that many will consider it a waste of time to teach girls to read and to write as well as boys.'

'Goodness, Kadar, I would be the last to think so!' Constance exclaimed. 'I find the philanthropic aspect of your plans admirable, although not without its challenges, particularly if your aspiration is to teach parents as well as children.'

'What do you mean?'

'Well, aside from the fact parents need to both work and look after their families, adults learn much more slowly than children, who take to education like a duck to water.'

'What would you suggest?' Kadar said, after a moment's silence.

'Your vision for universal education is laudable,' Constance said gently, 'but perhaps what your people really need are skills, rather than academic qualifications.'

Under the intensity of his gaze, Constance shifted in the saddle and bit her tongue. She had said more than enough and really, what did she know of such things? She was no prince.

Kadar sighed heavily. 'You are right. My ideas are sound in theory, but in practice...' He sighed again, pushing his headdress back from his face.

'I think you judge yourself very harshly,' Constance said, unable to bear his dejection. 'You told me that your people thought your brother a true prince, that he was a popular prince, but what did he do for his people in the years of his reign? You told me that he was having an expensive schooner built as a plaything, but I wonder if he ever built a single school.'

'Perhaps because there is no demand,' he replied with a very faint smile. 'Perhaps people are content with the status quo.'

'Why don't you ask them?' Constance said, indicating the fields, where the townsfolk were now openly watching them, abandoning any pretence of work.

Kadar had been facing away from the oasis. Now he turned his camel around to discover what seemed to Constance the entire town facing him, all of whom dropped immediately to their knees when their Prince faced them. 'It is

not the custom here to consult with the popu-
lace, only the council,' he said, studying the
rows of obeisant figures with seeming bemusement.

'You need your council's approval?'

'No, but it would make things much easier if
they were on my side—' Kadar broke off, staring
into the distance. 'I could pre-empt resistance by
demonstrating that my proposals have popular
support,' he said slowly. 'Though there is always
a chance, of course, that I will discover they do
not,' he added, frowning.

'Do you think in your heart that will turn out
to be the case?'

He shook his head decidedly. 'No. I know in
my heart that this is the right thing to do, and
my people will recognise that.'

Constance smiled. 'Then prove it.'

Kadar laughed. 'I will. Thank you. You are
wiser than any member of my council, Court
Astronomer.'

Heat suffused her cheeks. Seeing him transformed, knowing that she had played a small part
in the transformation, made her want to kiss him.
No, she must not think of kissing him, even if
only as a form of encouragement. 'I am glad to
be of service,' Constance said, dragging her eyes
away from his mesmerizing smile. 'Now, go and

demonstrate that you really are a different kind of prince from your brother.'

Kadar surveyed the serried rows of people, men, women and children, all still bowed, none daring to look him in the eye. *Show that you really are a different kind of prince*, Constance had said. Butrus would have ridden through them, gazing down from the height of his camel, taking this obeisance for respect, when really it was simply—what? Tradition? Fear?

Wrong, is what it was, Kadar thought. He did not want this kind of meaningless adulation. He wanted to be different. Truly different. He wanted to be the kind of prince these people deserved. Dismounting from his camel, he helped Constance to do the same. 'I want you to accompany me,' he said.

'But I can't speak the language, and you are the prince, Kadar. I—'

'I want you to accompany me,' he repeated. 'To set an example, Constance. Let them see, the women and the girls, that I practise what I preach.'

He could read her now as easily as a book. He could see her doubts flitting across her face, hear her protesting that she was no worthy example, almost as if she had spoken aloud. And he could spot the exact moment when she decided to do as he bid her, not because he demanded it but because she understood, at which point Kadar led his camel towards the throng, and ordered all of his people to rise.

Though he was accustomed to addressing groups of the most eminent men in Europe and Arabia, Kadar had never spoken to such a mixed gathering without the benefit of his usual meticulous preparation. Though his advice to diplomats and traders and politicians had affected countless lives over the years, it had been at arm's length, remote from the individuals themselves. But these people, these very people standing before him, watching him with trepidation and wide-eyed curiosity, they were a very different case. He was responsible for them. His decisions directly affected their lives. It was a humbling experience, and it was one which filled him with awe, and a fierce determination not to let them down.

His doubts fled. His nerves were vanquished. He needed no speech, no preparation. He knew, with absolute certainty, that what he must do was speak from the heart. 'People of Murimon,' Kadar said, 'I stand before you for the first time, proud to be your prince, and deeply aware of the privilege which has been conferred on me.

Though I have ascended to the throne under tragic circumstances, it is time to consign the shadow of Prince Butrus's death to the past, and to allow the dawn to rise on a new age for Murimon.'

He spoke not of what Constance had called his laudable plans. He kept to himself his more ambitious aspirations, and spoke only of what would immediately affect these people. A new school. Lessons for all who wished them. A port where the bountiful excess from this oasis could be sent out for the rest of the world to sample. 'I make no promises of wealth and fame and fortune, to you. I do not have the power to see into the future, any more than our court astronomer does,' Kadar said, nodding to Constance, who had been standing discreetly behind him. 'She can map the stars. She is proof that it is possible for anyone to reach for the stars, proof that we are grounded only by our own fears. But even a court astronomer has limitations. I do not know what the future holds, but I can promise you it will be different.'

Kadar drew breath. All eyes were upon him, but that proved nothing save that they were giving him his place as a prince. He had for the first time ever opened his heart to the scrutiny of public view. He wanted more than to be merely given his due. He wanted them to be on his side. 'I am sharing my dreams—some of my dreams—with you,' he concluded. 'But I will not impose them on you. I want you to share them. I also want to hear your dreams and aspirations. I will not be a prince who sits remotely on the throne. I will be your prince. Here. Now. Always. Listening.'

At first this was met with complete silence. Heart pounding, he waited. It started slowly. Whispers. Then murmurs. Then nods. And then applause. He resisted the urge to turn to Constance, resisted the urge to utter his relieved thanks aloud, and waited. When the applause died down, a man who was clearly the elder, came forward and invited him and the court astronomer to honour them by sharing a humble repast.

Graciously accepting, Kadar watched as the townsfolk dispersed to prepare the food, exhilaration giving way to disappointment as not a single person came forward to speak, save one, a tall, muscular man of his own age with a stern expression.

'Highness,' he said. 'I am Maarku. May I speak frankly?'

'It is what I desire above all else,' Kadar said.

Maarku smiled wryly. 'Highness, when a

prince asks a subject's opinion, it is the custom for that opinion to concur with the prince's, is it not? It is not considered wise to contradict a prince.'

'I don't want these people to pay mere lip service to my ideas,' he said. 'I want them to support them, and if they cannot, to help me improve them. Will you speak to them, encourage them to come forward?'

Maarku pursed his lips. 'Do you swear that there will be no repercussions if they tell you what you do not wish to hear?'

'I wish to hear the unvarnished truth, nothing more.'

'Then I will speak to the townspeople, Highness. Now please, bring your court astronomer and take some nourishment with us.'

Though she had not understood a single word of Kadar's speech, Constance had been struck by his very obvious conviction. There were none of his usual carefully considered sentences, no evidence of his measured tone or his cool, almost detached demeanour. The Prince Kadar who had spoken to his townsfolk that morning had been passionate, moving, emotional. It had been a revelation. He might only have been a prince for a few months, but Kadar patently loved his kingdom and his people. His desire to improve matters came from the heart and from his gut too.

Observing him now, as he sat with his usual careless grace, cross-legged on a blanket, surrounded by a group of young men so enthused that they were competing to have their voices heard, Constance felt a glow of satisfaction and admiration, and beneath it, something a little more concerning. She longed to remain here in Murimon to watch Kadar transform his kingdom. She wanted to witness his success, to see him become the radical Prince that he aspired to be. He would do it, there was no doubt about that. But she could not be part of it. And it was that, a yearning to be part of something she could never aspire to, and to mean something to a man she could never have too—yes, that was more than a little concerning.

But now was not the time for future regrets. Looking around her at her own little circle of people, not only women and their children but several elders, all smiling and gesturing and doing their best, despite the huge language barrier, to include her, added to Constance's glow of satisfaction. *We are grounded only by our own fears,* Kadar had translated for her from his speech. She had been just that, for most of her life, but no longer. Kadar's speech had been a turning point for her as well as for every single person here.

It was late afternoon by the time they left the oasis. 'I meant to show you many other places today, but there is not time now, and besides I need to seriously reconsider my plans in the light of what I have learned,' Kadar said as the last of their entourage of children waved a final farewell and returned to the town. 'Today has made me realise how egotistical were my ideas. I wished to bring my world to Murimon, when what is really needed is to improve this world first, make it ready. We need ship builders and road builders and teachers and engineers more than we need scholars. Practical men.'

'And women,' Constance said.

Kadar smiled warmly at her. 'And women, of course.' He brought his camel to a halt beside her. 'Today has been one of the most enlightening of my life, and you have been fundamental to that. I am very grateful, Constance.'

'I did nothing. It was all your own doing. Your speech had me spellbound, and I had no idea what you were actually saying! You were magnificent, Kadar. You should be proud of yourself.'

He shrugged, but she could tell he was touched. 'I have a lot to learn about being a prince, but today I made a start, I think.'

'Today, you took the first step—how did you say it?—out of the shadow of your brother's death towards a new dawn.'

'A small step.'

'But a significant one,' Constance persisted.

Kadar laughed. 'It feels that way at the moment, but I always find that the night brings true counsel. I'll see what I think in the morning. In the meantime, let us take a break from my kingdom's future, and enjoy the remains of the day.'

He urged his camel forward again, back through the mountain pass. Constance followed behind him, surprised, when they reached the head of the pass overlooking the port, that he then took a narrow path which led away from the palace, following the coast. They were traversing the ochre-coloured cliffs which bounded the beach where they had gone for their first horseback ride together, through the lines of olive trees and onto the scrubland which took over as the fertile topsoil disappeared. Below them now she could see the secluded crescent of the bay, the sand silver at the highest point, turning to gold where the sea was just beginning to creep in.

'It's a pity there is no way down,' Constance said, for her head was beginning to ache from the relentless sun. 'It looks lovely and cool down there.'

'My English Rose is finally beginning to wilt. Let us see what we can do to remedy that,' Kadar replied.

The path he turned onto was narrow, cut into the rock almost like a staircase, and surely far too steep for the camels to descend. But Kadar's camel was already on the vertiginous path, and terrifying as it was, the beach looked so appealing that Constance allowed her beast to follow, resisting the urge to screw her eyes shut, keeping them instead firmly fixed on the horizon. It took no more than a few minutes to reach the sanctuary of the sand, though it felt like an eternity. Letting out a sigh of relief, she slid down from the saddle, handing the reins to Kadar, who efficiently hobbled the two camels.

Her beautiful silk coat was quickly discarded, along with her boots and headdress. Kadar followed suit, removing his cloak, headdress and boots, running his hand through his hair. 'The water is the perfect antidote for hot feet,' he said.

'It does look very tempting.' Constance walked through the soft sand, which oozed around her toes, to the water's edge. Her trousers would get wet, but there was a limit to the amount of clothes she could discard. The first wave which washed over her feet was surprisingly cold. She jumped, staggered as her foot sank into the soft sand.

'Careful.' Kadar caught her arm to steady her.

They waded out further. The waves licked at her ankles and then her calves. Constance giggled with childlike delight. Further, and the water went over her knees, splashing her trouser legs, making them cling to her legs. They were deep enough for the tails of her tunic to trail in the sea.

'Far enough I think,' Kadar said, 'else I will have to teach you to swim.'

They stood side by side in the water. It was so clear she could see their toes on the seabed. Kadar's thigh against hers was warm. Her skin under the water tingled from the cold, yet there was a trickle of perspiration in the small of her back. 'I was going to say I've never been in the sea before, but that's nonsense, of course.'

She turned towards him as she spoke. Her toes brushed his and she stumbled. The wind whipped her hair over her eyes. She reached out blindly, flailing in the water, as some splashed on her face. And it was that, the spray on her face, the taste of brine on her lips, that made her panic, made her heart pump wildly, made her mouth dry, her legs shake. Screams. Tearing canvas. Crashing waves.

'Constance.'

Hands on her arms, steadying her. Her face pressed against the hard wall of his chest. The slow beating of his heart.

'You are safe. I have you. I won't let you drown. You are safe.'

Her heartbeat slowed. She forced herself to breathe. His hand was around her waist. The other was on her hair, smoothing it in a slow, profoundly reassuring motion. 'Promise?' she asked foolishly.

'I promise.'

Smoothing hands. Steady beating heart. His chin resting on her curls. 'Will you teach me to swim? Not now, but soon?' Constance asked. 'I don't want to be grounded by my fears,' she added ruefully.

'If I could give you a ladder to reach the stars, Constance, I would.'

'If you teach me to swim, I will overcome my fear of drowning, and be able to sail away to the ends of the earth if I choose.'

His arms tightened around her. 'Is that what you would like? To sail away to the ends of the earth.'

'It's a little more practical than climbing to the

stars.' Her arms were wrapped around his waist. 'I don't know what I want.' Her legs were pressed against his thighs. Warm skin, while hers was cold. He felt so solid. When had her fear melted into awareness? 'That's not true. Right now, I do know what I want,' she said, looking up, 'but I can't have it.'

'Constance.' Kadar pushed her hair back from her face. His eyes were dark with the passion she felt. 'Constance,' he said again, his tone a mixture of anguish and desire that left her in doubt that he felt exactly as she did. 'You know I want— You know how much I want you?'

'Yes,' she said simply. She touched his cheek, ran her fingers through his windblown hair. 'And I you, Kadar?'

He shuddered. 'Yes.'

He bent his head. She tilted hers. Their lips met but did not move. She could taste salt. She could feel his breath, rapid and shallow. The tide was ebbing, waves retreating now, rippling around her calves. Her heart was pounding, but she couldn't catch her breath. A kiss that was not a kiss. Did it count? Or not count?

'Constance,' Kadar said huskily, her name a caress. His hand smoothed down her spine, his fingers fanning over the curve of her bottom. 'We are playing with fire.'

And it was setting her alight. Something snapped in her. 'How far,' she asked, allowing her hand to mimic his, smoothing down his spine, feeling the rippling response of his muscles, flattening on the taut slope of his buttocks, 'how far may we go, Kadar, without getting burned?'

His laughter was a low rumble. 'I am already smouldering.'

His fingers curled into her flesh. She could feel the unmistakable ridge of his arousal against her belly. It excited her, this physical evidence of his desire, eliciting a shuddering response from deep inside her. Though their lips were still touching, they had not kissed. They had not even kissed, and she felt as if she would melt with wanting. 'I know we cannot,' Constance said, 'I know that, but if we could, Kadar, what would we do?'

His eyes flickered shut. When he opened them again they blazed, as if the fire they felt was raging was about to conflagrate. 'You should not ask such a thing.'

'But I am curious to know.' She curled her fingers into his hair. 'You told me, after we kissed on the rooftop, you told me that now you would stop wondering about kissing and start wondering about making love. I want to imagine that too, Kadar. I cannot have you, but I want to be able to imagine what it would have been like if I could. Don't you?'

He groaned. 'Yes.' Once again his lips brushed hers. 'Yes,' he said, 'I want to know.'

'Tell me then, for I know nothing beyond our kisses.'

'Do you have any idea what that does to me, knowing that you have not—that I would be the first?'

The naked desire in his face provided the answer. Here was Kadar, the man beneath the princely cloak, revealed just for her. Constance smiled, pressing herself just a tiny fraction closer. 'Yes,' she said, 'but I want to know more.'

Her words, her touch, her smile, seemed to release something in him. His mouth curled into the most sinful smile. 'Beyond our kisses,' he said, 'the kisses we have already shared, there are other kisses. Though I could never tire of kissing your mouth, of tasting you, of the touch of your tongue to mine, there is so much more of your delightful body to explore.'

Every bit of her body responded, as if Kadar's mouth, as if his hands, roved over her. 'Go on,' Constance urged.

'Your breasts. I would kiss your breasts. Not through your tunic as before, but my mouth on your skin, my tongue on your nipples, tasting you, teasing you. Tell me what that does to you, Constance.'

'Tingling. Hot. I feel hot.'

'Where?' Kadar asked.

She pressed herself against him, brushing the aching peaks of her nipples against his chest. 'All over.' She slid her hand between them, her palm flattened low on her own belly, the back of her hand just grazing his arousal, making them both shudder. 'Here,' she said. 'Especially here.'

Kadar shuddered, muttering something in his own language. 'Yes,' he said, 'especially here.'

He took several deep breaths, struggling to control himself. It was intoxicating, seeing the strength of his desire, seeing the effort he was making to contain it. And a challenge too. Constance felt light-headed, far beyond reason, intent only on feeding her body's urgent pleas for more and for more. There was only a breath between their lips. Their foreheads rested together. Her hair had fallen over her cheeks, tangled over his face, a screen from the world, a gauzy curtain to shield them from looking too closely, from facing consequences. 'What next, Kadar?'

'Your first time,' he said raggedly, 'for your

first time, it is better for you to be more...' He moved her hand from where it rested between her belly and his manhood, slipping it down, making her cup between her legs. 'Kisses,' he said. 'I would kiss you again, your mouth, your quite captivating mouth, and I would touch you, here.'

His hand covered hers. Her hand covered her sex. She was wet. Tense. Hot. No, not just hot. Every bit of her was burning. The gentle pressure of his hand on hers, the friction of her damp pantaloons against her damp sex, made her tenser, did strange things to her insides.

'Tell me,' Kadar said, his tone quite hoarse, 'tell me what that feels like.'

'As if I am being tightened inside. As if I might fly apart. As if...' Constance let out a low groan. 'As if I cannot— Kadar, I think I might— I cannot...'

'Yes, you can,' he urged, increasing the pressure, subtly coaxing her to increase the pressure, to increase the friction.

She had to clutch at his shoulder with her other hand. She was panting. She closed her eyes, unable to look, to think, to do anything save focus on that mounting pressure, that dizzying combination of intense pleasure tinged with fear as she climbed. Yes, that is what she was doing. Climbing. 'Higher,' she heard herself say in a voice that was not hers, 'higher', until suddenly she reached the top and there was nothing she could do but to jump.

Her climax made her cry out. Her knees buckled, and her grip on Kadar was so tight that she pulled them both down into the water. 'Now,' he said to her, his own voice hoarse, 'now I would enter you, now I would ride the waves of your climax, letting them take me high inside you.'

Another violent shudder shook her as he fell backwards into the shallows, pulling her on top of him, astride him, his hands cupping her bottom, her sex cupping his rigid arousal, separated only by two layers of saturated clothing. Constance shuddered again, cried out again, as her climax washed back over her. 'And now, Kadar? What now, Kadar?'

His chest rose and fell. His eyes were closed. But his mouth, it was his mouth which alerted her to the change in him. His lips thinned. When he opened his eyes, they were stormy, though not with passion. He sat up, lifting her gently from him. 'Now,' he said, 'we have managed to turn temptation into torment.'

Getting to his feet, he pulled her out of the shallows. She was soaking, covered in sand, her hair dripping, her body still thrumming, her mind utterly confused. 'Now,' Kadar said grimly, 'we know precisely how far we can go without getting burned.'

Chapter Eight

Following their encounter in the surf, in fact almost certainly *because* of it, it was almost a week before Constance found herself alone again with Kadar. She had seen him briefly at the coronation rehearsal two days ago, and she had twice bumped into him by accident, once on the roof terrace and once in the library, when they had both acted as if they had been scalded. Which she supposed they had. She could not regret what had happened between them on the beach, yet she wished she did not recall it quite so vividly or so often.

'Though wasn't that the point?' she muttered to herself as she gazed out at the port from the roof terrace, where she was sitting under the protection of the awning, writing up her copious notes from her many long nights of stargazing. It was human nature to want what one could not have. Was that the cause of this very persistent mutual attraction of theirs, which no amount of reasoning seemed to affect and no moral barriers seemed to keep at bay? Her decision not to marry hadn't affected her desire for Kadar, though it had made it, she secretly admitted, harder to ignore. Kadar's sense of honour, his determination to go through with his marriage seemed equally to have no effect on his desire for her. Passion, it seemed, had little to do with honour. Nor was it necessarily related to love. How odd that she hadn't thought of that before.

Returning to the desk to flick sightlessly through her notebooks, Constance pondered this. There was absolutely no question of love blossoming between them. Unlike her, he had experienced love once before, albeit an unrequited love. A forbidden love, for a woman who could not marry him. A love which had hurt him so much he was determined never to love again. It explained that way he had, of shutting one out. It explained look Number One, the Haughty Prince too. He didn't like to have his feelings probed. He didn't like to admit to having feelings. Which was why there could be no prospect of their falling in love. Even if she were foolish enough to do so, it could not be reciprocated. She would become the victim of unrequited love, just as Kadar had been.

Who was she, the mysterious woman who had broken his heart? Why couldn't they marry? She wasn't sure she wanted to know. She was certain Kadar would never tell her. Had their love affair blossomed here in Murimon? He had said only that it happened a long time ago. And that he would never allow it to happen again.

Constance closed her notebook. She had absolutely no reason to be jealous, and she, who was so determined never to marry, would be a hypocrite to judge this unknown woman harshly for refusing to marry Kadar. What mattered now was not his lost love but his new-found bride. Which brought her back in a full circle.

No, wait. She stared off into space, replaying her thoughts of the last few moments. *Her decision not to marry had not affected her desire for Kadar.* Had she really come to that most terrifying conclusion? With a sigh, she dropped her head onto her hands. It was all too much. Her eyes drooped closed. Suddenly exhausted, she lay her head on top of her notebook and fell asleep.

When she awoke, Kadar was standing over her. 'I thought you were working in the library,'

Constance said, rubbing her eyes. Today, his tunic was the colour of sand, his trousers cream. His hair was as ruffled as ever, but he looked tired. Dark shadows rimmed his eyes. Her first reaction was a ridiculous amount of pleasure at seeing him, quickly quelled and followed by a pang of regret. 'I didn't realise you planned to work up here today,' she said. 'I'll go.'

'No, please don't. I actually came up here to find you.'

Her heart sank. 'Has a ship arrived unexpectedly?'

'No ship, for which I am frankly grateful. I am in no rush to see you leave. I...' He rubbed his jaw. 'I want to put an end to this awkwardness between us. There is no reason why we must avoid each other's company. It would be exaggerating something, which meant nothing, out of all proportion.'

Something which meant nothing. Well, that put her in her place. 'I see,' Constance said.

'No, you don't.' He held out his hand. 'Come and sit by me.'

She did as he bid her, though she did not touch his hand, and she made a point of seating herself on a large cushion opposite him. As usual, she had kicked off her slippers, but she took care to tuck her bare feet under her tunic. 'I've been working on my star maps,' she said, indicating her work which was set out on the large desk.

'And I have been working on my revised plans. I would appreciate your views on them at some point. But that's not what I came to talk to you about.'

Kadar steepled his hands and treated her to his Sphynx look. She had almost forgotten how very off-putting it was. The silence stretched, begging to be filled. 'I'm glad there was no boat,' Constance said, 'because I've decided I'm not going to India to marry Mr Edgbaston.'

He looked as confounded as she by this statement, for though she had been thinking it, she had not meant to blurt it out. 'What made you change your mind?'

'I think I knew from the moment I set sail from Plymouth that it would be a mistake.'

'It might have been better if you had decided that before you set sail,' Kadar replied tersely.

'I thought you would be pleased,' Constance said, confused by his tone.

'Why would you think that?'

She flinched, reminded of that first night in the Royal Saloon, when she had felt as if she were being interrogated in a courtroom witness box. 'I was under the impression that you did not approve of my betrothal.'

'I have no right to approve or disapprove.'

His manner was beginning to irk her. 'You are entitled to an opinion, Kadar.'

'But I have been at pains to keep that opinion to myself. It is not for me to influence you.'

'But you do have an opinion,' Constance persisted.

Kadar folded his arms. 'It is quite irrelevant.'

'Right,' Constance said, folding her arms too and adding a glower for good measure. 'I see.'

This time the silence lasted so long that she had to curl and uncurl her toes to prevent herself from speaking, but she was finally rewarded. Kadar sighed. 'What is it you think you see?'

She *knew* he did not approve of her betrothal, but he was determined not to tell her so. Constance let out a little mewl of frustration. 'I think you think that I have changed my mind because of what happened on the beach, and therefore feel responsible. I also think you are worried that I now have—I don't know—expectations or something.' She threw another glower of formidable proportions at him, but Kadar was as stony-faced as the Sphinx again.

'Well, I don't,' Constance said, 'so you don't have to worry on that score. I have absolutely no expectations, and even if I did—which I don't— I would never, for a moment, allow them to come to fruition, because firstly, Kadar, for the avoidance of doubt, what I value more than anything is my independence, and secondly, *Your Highness*, not only am I perfectly aware that you are already betrothed to another woman, but I am also perfectly aware that even if you were not, or even if Murimon allowed you to have two wives, then I am undoubtedly the least suitable female you could possibly choose. So there you have it,' she concluded with a shuddering breath and a decidedly shaky tone, which she tried to counter by throwing her hair back and glowering once more, 'I trust I have reassured you?'

'I'm sorry.'

Two words, spoken with genuine remorse, and the last two words she had expected. Constance blinked and scrubbed her eyes. 'Why?'

A ghost of a smile and a shake of the head. 'You are right. I was egotistical enough to imagine that your decision was influenced by what happened between us on the beach.'

'"Something which meant nothing", you said. I did not need to be warned off, Kadar.'

He cursed under his breath—or at least she assumed that was what the vicious-sounding words were. 'It did mean something—to me, at least. That is why I have avoided you. What I meant was it must mean nothing because it simply cannot mean anything.'

'But I already know that.'

Another faint smile. 'Clearly,' he said. 'Forgive me. It has been a very long week, my coronation is only two days away, and I have been working long hours trying to— But that is no excuse for being so out of temper.'

'Actually, I think you have every excuse.'

This time she was rewarded with a much warmer smile. 'I have been debating with myself on whether it is best to leave matters between us as they are or whether to try to—to recover the situation,' Kadar said, in his more usual, considered manner. 'If you would rather I leave, then please say so.'

'No, don't go. I've missed your company dreadfully,' Constance answered, without any consideration at all. 'I don't want to lose something precious over some stupid—this obsessive passion that binds us.'

'Some would say the only way to satisfy an itch is to scratch it, just once,' Kadar said with a wry smile.

'I confess I have considered suggesting that.'

He laughed. 'I confess, so too have I, but I doubt once would be enough.'

Exactly the conclusion Constance had reached.

Realizing they were straying into very dangerous territory, she did not say as much, however. 'And it would also be very wrong,' she said instead.

His expression became immediately serious. 'Very.'

This silence was uncomfortable, but Constance could think of no way of filling it. She shifted on her cushion, adjusted her tunic over her bare feet, and tried very hard not to feel as if a door had slammed in her face. If there had been a clock on the terrace, its ticking would have been unbearable.

'So tell me,' Kadar said, for once the first to speak, 'why have you decided you will not marry your East India merchant?'

Constance spread her hands. 'Many reasons, but the main one is that I simply don't want to marry anyone.'

'Because marriage is a prison.'

'Did I say that? Yes, it is—for a woman. I've always known it, I've never wanted it, but I have never—not until I was cast upon the shores of Murimon—I have never seriously considered that I had any alternative, save to remain beholden to my father. Being here, experiencing this taste of true freedom—it has changed me.'

'When I first met you I had the oddest notion of wanting to set you free,' Kadar said pensively.

'I knew almost nothing about you, but I had a—a vision of you, a wild creature fettered by duty, and I wanted to sever the ropes which tethered you, I wanted—' He broke off, flushing. 'I am not usually so fanciful.'

'Well you have, in a way,' Constance said, snatching the hand back which was halfway to reaching out to touch him. 'Unfettered me, I mean. Not by kissing me, but by making me see that I am capable of standing on my own two feet. You made me realise that I am stronger than I thought I was, and you made me see that I am tired—I am very tired—of being used. Not only by Papa but in a way by Mama too.'

'Constance...'

'No, I'm not upset.' She sniffed. 'Only a little. I thought—I persuaded myself that she loved me. I'm sure she does, in her own way, but it's not enough, Kadar.' She pushed back her hair, meeting his gaze. 'I would never, ever force— blackmail—persuade— I would never make someone I loved do something I knew went against their deepest feelings, and that is what she did to me.'

She sniffed again, and rubbed her eyes with her knuckles. 'That is what I finally realised this last week, while I have been alone up here gazing at the stars. I don't owe my parents anything, I have done my duty by them for twenty-five years. I owe it to myself to make the next twenty-five or ten or fifty or whatever I am granted, mean something to me. Don't ask me what that will be for I haven't a clue, save that it doesn't involve either marriage or going to India, and it does not involve my relying on you to help me out either—well, except that I will need your assistance to get me back to England.'

Constance drew a breath, scrubbed at her eyes, and managed a watery smile. 'I'm not going to be grounded by my own fears ever again, but I am done throwing the unedited contents of my mind at you for now. It's your turn to speak.'

'Are you certain you wish to return to England?' It was not the question uppermost in his mind, but Kadar needed time to try to order his thoughts.

'Where else would I go?' she asked simply.

There was no obvious answer to this. Kadar shook his head. 'You have taken me quite by surprise.'

'And myself. I didn't plan to say any of this. Well, obviously I couldn't have planned to, since I didn't know I was going to see you, but even if I had—I mean I'm aware how preoccupied you must be with the coronation.'

'So you were going to share this change of heart with me afterwards?'

'Yes. No. I suppose so,' Constance said. 'I don't know. I assume it will be easier to transport me to England than to India, since I can sail relatively easily from here to Cairo?'

She was quite correct, Kadar realised with some dismay. If he handed the task to Abdul-Majid, Constance would be spirited away from Murimon before the coronation had even taken place. He should not be feeling dismay at the prospect, should he? Constance was a temporary encumbrance, nothing more. He should be relieved, rather than dismayed. 'You say you have no notion of what you will do, once back in England?'

'None at all.'

'Then you would probably benefit from some contemplation time.' Kadar nodded, giving Constance no time to reply. 'You are not expected in England. In fact, the addendum I sent to the Consul General stated that they should expect you in India some time in August.'

'So in fact I still have a month or so to consider in which form I shall rise from the dead,' Constance said.

'If you wish to take advantage of it?'

'I would not wish to inconvenience you.'

Kadar smiled. 'I believe we have had this discussion before. It would inconvenience me greatly to lose my court astronomer before she had completed her work.' Yes, that was it. Nothing to do with his wishing her to stay on any sort of personal basis, because they had quite firmly established that there could be nothing personal between them. 'So that is settled then?' Kadar said briskly.

Constance, however, frowned. 'Are we then to continue to avoid each other's company, or—or— I'm sorry, I'm still not sure what you think, Kadar.'

'I think that if a fire is not fuelled, it will quickly burn itself out.'

Constance considered this then heaved a sigh. 'Then we have no option but to do as you say, and refuse to feed the fire. I am sure that knowing we are doing the right thing will make it easier to endure.'

'It is also my hope.'

She laughed. 'Then I would like to enjoy what remaining time I have with you. We cannot have an *affaire*—goodness, how decadent that sounds! But we cannot have one, and even if we did, it would come to an end with my departure anyway. Worse, it might have come to an end before then, and think how uncomfortable that would be.'

'You make an excellent case for abstinence.'

'One you can endorse?'

'Yes. We are agreed, then.'

'Excellent,' Constance said, and he told himself he was imagining the hollow ring to her voice. 'Then I have a favour to ask of you. I would like to learn something of your language while I am here. I was wondering if there was anyone who could teach me.'

Himself, was the obvious answer, but he baulked at the idea of spending what little time he had with Constance engaged in such a dry activity as language lessons. 'The only other person I know with any sort of fluency in English is Abdul-Majid.'

She shuddered theatrically. 'Your chief adviser loathes me, and I'm pretty sure he would consider the role of teacher quite beneath him.'

'Abdul-Majid considers any role save chief adviser quite beneath him,' Kadar retorted. 'In fact I'm certain he considers himself superior to me.'

'You don't like him, do you?'

He took some time before he answered, and when he did, his words were deliberately ambiguous. 'His views are very traditional.'

'As are the views of many people in your kingdom, many of the people you talked to at

the oasis last week, but you were not so—so...'
Constance faltered. 'It is none of my business.'

'No, it is not.'

She bit her lip, studying him through narrowed eyes, that way of hers that made him uncomfortable. 'I call that expression Number One,' she said mysteriously. 'The Haughty Prince. You do it when you want to keep your thoughts to yourself, or when you don't want a subject to be pursued, which amounts to the same thing, more or less.'

Kadar was both impressed and irritated. 'I have nothing to hide.'

He should have known better than to try to call Constance's bluff in this way. 'Then tell me why you don't like him,' she said. 'He is a very influential man, he would be an excellent ally to have, yet you seem to make little effort to cultivate him.'

'Abdul-Majid,' Kadar said grimly 'is a man who cares only for privilege and position. He is a man who would sacrifice even his nearest and dearest in his pursuit of power. That is the source of my antipathy.'

'Would sacrifice, or did sacrifice?'

'Did sacrifice. His daughter, if you must have it.' He could not recall her face. He could not recall the colour of her eyes. He closed his own, trying desperately to conjure an image, but it was hazy. He felt himself a traitor. 'The subject is now closed,' Kadar said, making blindly for the terrace steps and the sanctuary of his library.

Alone in his chamber, Kadar stared down at the papers strewn over his desk representing Murimon's future, his utopian vision for his kingdom, and forced himself to think about the man who epitomised Murimon's past. In his previous life he had met many traditionalists such as Abdul-Majid, men who would do almost anything to stop progress, men who revered customs and traditions not for their value but for their simple existence, but he had always prided himself on his own sense of justice and fairness, and had never failed to give them a hearing.

Was his chief adviser so different? Yes, he and Abdul-Majid shared a tragic history, but that did not mean the man had nothing of any merit to say. He had years, decades, more experience of Murimon's ways than Kadar had. Constance was, sickeningly, correct, when she said it would be easier if the chief adviser was on his side. And yet, as he contemplated the time he would have to spend to persuade the man to support him, every instinct rebelled. He did not want the support of a man who had bartered power and influence for his daughter's happiness. He would not permit the man who had destroyed his youthful dreams to sabotage the new dreams set out on the desk before him.

No, he could not forgive him, but he could try to forget, close the door on the memories and the animosity between them, rid himself of the long shadow of the past. Butrus was dead. Zeinab was dead. Abdul-Majid was an old man. After the coronation, Kadar could find a way to retire him with honour. And in the meantime, he thought with a grim little smile, he would task his chief adviser with giving Constance language lessons.

His black mood began to lift. His plans lay before him, nearly completed. He had come to an arrangement with Constance which would permit him to enjoy a few more weeks in her company. What's more Constance had decided to free herself of the shackles of that cursed marriage—there, he could admit that was how he thought of it now. She would be free. Penniless and without family, but free. He could help her. He had contacts. He was certain he could help her. If she would let him.

His mood darkened again. In two days he would be crowned Prince of Murimon. In a matter of weeks, Constance's fate would be in her hands alone. She would be sailing for England and freedom, while he…

Kadar groaned. His coronation intended to mark the beginning of a golden age for Murimon, but it was also the countdown to the end of his own freedom and his impending marriage. And every day that it grew closer, his resistance to it grew stronger.

Chapter Nine

❦

'By anointing thy hands with this sacred oil, we give to thee, our king, the strength and the power to rule your kingdom and to defend our people from the unjust.'

The words spoken by the Chief Celebrant were almost exactly the same words which had been spoken at every Murimon coronation for centuries, and similar to the words spoken at the coronation of princes and kings of several other Arabian kingdoms too, so Abdul-Majid had informed Constance when he had provided her with a translation yesterday. She watched from her allotted position to one side of the Royal Saloon as Kadar's hands were anointed with frankincense. He was every inch the Prince today, dressed in a tunic and headdress of the finest silk, woven with gold. The long cloak fixed in place with an ornate golden clasp was also of gold, embroidered all over with an intricate and extremely elaborate geometrical pattern in jewel colours. It must be very heavy, for it trailed some twenty feet along the floor. At the centre of the clasp was a small red diamond, the companion of the huge Red Diamond of Murimon at the centre of his belt. Diamonds also glittered in his headband, on his boots and in the scabbard of the ceremonial scimitar tucked into Kadar's belt.

'By anointing thy head,' the Chief Celebrant was now intoning, 'we give to thee, our king, the wisdom to govern wisely and to rule justly.'

Constance was not the only woman present, which she knew was a clear break with tradition, and done at Kadar's insistence. The wives of all members of the Council, including Yasamin, stood with their husbands, and the huge retinue of palace servants, men and women, also stood together in one of the antechambers. But she was the only woman holding official office. Constance allowed herself a brief moment to admire the robes which Yasamin's grandfather had fashioned perfectly to her design. The tunic and pantaloons she wore were of celestial-blue silk the colour of the morning sky, beautifully made, but simple enough not to detract from the stunning beauty of her cloak. Midnight blue, the colour of the Arabian night sky, it had a high, stiff collar and very long pointed sleeves, the shape copied from a favourite picture Constance had once seen of the Arthurian wizard, Merlin. All of the main constellations were embroidered into the cloak which, if spread out, would depict as accurate a representation of the Arabian summer night sky as Constance had been able to draw. She was literally enveloped in the stars. She pulled the soft folds of the garment around her. Never, never would she forget this day.

The Chief Celebrant was preparing the special oil for the final part of the ceremony, mixing the secret ingredients into the frankincense of which even Abdul-Majid was ignorant. Any other man than Kadar would be lost in all the magnificent robes which he wore, his presence subsumed by the shimmer of gold and glitter of precious stones, by the fire that seemed to burn inside that huge diamond on his belt. But despite all his princely trappings, it was Kadar's own presence which shone through. There was authority in his stance and in his expression. In those fiercely intelligent eyes, there was strength, power, that certain something which singled out the true, natural-born ruler from mere mortals.

'By anointing thy heart,' the Chief Celebrant chanted, 'we give to thee, our Prince, the enduring and unquestioning love of our people, and in the name of those people, we do declare you Prince Kadar of Murimon.'

The audience fell in unison to their knees in obeisance, Constance following suit. She felt very strange, sneaking a look up at Kadar as the final words of the ceremony were spoken and repeated by all present, filled first and foremost with pride to be present on such a momentous occasion, privileged to be part of this ceremony, and almost overawed by Kadar's regal bearing.

But there was more to it than that. Behind that princely façade, there was a man whom Constance thought so much more admirable, for he was flesh and blood, a man who knew he could never be infallible, yet strived to come as close as he could to that state. A man of honour and integrity. A man of passion. Of all of this she was aware, and some of it only she, of all here present, knew.

Tears filled her eyes as the emotion of the occasion took hold of her. This ceremony tied Kadar to Murimon for ever. It heralded a new beginning for his kingdom, but it also marked the official end of his old life. His role from now on was Prince of Murimon. His future here, creating the kingdom he wanted for his people. A new dawn. Yet for her, it was the beginning of the end. It was an illusion, this being part of something, her role here as court astronomer. Soon, she would have to set sail into her future, to decide for herself what form it would take, what role she would carve for herself.

Her tears could no longer be held back. Here, in the Royal Saloon, at the end of this most moving and life-changing of rites, she could admit to herself that she cared for the man who was now Prince, cared for him rather too much. Never before had she felt this way about any man, because previously, she had equated such feelings with marriage, and therefore entrapment. There was no question of marriage here, and even if there were—no, she had not changed her mind on that. But it had not occurred to Constance until now that it was possible to feel two quite contrary things at the same time: a profound and deep-rooted affection for a man—no, she would not dare go so far as to call it anything more; and a fierce determination never to be any man's property.

Shaken, she rose to her feet with everyone else at Kadar's command. Confused, she listened as he spoke, noting how mesmerised his audience was by his words, noting that she was very far from being the only one with tears on her cheeks, noting the assurance with which the new prince spoke, knowing that his people hung on his every word, though she had no idea what those words meant.

Kadar concluded his coronation speech and, as the first cheers broke out, he made his way out of the Royal Saloon and Constance took up her position at the rear, behind the two lines of council members who would bear their prince's train. Her thoughts turned, as they had over and over again in the preceding nights, to two other women. The princess whom Kadar was to marry. And the woman who had broken his heart.

It was very late, or rather very early, when Kadar finally changed out of his coronation robes. He ought to be exhausted, for the day of his coronation had been an exceedingly long one, but instead he felt light-headed, wide awake, slightly detached from reality as he had all day, as if he had been watching himself from afar. It had all gone like clockwork, thanks to the ever-efficient Abdul-Majid, but from that satisfaction too he felt quite detached. He was officially Prince of Murimon, the foremost personage in his kingdom. He shook his head at the incongruity of it. As second son, he had never dreamt this day would come. Now he had everything which Butrus had ever wanted, and he was going to turn it into something which his brother could never have dreamt of. He had revealed only the outline of his plans to the council, and had repeated the exercise for the benefit of the people crowded into the piazza following his coronation. It was impossible to tell whether the apparent enthusiasm with which his words were greeted was merely a product of this most momentous of days. When the formal public exhibition of his plans was unveiled in the special room in the palace which was currently being prepared for just that purpose, then he would know more.

Would Butrus really be so appalled? Baffled, more like. Butrus would fritter away the huge Nessarah dowry on extravagant toys like the three-masted schooner he had ordered, on horses he could not hope to master, and on goodness knew what other luxuries. It was a large sum of money. It would take dedication and many years to spend it in such a fashion, but it probably wouldn't occur to Butrus that it might be spent in any other way. What was the point of changing traditions and customs and a way of life which had served for centuries? he would probably ask. 'Progress, Brother,' Kadar whispered softly.

Clad now only in a cotton tunic, he stared out at his kingdom from his rooftop terrace, breathing in the soft night air, listening to the waves gently breaking on to the shore in the distance. They were as different as night and day, he and his brother, but there were certain occasions, like now, when he missed Butrus. He didn't regret the years of his self-imposed exile, for he could not have stayed to witness—no, that would have been painful beyond endurance. But he wished Butrus could have come and visited him. Perhaps then, faced with a fast-changing Europe his brother would have opened his eyes to the need for change closer to home. 'Or perhaps not,' Kadar said wryly to himself. All Butrus had wanted was here. A kingdom to rule, a people to revere him, a dynasty to succeed him.

A dynasty to succeed him.

As soon as the celebrations were ended, the pressure for Kadar to marry would intensify. He had used his upcoming coronation as a shield, very effectively as it turned out. Now disarmed, he was forced to confront this next rite of passage square on. He was marrying for money and an heir. Yes, the money would benefit his people, and if that alone was the reason, perhaps he would not feel so squeamish. But dynastic purposes? The notion filled him with repugnance. Children were human beings, not heirs in waiting. They should be brought into this world for one reason only—that they would be

loved—and as the product of one thing only—
and that was love.

Oh, love, sweet perfect love. The province of
youth, of innocence, granted but once in a lifetime. He had sipped from that cup, had been
permitted a glimpse of paradise. Should he have
fought harder, pleaded his case more strongly,
simply taken matters into his own hands, overcome all her scruples and forced the issue by taking decisive action? But he had not, and it was
seven years too late for regrets. He would have
been happy, theirs would have been a perfect
union, but it was not to be, and now would never
be. As to this loveless union which his people
wished him to undertake, which his brother had
been about to embrace…

A noise on the steps made him turn. Constance, wrapped in a white robe, her hair floating
like a cloud behind her, appeared on the terrace
and stopped dead at the sight of him. Kadar held
out his hand. 'You're not disturbing me.'

She joined him in the ghostly predawn light.
Her feet were bare, as usual. 'Are you surveying
your domain now it is officially yours?'

Her very presence had a calming effect on
him. 'Yes, I find I've suddenly developed des-
potic tendencies.' He was rewarded with one of

Constance's captivating smiles. 'What brings you up here?' he asked. 'Couldn't you sleep?'

'Couldn't you?'

He laughed softly. 'Perhaps I am sleeping. Today has felt like one long dream.'

'You were magnificent, Kadar. It was a most moving ceremony. I have no doubt that you will provide your people with the prince they deserve and, judging from the reaction to the speech you made in the piazza, I think they agree with me.'

He was absurdly pleased, though he merely shrugged. 'You looked quite magnificent yourself today. Every inch the court astronomer. In fact the most impressive I have ever seen.'

'And how many other court astronomers have you met?'

He grinned. 'None! But I have to say, your ceremonial robes looked spectacular. The design using the map of the night sky was an inspired idea.'

'Yasamin's grandfather must take the credit for that. He made a wonderful job of bringing my suggestions to life.'

'When I said you looked magnificent I was referring to the person wearing the robes, not the robes themselves.' He turned to face her, pushing her hair back from her face, twining a long silky curl around his fingers. Looking down at her—big eyes wide open, fierce brows, soft mouth, that combination of strength and vulnerability which he had detected in her from the start—made something twist in his gut. Wanting, yearning, something stronger and more powerful than mere desire, overwhelmed him. He slid his hand further into her curls, letting their silky softness caress his forearm. It felt like an age before his lips touched hers, both of them watching, waiting on the other to withdraw, drawing nearer and nearer, until their mouths met, and even then, pausing. Then she emitted a soft sigh and melted into his arms.

When Kadar's lips met hers it felt so right that it left no room to conclude it might be wrong. This was a kiss that had been waiting patiently, suspended in the stars above them since that last kiss here on this terrace. Their mouths clung, their lips lingered, not tasting but drinking, savouring, a slow blurring of two people into one. Constance's eyes drifted closed. She could taste starlight in their kiss, something ethereal, brightly shining, yet it was a light which would slip through her fingers if she tried to catch it. A kiss which could not be earthbound, yet a kiss which felt so real.

She sighed as Kadar pulled her closer, wrapping his arm tightly around her waist. Her body nestled against his, her curves fitting into his hollows, her hands smoothing over the ripples of his muscles, relishing the tension in him belied by those pliant kisses, like wine now, heady, sweet, achingly sweet, bringing her body to life, making her melt against him, making her feel as if she could fly with him to the stars, where their kisses came from.

Deeper kisses, drugging kisses. His tongue sweeping over her bottom lip, hers licking into the corners of his mouth, and then tongues touching, that touch like a secret connection, making all the pulse points of her body into one shimmering constellation, her mouth, her breasts, her fingertips, her belly, her toes, and the beating pulse of that constellation throbbing inside her.

She could feel his arousal hard against her, but still their kisses were yearning kisses, kisses that longed only for more kisses and more kisses, kisses whose point was only kissing, and kissing, and kissing. Until desire rushed through her like a riptide, the fierceness of it startling her. And Kadar felt it too. So their kisses slowed, because they could not continue. And stopped, because they had to. And they stared at each other, dazed and dazzled. And then they let each other go.

'Thank you,' Kadar said softly.

Constance couldn't help smiling. 'No, thank you.'

He shook his head, kissing her brow, smiling back—a soft smile she had not seen before. 'Not for the kisses, that pleasure was mutual, I hope.'

'Very,' she said, unable to resist pushing his hair back from his brow, allowing her fingers to trail down his cheek, from smooth skin to rough stubble.

He took her hand, pressing another kiss on her palm. 'I want to thank you, Constance, for reminding me that I am not only a prince, but a man.'

'Kadar, when I look at you I always see the man first, the prince second.'

He laughed at that, keeping her hand in his, pulling her over to the mound of cushions which she kept by the telescope. 'I want to talk to you about something.'

'That sounds serious,' she said, seating herself with her back to the wooden frame.

He sat beside her, cross-legged. She had tried, but she had never quite been able to mimic that misleadingly relaxed-looking pose. His feet were bare. High arches, just like hers. She had noticed them before. Here? No, on the beach, the first day they rode out together.

'I've decided I'm not going to get married,' Kadar said, startling her from her reverie.

'What?' Constance stared at him in astonishment, thinking she must surely have misheard him.

'I can't do it. No, it's not that. I won't do it.'

Her jaw dropped. 'But why not? What made you reconsider—Kadar, have you thought of the consequences? The dowry—you said you needed it to implement your plans.'

'I do,' he said wearily, 'but I won't marry for money, and that is what it amounted to.'

'But what will you do?'

'I have no idea. The ramifications are too great for me to even contemplate right now. I intend to honour the pledges I made today. I owe it to my people to implement my plans, but not at the cost of betraying my conscience, which I would do if I married merely to obtain the funds to underpin my grand design. I must find another way. I will find another way—somehow. I don't know, Constance.' He raked his fingers through his hair. 'I have only just reached that conclusion, and have not thought any of it through. Today has been life-defining, but not in the way that I imagined. I'm sorry, it is none of your business, but I thought…'

'That I would understand,' she said, taking his hand between hers.

'Yes.' His fingers gripped hers. 'The situations are not the same, but there are… Not similarities but parallels.'

She smiled to herself. Even under extreme duress Kadar was so careful with his words. But his grip reminded her that he *was* under extreme duress. 'Tell me,' she said gently. 'Perhaps it will help to talk it through. Then you will know how to act.'

'I don't know where to begin.'

'Well, as with all good stories, one begins at the beginning.'

There it was again, that odd flicker, almost a blink, of his right eye. If she was not watching him so closely, if it had been night and not almost dawn, she would have missed it. It was followed by a long silence, while Kadar retreated behind his inscrutable look before finally spoke. 'Then I will begin with my trip to Nessarah,' he said. 'I journeyed there after I took my oath to this kingdom, after I had buried my brother. I went with every intention of breaking off the betrothal to the Princess Tahira. Assuming responsibility for my brother's kingdom was a huge shock for me as you know. I had no desire to assume responsibility for his intended wife in addition.'

'Even though you knew that there was a large dowry at stake?'

'Yes. At the time I thought only of myself, of my own feelings, which were— I was not yet thinking as a prince, Constance, but as a man. One who knew he would never marry. Taking a bride for the sake of her dowry, for the sake of my newly inherited kingdom certainly did not sit well with me. But I had not then considered the situation from my people's perspective, thought about what that money might mean for them, provide for them.'

'Is that what forced your change of heart?'

He hesitated. 'I will be honest with you. I think if I had not interrupted my journey to Nessarah, I would have acted with my instincts and broken the contract, but en route I paid a visit to an old friend in a neighbouring kingdom. Azhar had, by a strange twist of fate, also recently been crowned—in Qaryma they use the title "King." He too had spent his most recent years abroad making a different life for himself, though sadly our paths never crossed. He asked me what I intended to do now that I was Prince of Murimon, and I told him, somewhat flippantly, "Try to make a better prince than my illustrious and much-loved elder brother." Though I had no idea what that meant, it made me question whether my first act, of cancelling an alliance which Butrus had made, and which was very popular with his people, was the wisest of decisions.'

'But you told me you wanted to be different from Butrus.'

Kadar nodded. 'I do now, but then…'

'You had just lost your brother, you had gained a kingdom you never thought would be yours and you were contemplating the loss of all you had achieved for yourself since you left here,' Constance said, pressing his hand. 'You were shipwrecked, just like me.'

'Yes, I think I was. I was also— Azhar made me realise I was also being arrogant. It was he who reminded me that I had a kingdom to rule, and that nothing—not even what he called my precious books—must take precedence over that. His words made me see that I was being self-indulgent, putting my needs first. By the time I reached Nessarah, I had resolved not to break the betrothal, but to postpone the marriage. With hindsight I see that I was buying myself some time in order to reconcile myself to the situation.'

'Did you meet the Princess while you were there? Did you discuss the matter with her?'

'Nessarah is a very traditional kingdom. Women there wear the veil. In the palace, they live a separate life in the harem. My meeting with Princess Tahira was heavily chaperoned, though it was sufficient for me to be sure of her utter indifference to me—and I to her. It made me very uneasy, but again I was selfish, thinking only of myself, thinking all that mattered was to steel myself. Only recently, only because I have been drawing parallels between our situations, have I come to consider her feelings—or lack of them. It shames me.'

'Kadar,' Constance said tentatively, 'you must be very careful not to draw these parallels too closely. This Princess Tahira—it may well be that what you took for indifference was simply shyness or even understandable trepidation. She doesn't know you. She will have had no say in the matter, but she must certainly be feeling, at the very least, like a—a parcel, handed from one prince to the next without any consultation. You can hardly have expected her to throw herself adoringly at your feet.'

He laughed, but it was a bitter sound. 'You say nothing which has not occurred to me—recently, that is. Whatever her feelings, she had no more choice than you but to acquiesce. And like you, once we were married, she would have no choice but to feign affection, to play the amenable wife. Cupboard love, is how I believe you described it.'

And so she had, and it was the truth, but Constance felt distinctly uncomfortable. 'There is one big difference though, Kadar,' she said. 'You are a man of honour and integrity. Were you to marry this Princess, you would do everything in your power to make her happy.'

'Your faith in me is flattering, but you contradict your own logic. You imply that I could force the Princess Tahira to be happy, yet you insist that only you can be responsible for your own happiness. When it comes down to it, my decision is not based on the Princess Tahira's feelings for me or lack of them. My own feelings are the only ones of which I can be certain. I will sacrifice almost anything for my kingdom, but not my integrity.' He slipped his hand from hers. 'I thought you would endorse my decision. I thought that this marriage which my brother arranged was as repugnant to you as your marriage was to me.'

'That's the first time you've actually admitted to that.'

He smiled faintly. 'I didn't need to. You seem able to discern my innermost thoughts with ease.'

'You think so?' Constance exclaimed in surprise. 'I find your mind almost impossible to read. Especially when you do that—that Sphynx look.'

'I beg your pardon, that what look?'

She tried, but completely failed to imitate it, succeeding only in making her eyes roll and her mouth pucker as if she were sucking a lemon. 'Don't laugh. It is no laughing matter, and anyway you know perfectly well what I mean. You always do, my mind is an open book to you.'

'On the contrary. Your reaction tonight has surprised me.'

Constance bit her lip. The truth was, she was horribly relieved by his decision, and that, following the realization of just how much she had come to care for him, had set her completely off-kilter. 'When I told you that I was not going to India, your first reaction was defensive. You wanted me to assure you my decision had nothing to do with my feelings for you—I mean, nothing to do with the attraction between us,' she corrected herself hastily.

Kadar nodded slowly. 'You seek similar assurance that your presence here, our relationship, however one chooses to define it, has not influenced my decision?'

'Well, has it?'

He leaned back and stared up at the cool morning sky. The sun had not risen, but the stars were all gone. 'The contrast between my desire for you and my complete lack of desire for the Princess is one of the things which has made me reconsider, but it is not the main factor. It is quite simple really. I do not love her and I cannot in conscience marry a woman I do not love.'

'You don't know her, Kadar.'

'But I have known love, and I know that the princess could never hold a similar place in my heart. No one could,' he said. 'It is not possible to match perfection, far less improve on it. And even if it was, I doubt the fates would be so very cruel as to allow history to repeat itself in this twisted manner.'

'What twisted manner?'

But Kadar was rising to his feet, staring out at the horizon, where the sky was beginning to change colour, the first intimation of the sun's appearance. 'So you may put your mind at rest. My decision was mine alone.'

Constance scrabbled off the cushions to join him, determined not to allow him to shut her out, tugging on the sleeve of his tunic. 'Are you relieved to have come to a decision? Only I was vastly relieved, even though I still have no idea what the ramifications might be, and actually when I think about it I'm quite terrified, but I'm still more relieved than scared, and I expect at some point I'll be excited.'

She was rewarded with a warm smile. 'You know I can help smooth the path to your future if you'll let me.'

'No.'

'Constance, I don't mean money. I am not without influence.'

'I hadn't considered that.'

'Then please do.'

'Yes, but you haven't answered my question, Kadar.'

He laughed somewhat bitterly. 'Yes, I am relieved, but like you, rather daunted by the ramifications. I need to think about it very carefully, somehow find another way to discharge my duty to my people without compromising my own integrity. Then there is the Princess Tahira and her family. They will be expecting me to act on my promise to set a date for the wedding following my coronation. The whole thing will have to be managed with diplomatic sensitivity, observing every custom minutely, so for now it must remain our secret.'

'Well, I'm hardly likely to blurt it out to Abdul-Majid during one of our language lessons.'

Kadar shuddered. 'I should hope not. What sort of teacher is he proving to be?'

'Surprisingly *amenable*,' Constance said, choosing the word deliberately. She recited several phrases, and when Kadar looked impressed, several more.

'You are making very good progress. Your pronunciation is excellent. Have you a facility for languages?'

'I don't know. I can read French and German— oh, and Latin—but I've never had much chance to speak them. I am enjoying it though. We have been discussing books. Abdul-Majid is extremely well read. It is a pity you cannot bring yourself to like him, for I have found our discussions extremely interesting, and I gather that he has no one else who shares his passion.'

'He did have,' Kadar replied. 'Once.'

His wife? She waited for enlightenment, but he seemed to have nothing else to say on the subject, so Constance resolved to pursue it with Abdul-Majid herself. Besides, there were so many other more fascinating subjects whirling about in her head. She gazed out at the sunrise, distracted by its beauty. 'I could never tire of this.'

'Nor I.'

Kadar was not looking at the sunrise. Kadar was looking at her, and there was a heat in his eyes that was considerably warmer than the sun's rays. That kiss. Those kisses. She had thought them an end in themselves, but her traitorous body had other ideas now. 'I thought I saw a comet last night,' Constance said, because she had to say something. 'I thought it would be a good omen for you, on your coronation day.'

'They are more often seen as portents of natural disasters,' Kadar said. 'Earthquakes. Droughts.'

'And cats,' Constance said. 'There was an outbreak of the sneezing sickness in cats in Prussia following the sighting of a comet.'

Kadar laughed. 'That tale is new to me. A comet tale, one might say.'

He was still looking at her in *that* way. She suspected she was looking back at him in exactly the same way. 'Anyway,' Constance said, 'it transpires it was only a shooting star.'

'So no omen, good or bad.'

'You don't need one. It is written in the stars that you will be the best prince Murimon has ever had.'

They were not touching, but they were looking at each other as if they were.

'I thought court astronomers could not foretell.'

'I am certain of this prophecy, Kadar.'

'Constance.' He touched her hair. She lifted

her face. He bent towards her. A loud crash in the piazza below, where work had begun on clearing up the remains of the banquet, made them jump.

'It is morning,' Constance said. 'Your first official day as Prince of Murimon, and you haven't even slept. You must be exhausted.'

'I'm not tired.'

'You should be.'

'Yes,' Kadar said with a dawning smile. 'The festivities went on very late. What I need is a day of rest.'

'Yes,' Constance agreed in some surprise.

He laughed at her expression. 'I do not intend to sleep the day away. I mean to spend it away from here.'

'So only a day into your new role, and you are absconding already,' she teased.

'On the contrary, I shall be spending the day in contemplation before assuming the heavy mantle of power.' He cast a glance at the rising sun. 'If we are to make the most of it, we should leave as soon as possible.'

'We? But don't you want to be alone?'

'Constance.' He took her hand, pressing a kiss to her fingertips. 'We have both freed ourselves from a promise made mistakenly out of a sense of duty and honour. We will both have to face the consequences of that breach, and very soon.

But can we not take a day to ourselves, to briefly enjoy that freedom?'

What did he mean by enjoy? Now that the barrier of his betrothal was removed, there was nothing to stop them—is that what Kadar meant? Constance decided it was better not to ask. 'Yes,' she said simply. 'Yes, please. I would like us to do that very much.'

Chapter Ten

Kadar lowered the sail of the little dhow and leapt agilely into the shallows to pull the craft onto the beach. When she had first sighted the boat bobbing by the harbour wall and realised that his suggested day out involved going out on the water, Constance's nerve had almost failed her. But he had been true to his word, keeping them well within the relatively calm waters of the bay, sailing with an obviously expert hand, and she had very quickly relaxed, enjoying the freshness of the sea breeze whipping her hair, the faint spray of salt on her face, and refusing to allow herself to associate any of it with the day the *Kent* went down.

As the wooden hull bumped onto the sand, she rolled up the legs of her pantaloons and climbed out, relishing the lapping of the waves on her ankles, watching as Kadar pulled the boat higher up the beach onto the soft white sand beyond the tideline. He had said little on the journey here, merely touching her hand reassuringly every now and then when the boat scudded over a wave. It hadn't occurred to her that he would be able to sail, though when she had said so he had laughed. 'This journey would have taken days by camel. Our dhows are the camels of the sea here in Murimon. Everyone can sail.'

'I would like to learn,' Constance said wistfully. 'I would like to have a little dhow like this of my own to explore this beautiful coastline. I would stop on a whim at a sandy cove, and spend the night lying on the beach with the waves murmuring and the stars sparkling overhead.' She smiled, shaking her head at her own foolishness. 'I know, you are thinking it is a silly notion. Sailing is hardly a skill I am likely to need back in England.'

Kadar said nothing. Rightly so, England was a depressing topic on such a beautiful day as this. She didn't want to think about England. Today she and Kadar were cast adrift from both the past and the future. Castaways, Constance thought, giving herself a little shake. Just the two of them here, on this deserted beach with the promise of…

Stop thinking about that! Just enjoy! She

waded to the shore, gazing around her with delight. The tide was ebbing, leaving a long stretch of hard-packed golden sand in its wake. An odd formation of rocks which formed a natural harbour backed on to the cliffs behind them. Intrigued, Constance padded closer and clambered up a rough set of steps which had been hewn into the side. Not a harbour, but a huge rock pool greeted her, the waters a deep dark turquoise. Balancing on the narrow wall formed by the smooth rock, she made her way to the far side, where the rock sloped down into the pool like a little slipway.

'What do you think?'

She had been so intent on keeping her balance she had not noticed Kadar. Now she wobbled on the wall, which was fortunately only about a foot above the sand at this point. He caught her, helping her step down onto the beach. 'It's remarkable. Is it naturally formed?'

'Some work has been done to deepen it, and the steps you climbed were cut, but other than that, yes, it is completely natural.'

'It's wonderful.'

Kadar smiled at her. 'I'm glad you think so. It's perfectly safe too—as you can see, it is very shallow at this end.'

Comprehension finally dawned on Constance,

setting off a flutter of butterflies in her stomach. 'You brought me here to teach me to swim,' she said, eyeing the pool anew.

'This is where I learned to swim.'

'Really? Who taught you?'

'My father,' Kadar replied. 'When I was very young, four or five, he brought Butrus and I here in a dhow like the one in which I transported us.'

'So he taught you to sail too?'

'You look surprised. I told you, everyone sails here in Murimon.'

Constance shrugged, embarrassed. 'It sounds so *natural*, a father teaching his sons to sail and to swim. I thought— I was under the impression that you— Oh, it doesn't matter.'

She turned away, confused by her surge of emotion, and made her way across the beach to the boat, where Kadar had set out a blanket in the shade. 'This really is a lovely spot,' she said brightly, when he joined her.

He studied her with that look of his that made her uncomfortably sure he could read her mind. And so it proved. 'Your father…'

Constance flapped her hands. 'Oh, please, let's not talk about him, not today. Tell me about your father. Your brother.'

He hesitated, but then to her relief, decided to

do as she asked him. 'I told you that Butrus and I were very unalike,' he said, 'which no doubt led to the impression you seem to have gained that I was unhappy growing up here in Murimon. I was not. As children we were close, and when it came to what my father thought of as manly pursuits, whether it was riding or swimming or sailing or sword fencing—I have a facility for such things.'

'So your father was proud of you?'

'He was—satisfied with me,' Kadar said, choosing his words with his usual care. 'I met his expectations.' He picked up a handful of sand and allowed it to run though his fingers. 'Unfortunately, my father turned our games into challenges which naturally Butrus, as the heir, was expected to win.'

'I remember you said that you found it easier to refuse to race him on horseback.'

'Yes, but I was not always so sensible,' Kadar said, flushing. 'When I was younger, I confess that my own competitive spirit meant I took pleasure in besting my elder brother. It is not something I am proud of.'

'Sibling rivalry is a perfectly natural phenomenon!' Constance exclaimed. 'You would have been a very odd sort of child to have behaved in any other way.'

Kadar's laugh was bitter. 'A very odd sort of child is what my father thought me.'

'Because you chose your studies over these manly pursuits he was so keen on? Didn't he realise that it was his fault? That he was forcing you to into the library because that was most likely the one arena your brother wasn't interested in competing with you in?'

She had spoken indignantly, her heart touched by the image of Kadar's younger self which his words had conjured, but for a moment she thought she had overstepped the mark with him. He was staring out to sea, but his thoughts were clearly focused inward. 'Perhaps,' he said slowly, 'it is because you spend so much time looking at the stars through a telescope, that you see the world reflected in a different way. I mean,' he added, taking her hand, 'that I had not thought of my escape into my books in quite that way before. You may well be right, but if that is the case, my father did me a service.'

'All the same, it cannot have been easy for you to be so very different to Butrus. To be mocked for spending so much time lost in your studies, to hold yourself deliberately apart from life in the palace—you told me once that you were "temperamentally, intellectually, and in many ways ethically" unsuited to life at court.'

'It seems I am not the only one to recall conversations perfectly.' He sighed. 'I was not unhappy, Constance. Butrus and I would have grown apart regardless, because it is true, temperamentally we were very different.'

'But you must have been very lonely growing up.'

He stilled. Something flickered in his eyes. Grief? Pain? 'No, for I was fortunate enough to find a companion who shared both my interests and my views of life in court.'

'I am glad you had a friend. Is he still here, in Murimon?'

He flinched. 'He was a she,' he said bleakly, 'and she is dead.'

'Oh, Kadar, I am so sorry.'

He disentangled his fingers from hers and shook his head. 'We came here to enjoy a taste of freedom,' he said, getting to his feet, 'to escape from the past and the future, not wallow in it. Now, are you going to allow me to teach you to swim?'

The subject was closed, and compelling as it was, Constance did not want to spoil the day. She too got to her feet, eyeing the calm waters of the swimming pool with trepidation. 'What does one wear to swim?'

She was relieved to see Kadar's countenance clearing. 'I don't usually wear anything at all.'

'Oh.' Colour flooded her face, not because of what he said but because of the image it conjured, of those muscled shoulders, those long legs, his taut behind, wading into the pool. 'I hope you're not suggesting—that is I hope that you will not...'

'Modesty and decency will be observed,' Kadar replied, grinning. 'Though I warn you, you will be hindered by your clothing, and it really would be much easier...'

'Kadar!'

He held up his hand in mock surrender. 'Take off your tunic, but leave everything else on. Your clothes will dry quickly enough in the sun. Are you sure you wish to go through with this, Constance? I won't think any less of you if you don't.'

She gazed at the pool, and then out at the sea. The chances of her being shipwrecked again were slim indeed, but knowing she could swim would certainly boost her confidence when she next had to board a seagoing ship. Which would be soon. She didn't want to think about that. Neither did she want to be a hostage to her fears. 'You might not think less of me,' Constance said resolutely 'but I would.'

She unbuttoned her tunic and pulled it off before she could change her mind. The camisole she wore was made of muslin, a flimsy affair with narrow straps which left her arms and shoulders quite bare. No more so than a ball gown, she told herself, though if she were wearing a ball gown she would also be wearing corsets and a chemise. Her breasts were not actually exposed, though they were clearly outlined. She crossed her arms over them, relieved to see that Kadar had considerately turned his back to her.

He too had unbuttoned his tunic, and was in the process of pulling it over his head. He wore nothing underneath. Her mouth went dry as she looked at him. Broad shoulders, tapering waist. The sash which tied his trousers was low on his hips. Her stomach flipped as he turned around. His body was not that of a Greek statue, all powerful over-developed muscle bulging unconvincingly, but that of a true athlete, with an aesthetic quality to his musculature. Though it was there, under that smooth chest and flat stomach, there was no doubt about it.

'Ready?'

Her face flaming, Constance nodded, and marched determinedly over to the shallow end of the bathing pool.

Had this been a mistake? It would certainly be testing his control to the limit, Kadar thought as he watched Constance walking across the sand.

Though the material of her pantaloons and the tiny top she wore were not at all transparent, they were filmy, clinging to her curves, curves to which his body was responding with alarming speed. He dragged his eyes away from the beguiling contours of her bottom, forcing himself to concentrate on the swimming lesson ahead. Though she was concealing it well, Constance was afraid of the water, and with good cause.

He started by teaching her to float. Seeing her jaw clenched, feeling the rigidity in her muscles, banished all thoughts of anything other than teaching her to swim. She was not afraid, she was terrified, panicking when the water lapped over her face, but she was equally determined not to give up. Slowly, she gained confidence and began to relax. Within half an hour, she was taking her first tentative strokes herself, and when Kadar suggested she might be tired she laughed.

'I'm enjoying it,' she said, and executed several more splashy strokes.

Another hour, and Constance managed a full length of the rock pool at the deepest end, with Kadar by her side. 'I did it,' she exclaimed, clinging to the rock, breathing heavily with the effort, but flushed with triumph. 'I did it.'

'You did,' Kadar agreed, smiling. He had the

oddest feeling, as if his heart was swelling in his chest. Pride? Admiration? He wanted to kiss her. Desire, banished for the duration of the lesson, came rampaging back. Constance was effectively naked under the water. Now that he was no longer holding her, supporting her, his body recalled exactly how she had felt, all soft flesh yet surprisingly firm muscles. A body accustomed to effort. Her nipples had brushed against his arms when he held her. Hard peaks.

Stop! 'You have done very well indeed, but that is enough for now,' Kadar said, anxious to put some distance between them. 'Go and sit in the sun, dry out your clothing while I take a swim.'

She allowed him to help her into the shallows, though he kept himself immersed in the water and refused to allow himself to watch her as she waded ashore, diving back under as soon as he was sure she was safe. He swam powerfully, pushing himself to the limits, after two lengths of the pool losing himself in the rhythm of his swimming, emptying his mind of all thoughts but of the next breath and the next one, and the next.

Finally, exhausted, he rolled onto his back. Sunlight glinted off the water, dazzling him. He closed his eyes and floated, recovering his breath, lulled by the merest whisper of the waves breaking on the shore as the tide receded to its furthest point. When he opened his eyes, he had drifted to the far end of the pool. Constance was seated on the rock edge on the other side. She was leaning back on her hands, her face tilted to the sun, her eyes closed. Her hair was wild, a delightful tangle of half-dried curls. Her hands, her forearms and throat were tanned golden brown, but the rest of her exposed skin was a smooth creamy colour. Her clothing, like her hair, was half-dried, and clinging to her body. She might as well have been naked. And he was once again aroused. Kadar groaned. All that effort wasted.

'Constance, you should get into the shade.' She opened her eyes, turning towards him. Her smile was lazy, sun-kissed, unbearably sensual. She looked like a mermaid, perched up on the rock. 'The salt in the water will burn your skin as it dries. Get into the shade, please.'

She sat up, dangled her feet over the edge of the pool, and jumped in. Though the water was not deep, Kadar cried out a warning, hurtling himself through the water towards her. 'What are you doing? You could have…'

She laughed. 'Drowned? No, thanks to your expert tuition I will not drown. And now that I am wet again, I shall not burn.'

But he was burning. He had an armful of wet, warm, voluptuous mermaid, and his body was on fire. Her skin was still hot from the sun. 'The glare from the water,' Kadar said, struggling to keep his thoughts on practical matters, 'it makes it worse.'

Constance ignored him. 'I was watching you swim.' Her smile, that mouth, she should not be allowed to smile at him in that way with those lips. 'It was most impressive.'

'I have been swimming since I was a child. With a little more practice...' Her top was soaked through again. Her nipples were dark peaks beneath the fabric, her breasts clearly outlined, full and soft and—and they moved, when she did. He dropped his gaze. He could see the indent of her belly button too, and a strip of creamy skin where the top ended, above the sash which tied her pantaloons, mercifully below the waterline. 'Practice,' Kadar said. 'That is what you need.'

'You slice through the water like a seal, or an otter,' Constance said. 'Sleek. That is what I was thinking when I was watching you. Sleek.'

She was not looking at him. She was gazing at his chest. There was a crimson flush on her cheeks. The effect of sun, nothing more, he thought desperately. But he knew differently because she was looking at him in exactly the same way as he was looking at her. He shifted on the sand, and his foot grazed hers. He felt her shudder. He watched, mesmerised at the way her breasts juddered under the wet, clinging fabric and his resistance crumbled. He cupped her breast, running his thumb over her nipple. She shuddered again, and her flesh quivered. She flattened her hand over his chest, the cool flesh of her sea-damp palm stroking over his nipple, and Kadar groaned, pulled her tight up against him, and kissed her.

He tasted of seawater. Constance met his kiss with her own, matching his passion with hers. She was long past reason. While she had been swimming she had been far too focused on staying afloat to be distracted by Kadar's presence, but afterwards, watching him swim alone, she discovered that she had noticed after all. She remembered the feeling of his hands gently supporting her, his arm brushing her breasts, her newly buoyant body bumping against his thighs. When he floated on his back, she watched his chest rising and falling, the water droplets glittering on his skin. Her leap from the wall back into the pool was instinctive, a response to a primal craving she could not ignore, which was to touch him.

His tongue met hers. She pressed her body against him, her hands roaming feverishly over his damp skin. She was amazed that the seawater had not turned to steam, she was so hot. The world had turned blazing red with passion, and all she wanted was more. Kadar tore his mouth from hers, pressing kisses to her throat, to the wildly fluttering pulse at her collarbone, to the valley between her breasts. Her nipples were aching for his touch, for his tongue. He tugged the flimsy straps of her camisole top down her arms, rolling the fabric down to reveal her breasts. Colour slashed his cheeks as he gazed at her, his eyes dark with passion. She felt no shame, only a thrill of pleasure that she pleased him. He whispered her name before taking her nipple into his mouth and making her knees buckle.

He picked her up, wrapping her legs around his waist, and carried her to the hard-packed sand above the waterline in the shadow of the cliffs, setting her down beside him, and their kisses became deeper. She was wound taut, every part of her tingling, burning, and inside her, the thrum of arousal made her pant.

'Kadar,' she said, her voice both a plea for more, and for guidance. 'Kadar, what should I...?'

His breath was as rapid and shallow as hers. His chest was heaving. 'Constance?'

'Yes,' she said. She had no idea what she was agreeing to. Anything. Everything. She didn't care. 'Yes,' she said again.

He hesitated only briefly before undoing the sash which held her pantaloons at the waist, helping her to wriggle free of the pleated folds. She was beyond embarrassment. The blaze in his eyes was enough, and the slide of his tongue into her mouth was enough, and his finger slipping inside her was more than enough. Constance shuddered, clutched at his shoulders, shuddered again. 'You,' she said, grabbing him by the wrist to stop him before it was too late, 'you too.'

Her fingers were shaking on his sash. Her hand brushed his arousal, and he shuddered too, just like her. He struggled briefly with the knot, his teeth gritted. When it gave way she watched blatantly as he freed himself of the last piece of clothing between them, and discovered that there was a great deal of difference between a nude statue and a naked, flesh-and-blood man. She wanted to touch him, but she had no idea what to do, and there was a limit to her boldness, for she could not bring herself to ask.

And then Kadar kissed her again, rolling her onto her back. Cool damp sand beneath her, and hard, hot man looming over her. She was melting. His kiss was making her bones melt, and his fingers, sliding inside her again, were rousing her at the same time to new heights. She moaned. She shuddered. His tongue and his fingers thrust, and Constance wanted only to make him feel the same way, to take him with her. She wrapped her hand around his arousal, momentarily distracted by the softness of the skin covering the rigid length of him. She felt him tremble at the contact. Was that good or bad. 'Kadar?'

He covered her hand, showed her what to do. 'Slowly,' he whispered, his fingers sliding over her again. Slowly, she thought, as his touch made her tighten, slowly, she moved her own hand to the same pace as his, and slowly their tongues touched to that same pace. Kisses. Sliding strokes. Slow strokes. More kisses, and more stroking, more sliding, until she could not bear it any longer and let go with a cry, the pulsing of her climax echoed by a shudder running through him before he rolled away from her and his own release shook him.

It took her long moments before she returned to earth. Kadar was lying on his side, looking at her, his grey-green eyes heavy-lidded. She reached over to push a lock of silky hair away from his brow. 'Why are you frowning?'

'You know that I did not bring you here to— It was not a ploy to—to initiate any further intimacy between us,' he said.

She smiled. 'You did not initiate it.'

'Constance…'

'Of course I know that. I also know that you would not— It was a very considerate and chivalrous further intimacy,' she said, flushing.

He kissed her mouth softly. 'But be assured, the pleasure was entirely mutual.'

'Was it?'

'You know that I never say anything I don't mean.'

She knew her smile must be ridiculously self-satisfied, but she didn't care. 'Good,' she said.

Kadar laughed, pulled her against him and kissed her again. Their bodies were damp, gritty with sand, her skin was tight with salt and too much sun, but still the contact made her shiver with delight. She wrapped her arms around his neck, returning his kiss with enthusiasm, and it started again, astonishingly, the tingling and the thrumming, and she could feel him stirring against her as his hand sought her breast again, and her leg curled instinctively around his, and his member nudged between her legs.

Kadar pulled away instantly, muttering something under his breath. 'I'm sorry, I did not mean—*that* we cannot do.'

Registering the shock on his face brought her to her senses. She had not even considered the consequences of what they were doing, had been so carried away that she would have allowed him anything. Her naïvety took her breath away. The onus she had unthinkingly placed on him, the willpower he must have exercised to resist such innocent temptation. 'I didn't think,' Constance said, appalled. 'I was so—so—and I did not think. But you did, and I should thank you for being so careful.'

His expression softened. He pulled her to her feet, taking her hands in his. 'You have no need to thank me, Constance. That you trusted me is an honour.'

She had trusted him, implicitly. The knowledge made her uneasy. She had the horrible feeling that a very unwelcome fact lay waiting to be uncovered in the recesses of her brain. As if to emphasise the point, a tiny cloud covered the sun, briefly casting a shadow over the pool, giving her gooseflesh. 'Our clothes,' she said, using the excuse to slip from his hold, picking up the wet sandy rag that used to be her pantaloons and looking at it with genuine dismay.

She stumbled across the damp sand into the shallows and began to rinse the garment out, realizing then that her camisole was still wrapped around her waist. She was wriggling ineffectually, trying to free herself of it when Kadar's hand on her shoulder made her jump. He was wearing only his tunic, and held hers out for her. 'You must cover up or you will burn.'

'I can't get out of this thing,' Constance said pathetically.

'Stand still.' He ripped the now mangled strip of fabric from her waist, then pulled her tunic over her head, helping her slide her arms into the sleeves. 'Go and sit in the shade.'

'But my pantaloons…'

'Constance, I will tend to those. Go and sit in the shade by the boat. There is a flask in the hamper there, with lemonade. You need to drink, or you will get a headache. That is an order.'

She opened her mouth to protest and changed her mind. Besides he was right. Beneath the tunic, her skin was hot and prickly, and her mouth was dry, and her legs were a bit shaky, and the blanket was in deep shade now.

The lemonade was delicious. She drank two full glasses, pressing her forehead to the condensation on the outside of the flask with a grateful sigh. When she opened her eyes again, almost fully restored, Kadar was spreading out his trousers and her pantaloons on the rocks to dry.

'If I told Mama that a royal prince had done my washing she would never believe me,' she said, handing him a glass of lemonade.

'If you told your mother what else the royal prince had done she would hang me out to dry,' Kadar replied, sitting down beside her. 'Are you feeling better?'

'Yes, thank you. You were right,' Constance said with a mock sigh. 'Would you like to eat now? My first swim has made me ravenous. Does swimming always do that?'

'Many things can evoke an appetite,' Kadar said, smiling wickedly as he lifted the hamper out of the boat.

Together they laid out the food, which had been kept cool by a layer of ice packed around the metal box which lined the wicker exterior. There were pastries stuffed with nuts and pheasant, a salad of tomatoes, olives and orange, a rice pilaf scented with saffron and flavoured with dried fruits, and a delicious cake made with ground almonds, moist with lemon and honey. They ate in quiet contemplation, watching as the sun began its slow journey westward, the white-gold blaze slowly turning more golden, the tide turning, the waves growing white-crested, creeping their way slowly back up the beach towards the outer wall of the rock pool.

'Did your mother ever join you here?' Constance asked, when the remnants of the food had been returned to the hamper.

Kadar shook his head. 'She rarely left her quarters in the palace. Not because she was confined there, I hasten to add, but through choice. She was happiest in the company of other women, and seemed perfectly content to spend the day sewing, gossiping, reading. I think she would have preferred daughters to sons, though of course that would not have suited my father,' he added wryly. 'She died when I was ten. To be honest, I barely knew her.'

'How sad. Perhaps that is where you get your love of books from.'

Kadar shrugged. 'Perhaps. What about you?'

'What about me?'

'Does your mother like to read?'

'Goodness, no. Mama thinks reading is a waste of valuable time.'

'And your father thinks books are important only as a source of income,' Kadar said contemptuously.

'Yes,' Constance agreed, surprised by his tone. 'But my grandfather loved books.'

'And your father deprived you of that relationship too.'

'Yes.' Constance plucked at a thread on the blanket. 'No, that's not fair. My mother and I would have been welcome visitors, but Mama...'

'"Mama chose Papa, as she always does,"' Kadar quoted. 'Were you a very lonely child?'

'Odd,' Constance said, with a twisted smile. 'My parents thought me odd, so you see we have that much in common. Perhaps if I had been a boy my father might have shown more interest in me, and perhaps if I had been a boy, and my father had shown more interest in me, then my mother— But, there, that sounds horribly like self-pity.' She folded her arms, glaring out at the sea. 'I was a great deal more fortunate than most. You must not feel sorry for me.'

'I don't feel sorry for you, Constance, you are far too admirable for that, but I wish—I wish things could have been different for you, and I fear that your family will never appreciate you as they ought.'

'My family.' Constance gave a heavy sigh. 'I suspect I have put myself well beyond their appreciation. They will probably disown me. Let us not talk about that today, on our holiday.'

'Not today, but soon, we must discuss it. I can help you, Constance.'

'Perhaps.'

'And in the meantime, I am afraid we must set sail soon, if we are to be back in Murimon before dark, but if I may, I'd like to come up to the terrace and observe the stars with you later tonight.'

'I'd like that,' Constance said, closing her mind firmly on the alarm bells which were telling her that she would like it far too much. Tomorrow, she told the persistently tinkling warning bells as she headed over to the rocks to collect her pantaloons, tomorrow she would listen and heed their warning. Tonight it would be just herself and Kadar and the stars.

Chapter Eleven

Constance pushed aside the telescope eyepiece and wandered over to the parapet to gaze out at the horizon. Though her skin still tingled from their long day in the sun yesterday, the lotion which Kadar had had sent to her suite had worked wonders. Night was giving way to morning. The holiday was over. Kadar had retired to his bedchamber to snatch a few hours' sleep before he took up his formal duties. The stars were receding, the sky going through the first stages of its daily firework display, turning from inky blue to silver grey. Returning to the telescope, she flopped down on her cushions, feeling slightly sick. She could no longer ignore her feelings for him after what had passed between them on the beach. She was in love.

That profound insight was not the source of untrammelled joy it should be. Instead, it made her feel very, very foolish indeed. It simply hadn't occurred to her that she would fall in love. She had taken no precautions to guard her emotions until it was far too late. Kadar had given her a sense of purpose, a sense of worth, helped her take the first faltering step of this new path she was about to follow on her personal road to freedom. Kadar had seen something in Constance that no one else had seen. So, yes, gratitude formed part of what she felt, but there was a lot more to it than that.

From the moment she set eyes on him she had known he was different from any other man she had ever met. She smiled now, recalling that shockingly primal gust of desire which had gripped her. Her body had known in an instant what it had taken her mind and her heart several more weeks to acknowledge. This man was made for her. The unspoken bond that existed between them, the desire which had beguiled her into a false sense of security was not something which would fizzle out. It was a symptom of a long-term malaise. She was in love, and though she had known Kadar less than a month, she knew with sickening certainty it was a love that would last a lifetime.

Constance groaned. She loved him, and despite the fact that it changed nothing, deep inside her was a determination that it changed everything. She, Constance Montgomery, was in love. She wrapped her arms around herself, closed her eyes and allowed herself to dwell on this astounding fact. It was true, love knew no reason, cared not for logic. She loved him. For a moment, being in love was all that mattered.

But only for a moment. Opening her eyes and sitting up with her back against the telescope, Constance prepared to administer a harsh dose of reality to herself. 'Facts,' she muttered, 'facts. And the first and foremost of these is that these feelings have absolutely no impact on your future.'

Her instinctive protest against this statement startled her. Love appeared not to care for harsh reality. She would simply have to try harder. 'Fact one,' she began, drawing up a mental list, 'I can't stay here for ever. Yes, the position of court astronomer would grant me all the freedom I could wish for and more, but is it a position I would wish to hold when Kadar's passion for me has cooled, as it inevitably must?'

It was tempting to answer in the positive, tempting to tell herself that they could return to their original official footing of court astronomer and prince, forget that they had ever been a man and a woman in the throes of passion, but she knew it for a lie. Her passion would not cool. It would be folly to remain here, counting the weeks or months, waiting for Kadar to turn his attentions elsewhere as he surely would— fact two. And fact three—all the time she'd be waiting, vainly hoping that he would fall in love with her. And fact four—he would never fall in love with anyone again because—fact five—you can't improve on perfection. He'd said so himself, and emphatically at that.

Which really was the insurmountable barrier of facts, Constance thought sadly. Even if all the other practical considerations, such as her complete unsuitability as a royal bride, and her determination never to be a bride were set aside, Kadar would never marry her because Kadar would never love her.

'And so concludes my list.' She got to her feet, padding over to watch the sunrise. As ever, the spectacle took her breath away. This morning the horizon was streaked with wispy cloud, filtering the rising sun's rays into bursts of gold through a softer silver-gold shadow. Long fingers of light danced off the Arabian Sea, turning it the colour of melted butter.

Who was she, this woman who had broken Kadar's heart, this woman that no other woman could ever measure up to? Relieved to be distracted from her own weighty heartache, Constance turned her mind to Kadar's. What did she know? Very little, it seemed to her at first. Some years ago, Kadar had fallen in love with a woman named Zeinab who for some reason could not marry him. A perfect love, he had called it, so perfect that he believed he would never find such a love again, so painful in its loss that he never wanted to risk such loss ever again.

Dispirited, Constance returned to the desk and opened her notebook. Perhaps if she documented what she knew, like a star map, it would start to make sense. A star-crossed lovers' map. It would be amusing if it wasn't so tragic. She drew a heart shape around two stick figures representing Kadar and his love. What else did she know of his past? She drew a book. Yes, and there was his friend, who shared his love of books. A girl who had died, he had told her on the beach. And then he had closed the subject. Just as he had on another beach, talking of another female, now she came to think about it. His brother's wife, who had died in childbirth.

The lead of her pencil snapped on this second stick couple she had drawn representing Butrus and his wife. She stared down at her little diagram in horror. Dear heavens, surely not?

I doubt the fates would be so very cruel as to

allow history to repeat itself in this twisted way.
Kadar's words, spoken on this very terrace the
night after his coronation. Constance picked up
another pencil and drew a shaky triangle to con-
nect all three women on her chart. Kadar's childhood friend. Kadar's lover. Kadar's brother's wife.
She drew a circle in the centre of the triangle and
wrote one word. *Zeinab?*

Pity mingled with an immense sadness. Seven
years ago, Kadar had left Murimon. Seven years
ago, his brother had been crowned. And married.
A tear fell on to her notebook. Had Zeinab loved
him? No question, Constance thought, her own
new-found love making her absolutely certain.
What woman would not fall in love with Kadar?
Yet he had been forced to watch her marrying
another, and his own brother to boot. No wonder his heart was broken. No wonder he had left
Murimon. Such an honourable man. Such a terrible tragedy.

The sun was fully visible over the horizon
now. Constance sniffed, blew her nose, and
stared down at her diagram. No wonder Kadar
was so determined never to love again. She
slowly closed the notebook over. And then to
return from his exile and the entanglement of
another bride intended for his brother. History
repeating itself in a very cruel manner indeed.

He must think himself doubly cursed. No surprise at all that he could not force himself to go through with it.

But she couldn't bear to picture him living alone for the rest of his life any more than she could bear the thought of him forcing himself into another arranged marriage for the sake of his kingdom. What she wanted above all was for Kadar to be happy, but Kadar seemed intent on courting unhappiness. The spectre of the past was still haunting him, no matter how much he denied it. But how best to help him exorcise his demons? And was she considering doing so in the vain hope that if Kadar laid his ghosts to rest he might miraculously find some way to love her?

No. No, she could not be so utterly blind to reason as to contemplate that. So desperate as to avoid harsh reality. Constance yawned, exhausted from the emotions of the last few days. Returning to the cushions under the awnings, she wrapped her arms around herself and closed her eyes. It could never come to pass, but where was the harm in dreaming, imagining how it might be. She pictured herself on the beach. The sand was gritty on her back. Kadar was naked beside her. He was kissing her. Touching her. Loving her.

* * *

Kadar prowled restlessly around the room where his plans for Murimon had been brought to life in the shape of a large model of the kingdom which took up most of the available space. It showed the locations of all the new schools and the huge development that would be the new port, the wharves and docks, and even the location of a ship-building yard proposed for future development. Lining one wall were detailed drawings and more explanatory information in written form. There would be representatives from many of the towns and villages on hand to explain to those who could not read, to attempt to answer questions, and to pass on those which they could not. His own idea, which Maarku from the Great Oasis had embraced with enthusiasm, co-ordinating the representatives on his behalf. The room was to be unveiled to the council in a few days' time, opened up to the people next week. He should be feeling triumphant, but now Kadar was wondering if his utopia was simply a pipe dream.

It would be extremely difficult to achieve without the Nessarah dowry. Some harsh and unpalatable choices would be forced upon him. New schools or deepen the harbour? This would allow more varied goods to be imported, but who would be able to afford to purchase them? Which of Murimon's children to bestow the gift of education on first? And which adults? Or any? Better education would lead to increased wealth but being forced to stagger its introduction due to lack of sufficient funds meant only some would be beneficiaries. There would be rivalry. Resentment. Inequality. The very things he wished to eradicate. How to be a fair prince and provide equally for all? Kadar ran his fingers along the boundary of his model kingdom. It struck him that in one sense, it would be considerably easier and much fairer to make no changes at all.

No, that was not an option. And nor, despite the fact that her dowry would eliminate the need for this painful dilemma, was marriage to the Nessarah princess. A prince first, and a man second. A month ago, returning from his first visit to Nessarah, he remembered thinking just that. His duty was first and foremost to his kingdom. But he also had a duty to be true to himself. He would not marry a woman he didn't love, not even to launch Murimon into the nineteenth century. He would summon Abdul-Majid, set in train the delicate, rarely used but none the less established protocol for ending the betrothal, and he would then set about making the difficult choices which must be made as a consequence of his actions.

But though he was relieved to have formulated a workable strategy, Kadar was in no mood to set about executing it. Closing his eyes, he surrendered to the temptation of replaying yesterday's lovemaking in his head. Constance beneath him, on top of him, the sound of her voice, a whispery, throaty gasp as she climaxed, made his member stir to life. Captivating Constance, he had called her once and she was—utterly captivating. The way she smiled. The way she kissed. The way she bit her lip when she was trying to decide whether to press him on a subject she knew he would prefer closed. The way she saw past his words and into his mind—though that was most certainly a double-edged sword. No one had ever been able to do that. Not even Zeinab.

Startled, Kadar looked around the room foolishly, as if someone else had spoken her name aloud. He rarely permitted himself to speak it. Until recently, he rarely permitted himself to think of her at all. He could see her as the child he had first known, a serious little girl with a passion for horses and books, but he still struggled to remember the beautiful young woman she had become. He could recall her voice, smoky, soft, and he could recall the way she walked as if she were floating beneath the layers of rich silks and gauzy lace she was fond of wearing. Yes, he remembered now, teasing her that she had grown to prefer fashion to books. He had hurt her. Tears had filled her eyes—and he also remembered their colour now, a very pale brown, like the sand at low tide. She had allowed him to kiss her then. He remembered that too, the innocence of her kisses. Not passionless. Innocent. She had never allowed herself to succumb to passion. She was more honourable than he—that was all. If things had been different, he didn't doubt that she'd have allowed her passion full rein.

He had never once pressed her. Those chaste kisses were all that they had shared. She was too precious, too sweet, too fragile. He had been afraid to overwhelm her with his desire. Though he had never once had any difficulty in restraining himself.

In stark contrast to his lack of restraint on the beach with Constance. It had taken every single ounce of control not to take what she had offered, not to thrust into her, to feel her flesh enfolding him, holding him, to push higher inside her, and higher, to feel that delicious frisson as he thrust and withdrew, thrust and withdrew, to feel her tighten around him, to experience that painfully delightful tension as he held himself back until she came, the pulsing of her climax sending him over the edge.

Kadar groaned. He was hard. How could he ever have imagined that what they had done would be enough to sate his need of her? He was very far from being sated, either of her body or of her mind. Captivating Constance. Clever Constance.

Outside, the sun was coming up. He ought to be turning his mind to the diplomatic disaster looming over him. He ought to summon Abdul-Majid, but the need to be with Constance was overwhelming. Waiting only for his all-too-obvious desire to subside, Kadar made his way to the roof terrace.

She was sound asleep. Her bare feet were showing beneath the loose pleats of her pantaloons. He sank quietly onto the cushions beside her, curling himself into her back, breathing in the scent of her. Smoothing back her hair, he pressed a gentle kiss to the nape of her neck, wrapping his arms around her waist. She stirred, snuggling her *derrière* against him, and he too stirred, in a very different way. Not what he intended at all. Reluctantly, he loosed his hold on her and tried to edge away. Constance turned around, her eyes slumberous, her mouth curved into a soft smile. 'Am I dreaming?'

He knew he ought to move, but he could not bring himself to. Instead, he said her name, planting a kiss on her lovely lips. She sighed. She ran her fingers through his hair. 'I've missed you.'

His hand had slid back around her waist. Her breasts were soft against his chest. He flattened his palm over the curve of her bottom. She sighed again, snuggling closer, her thigh brushing his erection. 'I've missed you too,' Kadar said, speaking his mind, for once, without thinking.

He kissed the faint line of the scar on her brow. Her fingers fluttered over his neck, his shoulders, slipping inside the collar of his tunic. Skin on skin. Kadar shuddered. Constance tilted her head in mute invitation and all thoughts of resistance fled.

She tasted of sleep and sunshine. They kissed slowly, gently coaxing the heat between them into life. His lids were heavy, closed to reality. His senses were filled with Constance. Her soft curves. Her sweet mouth. Her sinful tongue. They kissed lingeringly, whispering their pleasure, hands tracing the shapes of their bodies, remembering, savouring, arousing.

He slid his hand inside her overdress to cup

the weight of her breast through her tunic beneath. Her nipple was a tight bud. He traced circles around it, relishing the way his touch made her shudder, sigh, her lips cling. She was lying on her back now, he was draped half over her, his leg between hers, his shaft rigid on her belly. Their kisses were passionate. He lifted his head, seeking her breast, and their gazes locked. Her eyes were cloudy, dark with desire, no doubt reflecting his own.

It came slowly but surely, the awareness of what they were doing, the dangerous path down which they were travelling. Her eyes began to clear, again no doubt reflecting his. She moved fractionally. He moved too. They sat up. They adjusted their clothing. The stared out of the awning, at the pale blue of the noon-day sky.

If only it had been a dream, they would not have stopped, Constance thought. Kadar had got to his feet, was perched on the edge of the desk. Pushing her hair back from her face, she sat up. 'Have you reached a conclusion regarding your plans, how best to terminate the betrothal?'

'It is the recognised custom that if a betrothal is ended, a gift of compensation must be made to the injured party.'

'What form might that take?'

Kadar shrugged. 'No doubt a weighty purse of precious stones. Abdul-Majid is the expert on tradition and protocol, I shall consult him. He will most likely be delighted to know that my radical plans for Murimon must be significantly pared back.'

'I think you may be surprised by his reaction,' Constance said, taking her seat behind the desk. 'It seems to me that he admires you, that he may even believe you are a better prince for Murimon than Butrus.'

Kadar sat down opposite her, picking up her notebook and flicking idly through the pages of her carefully plotted celestial observations. 'Constance, he is merely trying to ingratiate himself with me through you. He has a fondness for expediency that—what is this?'

He was holding her notebook open. Glancing at the page, Constance's stomach lurched. How could she have forgotten that stupid drawing! 'Give me that.' She leaned across the desk, but he snatched it away from her. 'I was curious,' she said. 'No, not only curious. I wanted to know—to understand why you are so—what it is that makes you so—' She broke off, afraid that if she articulated her thoughts he would detect the strength of feelings that lay behind them. 'I would have asked you directly, if I'd thought you would have answered.'

He said nothing, gazing down at her diagram, but she could see that telltale flicker in his eye. What to do? She should have torn the page from her notebook and burned it, yet there was a part of her that hoped it would force him to talk, and that by talking—what? Effect a lancing of the wound?

He rubbed his eyes wearily, and Constance wanted nothing more than to hold him, to smooth the lines from his brow and kiss away all his cares. She wanted to tell him that it didn't matter, but it did. She wanted to reassure him that he didn't need to talk about it, but he did. 'I simply want you to be happy,' she said, opting for the truth. 'That is all I care about, Kadar. I want you to be happy.'

He believed her. He could even echo her thoughts. Looking down at the sad little cartoon depiction of his doomed love affair, he felt oddly detached. He felt pity for the star-crossed lovers, yes, and sorrow for the loss of their perfect love, but both emotions were second-hand, as if the story belonged to someone else and not him. As if the little stick man was some other foolish youth, not he. It felt so much longer ago than seven years.

He could still barely recall her face, and the love that had once filled his heart, that had made her the centre of his universe—no, that was long dead. A shadow. An echo. A ghost.

Was he tired of carrying that ghost on his back, tired of the burden of the past weighing so heavily on the present and the future? Staring down at the childish images, Kadar realised that he was. Would it help to share his burden with Constance, with her big brown troubled eyes and her lovely mouth currently curved uncharacteristically downwards? Constance, the only person he had ever known who could read his thoughts. Constance, who refused to allow him to intimidate her, who pressed him and pressed him until he told her truths he never shared with anyone. Constant Constance, whose upside-down way of looking at the world had several times reflected it back to him from a new perspective. Would she be able to do so again? He was prepared to take the risk.

'It is obvious from your idiosyncratic diagram that you have grasped most of the salient facts,' Kadar said. 'However, one significant component is missing.' He picked up a pencil and added another stick man figure. As an afterthought he gave the figure a long pointy beard and drew a line from him to the circle in the middle of the drawing.

Constance looked perplexed.

'Zeinab was Abdul-Majid's daughter.'

Constance's mouth fell open. Her eyes widened. '"He did have, once..."' she said in a hollow voice. 'I mean—someone who shared his love of books. That's what you told me. You meant her, didn't you? His daughter. Zeinab. Oh, Kadar, I had no idea. No wonder you— Was it he who forbade the match?'

Yes, he wanted to say, because that is what he had always believed, it is what Zeinab had told him. But he hesitated. Was it true? 'It was complicated,' he said instead.

'And I've interrupted you. I'm so sorry.'

Constance folded her hands together on the desk. She was biting her lip, which she always did to remind herself not to speak. Her hair was flattened on one side, where she had been sleeping on it. Had she any idea how endearing she looked? Did he really want to entrust her with this sad little tragedy? Would it diminish him in her eyes? She would judge him, but wasn't that what he wanted—not so much to be judged as to have the facts scrutinised, reflected by her perceptive mind that operated like some sort of internal telescope, before being re-presented to him in a different form. He did trust her. Completely. He smiled at her crookedly. 'I will begin where all good stories should begin,' he said, echoing her own words, 'at the beginning.'

'Zeinab was raised here in the palace,' Kadar said. 'We knew each other as children. She was very beautiful, very intelligent. We shared a love of books and horses. We were—we were very like-minded.'

'Perfectly matched, you mean?'

Kadar frowned. 'It is what I thought—how I always thought of her.'

'And for the seven years of your self-imposed exile, you had no evidence to counter that belief, and now she is dead and you will never know.'

'Yes,' Kadar agreed, with another frown, lapsing into silence.

And thus her perfection is enshrined and set in stone, Constance added silently to herself. 'So,' she prompted gently, 'two like minds, spending so much time together, it is hardly surprising in such a claustrophobic atmosphere that friendship blossomed into love.'

His frown deepened. 'We knew it was forbidden. Zeinab was betrothed to Butrus from a very early age.'

She had not anticipated this. Touched to the

heart, Constance reached impulsively across the desk to take his hand. 'I'm so sorry. To love someone, and to know that you can never have them is so very dreadful.'

Too late, she realised that her own newly discovered feelings were horribly present in her voice, in the tremor, in the thickness caused by the tears which clogged her throat. She could only hope that Kadar was too caught up in his own thoughts to notice.

Apparently not. 'A rather odd response from someone who equates love with servitude, if I may say so,' he said.

She blinked at him, her fingers straying to her scar, a habit she thought she had cured herself of. 'I meant—I believe I referred to love that was one-sided,' she said. 'You and Zeinab loved each other. A different case entirely, and all the more tragic. That is why I sound a little emotional. You did love each other, didn't you?'

'Why do you ask?'

'Your brother. I can't fathom why Butrus would marry the woman you loved, who loved you back.'

'Because Butrus was unaware of our feelings for each other.'

'Surely he must have guessed when he saw you spend so much time together.'

'Our love was illicit, Constance. We were very careful to keep our assignations secret, our true feelings hidden.'

She tried, but could not imagine someone as honourable as Kadar involved in the subterfuge of an illicit love affair. Or involving the woman he loved in such subterfuge. 'I have learned that you are a man of great integrity, and you are also a man who likes to consider his options and to plan for them. I doubt you were so very different back then. You must have considered the future, Kadar. I cannot imagine that you simply allowed the matter to drift along, hoping that fate would intervene or—or something.'

'I was very different, Constance. I was naïve enough to imagine that nothing mattered save our love for each other. I wanted Zeinab to marry me at any cost.'

'Would the cost have been so great? Your father was not a despot. If you had explained the sincerity and depth of your feelings, wouldn't he have understood?'

Kadar looked distinctly uncomfortable. 'I could not persuade Zeinab to take the risk,' he said. 'If he had refused, and Zeinab was still required to marry Butrus—to have a husband know that you are in love with his brother...'

'But then if Butrus knew you were in love,

wouldn't he have gladly relinquished his claim on her?' Constance persisted. 'I assume he harboured no deep feelings for her himself?'

'No, he was indifferent towards her.'

If she did not know him better, she would have said that Kadar looked—uneasy... No. Slightly panicked, perhaps?

'Zeinab reckoned that Butrus would be even more set on marrying her if he knew that I loved her. The fierce sibling rivalry between us meant that...'

'She believed he would marry her just to spite you?' Constance covered her mouth, but it was too late to pretend she was anything other than incredulous.

Kadar nodded his head in affirmation, swallowed, and gazed down at his hands. 'Whether she was right or not,' he said slowly, 'that's what she believed. And that is all that mattered to me at the time.'

Constance bit her tongue. Kadar would not wish to hear her most uncharitable thoughts on Zeinab, and she did not wish to voice the jealousy she was convinced lay at the root of them.

Her silence for once spurred him on. 'Besides,' Kadar said, 'it was not only a question of my father but her father too. Abdul-Majid's ambition was for his daughter to be Princess of Murimon. It would secure his pre-eminent position within the court hierarchy.'

The last piece of the puzzle. 'And so he sacrificed her,' Constance said. 'That is what you said, that Abdul-Majid had sacrificed his daughter for the sake of power.'

'Yes. He did. That is what I meant.'

'He knew, then, that his daughter was in love with you?'

'And he insisted that she marry my brother. Now you understand the kind of man he is.'

Did she? Abdul-Majid did not strike her as a power-mad despot, but she hardly knew him, and was in no position to judge. Was Kadar, or had his judgement been skewed by his emotions? 'So Zeinab would not permit you to do the honourable thing and declare your love. That must have been very difficult for you—no, it must have been almost impossible.'

'You give me far too much credit Constance,' he replied stiffly. 'I wanted to elope. It was not only an utterly naïve and foolish idea, it was a selfish and most dishonourable one. Zeinab made me see that. Zeinab persuaded me that love stolen under such circumstances could never flourish.'

'And so she strangled it at birth, by agreeing to marry your brother.'

Once again she had let her feelings get the better of her. Kadar flinched. 'You have no right to judge her.'

'I beg your pardon,' Constance said, thinking that it was about time someone judged the perfect paragon Zeinab. But how to force Kadar to see that his goddess was probably tarnished? And how to be sure that her own motives for doing so were noble and not self-serving. 'So Zeinab married Butrus. Were they happy?'

'I left Murimon immediately after the wedding.'

No answer, Constance thought, and Kadar must have read this thought because he shrugged. 'I believe my brother remained in ignorance of his wife's true feelings.'

She waited. Kadar tapped his finger on the desk. 'I honestly don't know,' he said. 'What I do know is that Zeinab was a woman of honour. She entered into that marriage determined to make it work.'

'But you suspect she must have endured unhappiness. That is why you were so against my marriage,' Constance said, touched, 'though I was not in love with another man when I agreed to it. If I had been, I would never, ever have consented to marry another.'

Once again her words were fuelled by her

new-found love, and once again Kadar was subjecting her to his Mind Reader look. She must not wear her heart so obviously on her sleeve. Luckily he couldn't literally read her mind.

'How can you be so certain of that when your experience of love is confined to an adolescent infatuation with a groom and a brief flirtation with a Russian acrobat?' Kadar asked, once again proving her wrong.

'Don't forget the blacksmith,' she said in an effort to distract him. 'I never claimed to be in love with any of those men.'

'Which makes you singularly unsuitable to judge Zeinab.'

He was right. Constance slumped back in her seat, as if the air had been punched out of her body. 'I'm sorry. You are quite right, I have no right to judge her. I wished only to help you, and all I have done is make you angry.'

'I'm not angry, Constance.' Kadar picked up the notebook again, rifling through the pages until he came to her diagram. He drew a question mark above the head of the bearded figure. 'And you have helped, despite what you think,' he said.

'How?'

'By pointing out that I have no way of knowing whether Zeinab was happy with her lot or not. I assumed—but I don't know for certain. There is one person who does, though, and I intend to ask him.'

'Abdul-Majid.'

Kadar shut the notebook with a decisive snap and got to his feet. 'Once the past is put to bed I can focus on the future. Now if you will excuse me, I have a betrothal to cancel, and plans to revise.'

Chapter Twelve

~~~~~~~~~~~~~~~~~~~

Anxious as he was to confront Zeinab's father, experience had taught Kadar the value of contemplation. He was, as Constance had adroitly pointed out, a man who liked to consider and to plan. Picking up the key of his orrery, he wound it up and watched the planets slowly begin their orbits of the sun, the tiny representation of the moon rotating around the earth. His thoughts drifted away from the past to the present and his court astronomer.

Constance had said that she missed him. When he'd told her he'd missed her too, he hadn't been referring to their mutual passion. He had missed *her*, though there had been times during their last conversation when he hadn't recognised her. Her thoughts and feelings, usually written so plain on her face, had been guarded, yet there had been other moments where she had seemed to him oddly overemotional. And judgemental too, implying that Zeinab had lacked the courage of her convictions, that Zeinab had not loved him enough. And that he had been too trusting.

Had he, as Constance implied, put his lover on a pedestal? Idealised her? Created an impossibly perfect version of reality? Kadar propped his chin on his hand, frowning as the planets orbited to the sound of the mechanical cogs turning the mechanism. Had it been a cathartic experience to discuss it with Constance? It had certainly raised questions he had never before asked himself, and he found that he now wished to seek answers to those questions.

The moon had ground to a halt again, as it was prone to do. He flicked it with his little finger, setting it off on its journey around the earth. Anningan, chasing his lady love, Constance had told him. Had he been more in love than Zeinab? Had he misread a lack of love as a desire to do the honourable thing? If she had run away with him, would they have been happy? With Zeinab by his side, would he have achieved more or less in life? She had never been strong, not like Constance. Zeinab was a delicate and fragile desert flower, requiring nurturing, careful tending. Not that she had been weak, but it was true, she had been inclined to bend her will to the wind, he recalled now. Resistance made her wilt. With Zeinab as his wife, he would not have been able to pursue success so single-mindedly. But with Zeinab as his wife, would he have wanted to pursue such success?

Had she loved him less than he her? Another potentially painful question, yet it merely roused his curiosity. She was dead, and so too was whatever love they had shared seven years ago. Seven years! It seemed like a lifetime, so much had changed. He had changed. He tried, but he could not remember what it had felt like, that love he had once thought so precious, so perfect. If he could meet Zeinab now, what then? Would their love blossom afresh? The question seemed treacherous, the answer treason, for into his head came a vision not of Zeinab, but of Constance. Captivating Constance, whose body he craved, whose passions equalled his. Kadar smiled, forgiving himself. To compare the two women was foolish beyond belief. Love and passion. Two very different emotions.

The orrery came to a stop, Jupiter halting with its usual jerky click. There was only one man capable of answering his questions. Could he trust him to tell the truth, or would Abdul-Majid's propensity for expediency lead him to tell Kadar only what he thought he wanted to hear?

He had been deeply unhappy in those early days after fleeing Murimon. Slightly disgusted at his younger self, he recalled taking perverse comfort in imagining Zeinab being equally unhappy. It had become a habit with him to think of them both nursing their broken hearts and shattered dreams, but truly, when he searched his memory, his conscience, the anguish of those first months had not persisted. The heartache had faded, leaving only a steely determination never to suffer it again.

And Zeinab? How often had he thought of Zeinab? Not the love he had lost, but the princess, the wife, the woman living out her new life in the kingdom he had left behind? The harsh truth was that he had not thought of her at all, had not tried to imagine that life, had taken every care, in his limited correspondence with his home, not to discover what life might be like for her. Had she been content with Butrus? Had she made his brother happy, or had the lack of a child made them both miserable? Only Abdul-Majid knew.

The time had come to find out, because Constance was right—once again Constance was right, he corrected himself with a rueful smile.

Whatever the truth, the time had come for him to face it and then put it firmly behind him.

'Very well, Highness, I shall attend to the matter immediately. The question still remains as to appropriate compensation to the princess's family for the breach of contract.'

Kadar took a sip of mint tea, nodding his assent when Abdul-Majid offered to refill his glass from the chased silver pot which sat on the huge tray in the middle of the low marble table. This was his first visit to his chief adviser's suite of rooms since his return to Murimon. The bookshelves lining the walls were perhaps a little fuller, the rugs which covered the marbled floor a little more worn, but they were the same bookshelves, the same rugs which had been here when Abdul-Majid had been his father's chief adviser. This table—how many times had he drunk sherbet at this table as a boy, after lessons? How could he have forgotten those lessons in Ancient Greek and in Latin? The histories of the pharaohs and of the ancient Arabian tribes? Lessons learnt from scrolls so delicate that he had worn fine silk gloves to prevent the heat from his fingers damaging them. Abdul-Majid had been a patient and talented tutor. How could he have forgotten that? But nothing had actually changed, and that was the irony. The room was the same. No doubt Abdul-Majid's determination to keep things as they were had not changed either. 'I was thinking,' Kadar said, 'that instead of jewels, we could offer Nessarah what they would have gained through the marriage alliance. Access to our port,' he clarified, seeing the confusion writ on the older man's face. 'Favourable trading terms for both exports and imports.'

'It is the tradition to offer precious stones, Highness.'

Kadar sighed. 'Can you not see your way to break with tradition this once?'

'As it transpires I think it a most excellent suggestion, Highness, and one which is likely to be well received. A proposition which I would be glad to broker on your behalf. From Nessarah's perspective, such trade is of far more value than some shiny baubles, and from our perspective— well, who would not wish to increase their trade with such a wealthy kingdom?'

'Precisely,' Kadar said, trying not to sound as disconcerted as he felt.

Abdul-Majid tugged at his beard, forming his mouth into what might have been a smile, but it was difficult to tell. 'I am an old camel, but it is still possible for me to learn new tricks, Sire. Tragic as the circumstances surrounding your succession, for Murimon your arrival is most timely. If we do not rise to the challenge of this new century, then we will fade into obscurity.'

'Are you saying that you approve of my plans?'

'I am saying that I understand the need for them, Sire.' Another tug of the beard, another slightly ingratiating smile. 'My days of influence are over. It is time, as Candide says, for me to cultivate my garden. You do not need my approval, Highness, but if you ask do I think your plans are what Murimon needs, then my answer must be in the affirmative.'

'When Butrus died, you told me that what Murimon needed was stability, a royal wedding, a new dynasty, yet you do not seem overly upset or indeed surprised at my decision to cancel the betrothal contract you negotiated for my brother.'

'Prince Butrus was happy to rely on others to look after his best interests, Highness. You have always struck me as someone who prefers to make his own decisions, whether right or wrong.'

As ever with Abdul-Majid, there were two conversations going on, two sets of meanings to be attributed to his words. It was precisely the kind of conversation which Kadar had presided over countless times on behalf of the great and the good. The seeds of his own diplomatic skills had in fact most likely been sown by the man sitting at the table with him, but Kadar decided the time had come for frankness, not finesse.

'Was my brother happy in his marriage to your daughter? No, don't shake your head and shrug your shoulders, Abdul-Majid, I want an honest answer.'

But Abdul-Majid shook his head and shrugged his shoulders anyway. He took a sip of tea. And then another. And then he did something he rarely did. He met Kadar's gaze square on. 'He was content, as far as a man such as your brother could ever be happy with a woman who could not give him a son to succeed him. There were, as you would expect with Prince Butrus, other women, but he was discreet. I doubt my daughter suspected, else she would have confided her suspicions to me.'

'Do you really think she would have spoken to you of such a thing?'

'Yes.' The affirmative was spoken with absolute certainty, but immediately Abdul-Majid's voice gentled. 'My daughter trusted me, Highness. I always knew what was in her heart.'

Like Kadar, Abdul-Majid was a man who chose his words carefully. Was this an admission of guilt? 'You must have known then that she loved me,' Kadar said, although what had been a statement of certainty for so long was now most definitely posed as a question.

His answer was painfully slow in coming. Once again, Abdul-Majid chose his words with care. 'She did love you, Highness, but Zeinab was— My daughter was accustomed from a very young age to the knowledge that one day she would be crowned Princess of Murimon. She could not help but be attracted to the influence and the riches that position would provide.'

'The lemon does not fall far from the tree,' Kadar said drily.

Abdul-Majid acknowledged this with a shrug and a nod. 'She was my daughter. We were more alike than perhaps you realised. But you must not think her guilty of deceit, Highness. Her feelings for you were genuine, if not as strong as yours for her. Nor was her resolve as resolute as yours in the face of opposition.'

'I would never have tried to make her do anything she didn't want to do. Quite the contrary,' Kadar said, recalling his conversation with Constance. 'So many times I begged her to allow me to speak to my father, but she would have none of it and I acceded to her wishes.'

'For which I am glad. Sire, I am truly sorry to have to say so, but what you wanted could never be permitted to happen. You would only have succeeded in making things worse for both of you.'

'I asked her to elope with me, did you know that?'

'I did, and that would have been another huge mistake on both your parts. I told my daughter as much. Zeinab was a delicate desert flower who could only flourish in the cossetted confines of the palace. She was born and bred for court life, not living a nomadic life with you, surviving on your wits. She knew that in her heart, which was why she chose to marry Prince Butrus. Highness, the stark truth is that you were not capable of making each other happy.'

'A delicate desert flower,' Kadar said, with a twisted smile, remembering his own thoughts.

'As you say.'

'And did she bloom under my brother's tender care?'

The older man sighed, dropping his eyes to his empty glass. 'The lack of a son and heir was a tragedy which affected them both, but she was as content as it was possible for a wife to be, under such circumstances.' He looked up, his eyes damp. 'It has been a great source of regret to me that this has caused a rift between us, but I am, despite what you may think, first and foremost a father, even before I am a loyal servant of the crown. My intervention was with my daughter's best interests at heart. I would do so again, Highness.'

'I would like to think you would,' Kadar said, getting to his feet. 'If we could have had this conversation seven years ago—ah, no, that is unfair of me. I doubt very much I would have listened. I would more likely have acted in the mistaken belief that I was playing the knight errant, and I suspect the repercussions would have been as you said. Unhappiness. For all parties. I thank you for your honesty.'

'And I must humbly thank you for your gracious understanding, Highness, and beg your forgiveness.'

'Even though you would do it again?' Kadar laughed shortly. 'Let us, as the English say, draw a line under the matter. It is done, and I am done with it. The future is what matters. Will you draw up the necessary papers, setting out the terms of our offer to Nessarah?'

'I will do more than that. I will personally deliver them and obtain their agreement, Highness. After which I think it is best that I retire from this positon. You will wish a younger man, a man you have chosen yourself, to be your trusted adviser.'

'So you'll go and cultivate your garden, just like Candide?'

'It is as Cicero said, Highness. If you have a garden, and a library,' Abdul-Majid said, indicating the bulging shelves, 'a man has everything he needs.'

'Except your daughter to share it,' Kadar said sadly.

'But she does, Highness. She is here with me, every day in my heart.'

Constance spent the night as usual working on her star maps, but for once the heavens could not hold her attention. Time and again, her mind strayed from tracking constellations to Kadar's decision to track down the truth of his past. Had he spoken to Abdul-Majid? Was he now avoiding her because it had been an unsatisfactory meeting, because it had changed nothing, or changed too much, or because there had been no meeting at all? Perhaps he had thought better of it. That might be best. She had been so certain that she was doing the right thing in forcing him to confront the past, but now she was terrified that the only thing it would do was cause him more pain.

Finally, as dawn broke, her patience snapped. Quickly changing into her riding clothes, Constance saddled up her lovely mare and headed for the beach.

She found Kadar seated on the sands nearest the port. It was obvious that he too had been up all night. Her heart ached when she saw him. Hearts did really ache, who would have thought it? And arms ached too, when they were prevented from throwing themselves around a beloved, and lips too, when they were not permitted to say that they would make everything better. 'I was worried,' she said. 'I am sorry, I know if you'd wanted to talk to me you would have found me, but—should I leave you to your musings?'

He shook his head, patting the sand beside him. 'I have grown weary of solitary contemplation. Your presence is most welcome.'

Thoroughly relieved, for she wasn't at all certain she'd have been able to leave him, Constance tied her horse up alongside Kadar's and joined him on the sand.

He picked up a stone and held it out for her inspection. 'Flint,' he said, 'and perfectly flat, see? Ideal for skimming, something Butrus could always do with much more skill than I. I'd forgotten.' He threw the stone, smiling faintly when it sank after four skips. 'Butrus would have managed six or seven. He did twelve once. A record neither of us ever surpassed. Here, try.'

He handed Constance a stone, showing her how to hold it. 'Two,' she said, 'pathetic.'

'Try again.'

This time Kadar guided her arm, and the stone skipped three times, earning her another faint smile before he returned his gaze to the sea, or, more likely from the distant look in his eyes, towards the past, seemingly unaware of her presence at his side. Constance bit her lip, determined not to resist the urge to fire a barrage of questions at him.

After what felt like an eternity, he turned back to face her. 'Butrus was genuinely delighted when I came back to Murimon. So full of *joie de vivre*, so pleased to have me home, looking forward so much to his future with his new princess and hopefully, at some point, a son and heir. Thank the stars he had never, ever had any idea of the feelings which existed between Zeinab and I. Or rather,' he added with a grimace, 'the feelings I thought existed.'

For once, he made no effort to hide his emotions. There was sorrow in his eyes, and regret, but overall, what Constance discerned was something more akin to shock. Her heart in her mouth for fear she would say the wrong thing and cause his defences to reform, she instead squeezed his hand tightly.

Kadar picked up another stone and threw it.

Four hops. Another. Six this time. 'Your questions served to make me doubt my previous certainty,' he said. 'When I saw Abdul-Majid yesterday I was prepared to hear a slightly different version of events. But what he told me—well, I will tell you exactly what he told me.'

Constance listened as he recounted the conversation, alternating between outrage and pity and sorrow, and fighting with all her might to keep every emotion from her face. 'Oh, Kadar, I am not surprised you needed to be on your own,' she said when he finished, 'you must feel as if your world has been turned upside down.'

'You'd think I would, wouldn't you, but the strange thing is that I feel as if it's actually been put to rights,' he replied with an odd little laugh. 'I deeply regret the time I could have spent with Butrus, I regret the seven almost silent years of my self-imposed exile, but very little else.'

'Because you didn't waste those years?' she hazarded.

He kissed her hand. His mouth was cold on her skin. 'Clever Constance. Yes, because they made me who I am now, and because they also prepared me for the challenges of being the type of prince I want to be. But that is not to say that I think Abdul-Majid did me a favour.'

'Far from it,' she said indignantly. 'It is one

thing to understand his motives, quite another to endorse them.'

'Constant Constance.' Kadar threw another stone, not skimming it, but hurling it as far out into the waves as he could. 'I can always rely on you to be on my side.'

'You know you can, Kadar.' *Even though she could not be by his side for much longer.* Her love for him was so huge she felt as if she could hardly contain it, and for the briefest of moments she made no attempt to, allowing her feelings to show in her eyes as she reached over to smooth his rebellious hair from his brow. 'You know you can,' she repeated softly.

'Yes.'

Kadar leaned towards her. He touched her cheek. Her lips parted for his kiss, but at the last moment he pulled back, picking up yet another stone from the pile he had amassed by his side. 'The most surprising thing I learned,' he said, his tone bright but brittle, 'is that Abdul-Majid is, as he claimed, a father first and foremost. A very loving father, though I am not sure that he understood his daughter as well as he thinks. Zeinab could easily have told Abdul-Majid what he wanted to hear, just as she told me what I wanted to hear, and no doubt her husband too.'

This latest stone followed the other into the

sea, and Kadar let out an exasperated sigh. 'Am I being unfair?' He did not wait for an answer. 'Were my own motives really as pure as I thought them? I loved her, or I believed it was love, but how much of that attraction was the illicit thrill of the forbidden?' His gaze had returned to the sea and inwards. 'Were my feelings for Zeinab a figment of my youthful imagination, built on sand with no firm foundation?'

His tone was questioning, as if he were debating some legal matter rather than one of the heart. 'What on earth did Abdul-Majid say to lead you to that conclusion?' Constance asked.

'Nothing at all. If you must know it is you who has led me to that conclusion,' he answered, turning around to face her. 'You see, I had no difficulty in restraining my passion for Zeinab and yet I have enormous difficulty in restraining my passion for you.'

Her heart began to thump very hard. What was she to make of this startling revelation? Dear heavens, what she mustn't do was make too much of it. For her, passion was an expression of love, but for Kadar—no, she must not make too much of it. 'Passion is not love,' she said, somewhat disingenuously, for she longed to be contradicted.

'No, it is not,' Kadar said, unwittingly twisting a dagger into her poor heart. He lobbed yet another stone, this time half-heartedly. It landed with a plop in the shallows. 'Enough,' he said, getting to his feet. 'I have wasted a whole night on speculation. To continue would not only be pointless but destructive too. Zeinab has gone, and with her the opportunity to know with any certainty.'

He held out his hand to help her up. 'In my heart I am relieved Abdul-Majid intervened as he did. It gave me the impetus I needed to leave Murimon, to broaden my horizons. To make me the man I am today, as I said. In the end, Butrus remained blissfully ignorant and Zeinab—well, I can only hope that she was content with her decision. My story is not tragic, Constance. The true tragedy lies in the untimely deaths of both my brother and his wife. But those too are in the past, and their version of my story lies buried with them. What matters to me now is to deal with the consequences, and to take charge of my future.'

The relief was overwhelming, though her joy must be bittersweet, for Kadar's beginning must mark their ending. 'I am so glad. I want you to be happy,' Constance said, the words heartfelt. 'It is all I want, but I was so afraid that I was wrong, that...'

He touched her cheek. 'You were right. I can

finally be free of the past and look forward to whatever the future holds for me. Clever Constance.'

'Considerably relieved Constance,' she said with a weak smile.

'Captivating Constance.' Kadar slid his arm around her waist, pulling him towards him, his expression lightening. 'Now we have both, in our own ways, found freedom, I think a celebration of this momentous event is warranted.'

'What do you mean?'

'A short hiatus,' Kadar said with a smile that was unmistakably sinful. 'A break with the past, a suspension of time before we embrace our respective futures.'

'We cannot suspend time,' Constance said, trying and failing not to be beguiled.

'We can suspend reality,' Kadar said, tightening his hold on her. 'Or at least escape from it. What do you think?'

Her face was heating with what she was thinking. 'I think that it would be unwise,' Constance said, because it was what she ought to say. 'We have been at such pains to avoid speculation, to respect the proprieties, why now, when my time here is coming to an end…'

'Precisely because your time here is coming to an end, as is my betrothal. Because I have the rest of my life to behave with propriety, but I have very little time left with you to behave with abandon.'

'Abandon.' A shiver of delight ran up her spine. 'I would very much like to behave with abandon,' Constance said. And there was so very little time left to do so. Such a heartbreakingly tiny amount of time. But that was better than none. 'If you are certain it is not unwise, that we will not give in to temptation?'

'I am sure it is very unwise, and I make no such promise.'

'Then let us be unwise,' she said fervently.

'Then so it shall be. A hiatus,' Kadar said. And finally, he kissed her.

The next morning, Constance, perched on one of the wooden bollards used for securing the various craft to the quayside, watched on as Kadar readied their dhow to set sail.

He seemed unburdened, after yesterday's astonishing confessional on the beach. She would not have dreamed such intimate revelations possible from the man she had first encountered, whose every feeling had been guarded, whose every word was considered. And to have entrusted her with such deeply personal thoughts, such—such painful thoughts. She was beyond honoured. She could have no more doubts that he would find happiness in his future now, and that knowledge must bolster her resolve to leave Murimon in pursuit of her own happiness. She was under no illusions. Kadar's road to freedom and her own would never converge. Tempting as it was to postpone her own journey, every day she spent in his company increased her love for him, and increased the heartache she would suffer when she left him. She had to leave while she still had the will and resolve to do so.

This fact lurked like a tempest on the horizon. But today the sky was a perfect blue and the water was a sparkling turquoise and Kadar was smiling up at her from the dhow, his bone-melting smile, and her bones and her heart were duly melted. A hiatus. Yes, she intended to enjoy her hiatus to the full.

'Ready?' he called, and she got to her feet.

Kadar was dressed in plain white cotton trousers and tunic. His feet were bare. Constance removed her own slippers, casting them down ahead of her into the boat. His eyes were more green than grey today, taking their colour from the sea, she thought fancifully as she took his hand and clambered down from the jetty into the dhow. She was also dressed simply, apricot pantaloons and camisole, a darker orange overdress trimmed with apricot braid, her hair tied back with a matching ribbon, though she doubted it would remain confined for long, once they set sail.

This dhow was painted white, trimmed with blue and yellow, low in the water at the aft, rising in a sleek curve to the pointed prow. The white triangular sail which sat at an angle on the central mast was already set, though the sailcloth was not yet filled by the wind. Though the boat was diminutive compared to some of the other commercial craft moored in the harbour, now she was on board, Constance could see it was considerably bigger than the little boat they had sailed to the swimming beach in.

'Won't you need help to sail this?' she asked.

'I have all the help I need,' Kadar replied, laughing when she looked around her, as if there was another crew member lurking somewhere. 'You did say that you wanted to learn, didn't you?'

Her heart gave a little skip of excitement. 'I'd love to learn,' Constance said, eyeing the sail, which seemed much bigger now she was standing next to it. 'But why this dhow? Wouldn't it be easier for me to learn in something smaller?'

'The other boat is only really suitable for sailing close to the coast,' Kadar replied.

It took her a moment to understand his meaning,

and when she did, she dropped onto the narrow seat, her stomach fluttering with apprehension. 'We're going out to sea.'

'Not if you don't want to, Constance.' Kadar sat down opposite her. 'You told me that learning to swim would overcome your fear of drowning, but I thought you'd like to prove it to yourself before you sail away to the ends of the earth as you said you wished to do.'

She smiled faintly at the memory. 'Only because you couldn't give me a ladder to reach the stars.'

'If I could I would, I promise you, but even princes have their limitations. I can promise you a night lying on the beach with the waves murmuring and the stars sparkling overhead, just as you wished for,' Kadar said. 'If you think you can brave the voyage?'

A trial run for the longer sea voyage to come. His thoughtfulness brought a lump to her throat, but at the same time she felt as if her heart was being squeezed at this evidence that he accepted her departure was both inevitable and imminent. He was now free to embrace his own future. Which, after all, is what she wanted for him, even though that future did not include her. She knew that. Yes, she knew that perfectly well.

'Constance? It is too much. I'm sorry...'

'No.' She would not permit such thoughts to blight this day, and she would make very sure that Kadar was not even aware of her having thought them. Having vanquished the ghosts of his lost love, she had no desire to burden him with the guilt of failing to return hers. 'No,' she repeated firmly, rising from the narrow bench. 'I want to learn to sail, and I want to face down my fears.'

'You're sure?'

'I'm certain,' she said with a great deal more confidence than she felt.

'Courageous Constance,' Kadar said, kissing her hand.

'Let us hope that I don't prove to be Catastrophic Constance,' she said, 'the captain's capsizing crew member. Now, let us set sail before my courage fails me.'

She need not have worried. Kadar was an expert sailor and an excellent tutor. From the moment they sailed out of the harbour and the breeze filled the lateen sail, he entrusted her with the tiller, assuring her that the boat was almost impossible to capsize. For the first half hour, she felt as if she were doing her best to prove him wrong as she guided them flawlessly at precisely the wrong angle into every oncoming wave, tip-ping dangerously into the swell as they reached deeper waters, and at one point sending a wave crashing right over them both, drenching them in spray.

'Kadar,' she shrieked, terrified and exhilarated, her hair dripping wet, her hand slippery on the smooth wood of the tiller. 'Please take over, I have no aptitude for this.'

But he shook his head, continuing to sit with apparent confidence by her side, tending sporadically to the sail. 'How will you develop aptitude without practice?' he asked her.

His hair too was dripping. His thigh was pressing against hers. His tunic clung to his chest. His smile made her heart turn somersaults. The sail whipped in the breeze, and the waves crested around the slim hull, which rose and fell with a soft smack on the swell, as Constance finally began to steer with more confidence. Spray stung her cheeks. Her ribbon long lost, her hair flew around her, thick with salt and doubtless tangled beyond redemption. The dhow scudded over a larger wave, lifting her from her seat and dropping her back down with a thump.

'I feel as if I am flying,' she exclaimed, laughing with the sheer exhilaration of it. 'This is truly wonderful.'

Kadar, laughing with her, wiped the spray

from her face. 'You certainly seem to have lost any remaining fears you had of the sea.'

'Oh, I don't fool myself into thinking that I would be able to swim far in this swell, but I know enough now to keep myself afloat, thanks to you.' Constance lifted one of her hands briefly from the tiller to touch Kadar's knee. 'You did that. I was shipwrecked, cast adrift in this beautiful, strange, exotic land, and I have not only survived, I'll never be the same. Thanks to you, I am a new, stronger Constance.'

'Confident Constance,' he said. 'No longer afraid of anything.'

Save leaving you. 'Save capsizing this dhow,' she said, hastily replacing her hand on the tiller as a cross-wind caught the sail, the struggle to re-gain control banishing this melancholy thought. Confident Constance, Kadar had said, and there had been a touch of pride in his voice that made her determined to live up to his expectations.

'Yesterday,' she said, 'you told me that you regretted the years which separated you and your brother. It made me think of how much I regretted the years in which I allowed my parents to deprive me of my grandfather's company, but it also made me realise—oh, I have wasted so much time nurturing resentment, in railing at my father's failings and my mother's blind loyalty. I wasn't exactly unhappy, but I could have been so much happier. Being here, thanks to the freedom you have given me, I see that I don't need to accept the hand fate has dealt me. Like you, I can take charge of my own destiny. Like you, I am done with the past. I want to be Courageous Constance. I don't want to let you down, Kadar.'

'It is not possible. You have only to be yourself in order to succeed.'

If she chose to, she could read tenderness in his expression as well as admiration. How much she wanted to. 'Well, then I will succeed,' Constance said, hoping that the tears which spilled over onto her cheeks would be mistaken for sea spray. 'I am determined to be myself. Free, under any circumstances. I know it's not going to be easy, because my circumstances can't be anything other than constrained, but they will be my choice, those constraints, and that is what matters.'

'I have no doubt that you will succeed in whatever you do,' Kadar said, kissing her cheek, 'but you know that I can help you, remove some of those constraints.'

That look again. It was *not* tenderness. 'No,' she said, determinedly focusing on the sea ahead. 'Please,' she added, when he would have protested. 'This is our hiatus. Let us have no more talk of the past or the future.'

He nodded, though reluctantly, and another whip of cross-winds forced him to turn his attention to the sail. Her future would be hers alone, without Kadar. Her choice. She loved him, and she could choose to make a slave of herself to that love, but she would not. Another thing she had learned here. Such a marriage would indeed be a prison, unless he loved her back—then their marriage would be without bars. But he did not love her. Her time here had always been an interlude for both of them, and that interlude was coming to an end.

But it was not over yet. When Kadar returned to her side, slipping his arm around her waist, she nestled closer. 'Thank you,' she said. 'For today. Now I really can sail away to the ends of the earth without fear, if I choose.'

He pressed a swift kiss to her lips. 'Never mind the ends of the earth. Do you think you're ready to steer us onto landfall?'

He gave her no chance to decline, placing his other hand on top of hers on the tiller. At first she thought they were headed for the huge grey outcrop of rock that rose rather like a loaf of bread from the sea, but as they sailed towards it, she could see a cluster of smaller islands sheltering in the lea of the larger one. Some were simply huge crags, others were smaller, no more than a sandy shore and a clump of rock, forming a chain around a larger, central island.

'That is where we will land,' Kadar said, his hand now firmly guiding hers through the narrow channel, where the water turned from azure to turquoise, clear enough and shallow enough for her to see the bottom. 'Hold her steady,' he said, 'and aim for that gap in the rock there.'

She did as he bid while he tended to the sail, returning to help her steer just as the inlet loomed up with frightening speed. A natural harbour, it seemed to be, with the rock forming a jetty, against which the dhow came to rest. Kadar jumped lithely out, quickly securing the vessel, leaning down to help her ashore. Constance staggered, her sea legs turning to jelly on the land. He took her by the hand, leading her up a rough-hewn set of steps. 'What is this place?' she asked in wonder.

'It's known as Koros.'

Behind her, on the other side of the harbour, scrub grew out of the rocks. At the top of the steps they came to a wall constructed of white stone, and Kadar ushered her through a doorway, at which point Constance stopped in her tracks, speechless with wonder. The wide flat space looked to be an ancient marketplace or forum. The remains of the tall pillars which would have formed the arcade stood in two lines, some as tall as twenty feet, some a mere three or four, the height of a single stone block. Remnants of the pillars lay on the ground, along with other long, flat stones which must have formed other parts of the building. The forum stood open on three sides to the sea, but it was built up on one side, a steeply angled wall with a set of stairs leading to another, higher and narrower terrace.

It was here that the tent was pitched in the shelter of a group of palm trees, looking outrageously exotic. Scarlet trimmed with gold tassels, it was enclosed on three sides, the front open to face out to the sea. Constance clasped her hands together, quite overcome with delight as she stepped inside. The tent was lined with silk, the floor covered with rich rugs, scattered with heaps of plush velvet cushions. Lamps were hanging from the ceiling in readiness for the night, and a wide, low divan stacked with blankets, also in readiness. She shivered in anticipation, wondering what other delights night might bring, but there was too much to distract her for her to dwell on it. A low table was set in the cooler part of the tent, where the palm trees overhead protected it from the heat of the sun. Beside it sat several huge hampers. The kind designed to keep the contents cold, she saw, gratefully accepting a drink of lemon sherbet which Kadar poured for her.

'How? Where are they all?' she asked in wonder, looking around her for the retinue of servants it must have taken to set up.

'There's no one else here now,' Kadar replied, clearly pleased by her reaction 'It was prepared for us at first light.'

'You ordered all of this especially for me? But what if my courage had failed me?'

'I knew it would not. Do you approve?'

'I love it. It's magical.'

'There's more,' he said, taking her hand again and leading her back out, down another set of steps that led directly to the beach, where a huge hammock was strung out between two more palm trees.

Constance jumped into the air with delight. 'Kadar!' She threw her arms around him. 'This is what you meant when you promised me a night lying on the beach with the waves murmuring and the stars sparkling overhead.'

'According to legend, the sea people, whom you know as mermaids, lived here. Unlike other mermaids, our sea people can live and breathe on the land, provided they stay within sight of the sea. Here, so they say, the mermaids brought the sailors they lured onto the rocks. Only the most handsome, the most virile, the most lustful sailors of course, for these sea sirens had insatiable appetites,' Kadar said, with a wicked smile. 'The children of these unions could live underwater. Eventually though, the sailors learned to avoid this place, and the sea sirens no longer had a fresh supply of young men to satisfy their appetites, so they returned to the sea with their children. Though they say that on a stormy night you can hear them calling from that island over there, singing their siren song in the vain hope that some sailor ignorant of the legend will listen and be drawn in.'

Constance shivered, eyeing the forum with fascination. 'What happened to the sailors they left behind?'

Kadar laughed. 'Do not be imagining you will encounter their ghosts. I'm afraid the reality is rather more mundane. This was an ancient trading post, abandoned about a thousand years ago.'

'I prefer the legend of the sea sirens,' Constance said.

'So do I. Looking at you, I could easily be persuaded that one of them had returned.'

Her heart began to thump as she looked at him. 'I have certainly lured the most handsome, the most virile, the most lustful sailor to my den.'

Kadar's eyes darkened. The air around them positively crackled with awareness. 'Do you think your appetite is insatiable?' he asked, his voice husky.

Constance put her arms around his neck, pulling him towards her. 'I don't know,' she said. 'But I'm willing to find out.'

Chapter Thirteen

Kadar had been teasing when he had compared Constance to a mermaid but it turned out his words were prophetic. He could not resist her siren call. He closed his eyes and he kissed her, and Constance let out the softest, most yearning whisper of a sigh and kissed him back, and he was lost. He kissed her—her mouth, her eyelids, her cheeks, her mouth again. And again. Captivating Constance. He was captivated. Her kisses were so sweet, and then the sweetness darkened into sinfulness. So sinful, her lips and her tongue, kisses he wanted to drown in. And it was obvious that she wanted him just as much as he wanted her. It was there in her kisses and in her touch, in the way she pressed herself against him, her hands fluttering and clutching and stroking feverishly, over his tunic, under his tunic, her skin on his, making him burn.

She wanted him, and he wanted her. He told her so, again and again. And she told him back. His name. Her little ragged sighs. Her searing kisses.

Kisses that had them staggering together across the sands, back up the stairs to the tent. Kisses that continued as they fell together on to the low divan, toppling the neat stacks of cushions and blankets. Kisses that made him achingly hard. He unfastened the buttons on her overdress, placing kisses on her throat. In the valley between her breasts. He pulled her camisole top over her head and kissed her breasts. Soft, creamy, full, the nipples dark, peaked. His hands on them. His mouth. And Constance's panting response, her urgent little cries for more and more and more.

He knelt between her legs and untied the sash holding her pantaloons, easing them down. Kissing the underside of her breasts, down the taut muscles of her belly. Bestowing kisses on the soft, warm flesh of her thighs. She stilled. She arched under him. Her eyes flew open. Kadar gazed into Constance's eyes and she smiled. Such a wanton smile, smoky with passion, and as sinful as the lush curves of her body. He became impossibly hard. And then he eased her legs further apart and kissed her again, the sweetest, most intimate of kisses, and the world turned fiery crimson, leaving no room for anything but their all-consuming passion.

She was wet. She was fevered. She was already close. He licked into her. He licked around her. He circled her with his tongue and slid his fingers into her. And then he repeated each deliciously intimate action. He could feel her climax building, see it, taste it. His name on her lips was a plea now, but still he teased her, slower and slower, until neither of them could bear it any longer.

Constance's climax swept her up like a powerful wave, threw her high, and then held her there, pulsing forcefully around her, making her cry out, holding on tight to Kadar's shoulders for surely if she let go she would fall. But even as the waves began to ebb she was caught up again in another fierce need that made her sit up, wrap her legs around him and kiss him savagely. Driven by a different force she dug her fingers into his arms, plunged her tongue into his mouth. She wanted more. She slid from the divan on to the floor of the tent, rolling him onto his back, claiming him with the ferocity of a wild animal. His tunic had long ago been discarded. His trousers quickly followed.

Naked, fully aroused, he was magnificent.

She touched him. She couldn't prevent herself from touching him, wanting to have all of him, the memory of all of him, to take away with her, to have always, in her mind and in her heart. Lying beside him, toes touching, knees touching, thighs touching, she wrapped her hand around the thick, hard, silken girth of his arousal, pressing her lips, her tongue, to his nipples. Kissing and stroking and licking. Slow strokes, mimicking the actions he had used to tease her to the edge. But that wasn't enough either. She wanted everything.

She kissed his mouth again, rolling closer, releasing her hold of his shaft to press herself against him. He moaned. And then he pulled himself away. No! She wrapped her arm and her leg around him, and deepened her kiss. He moaned, kissed her back with equal fervour. She could feel him pressing between her legs now, and she wanted to know, she wanted to feel him inside her, have him possess her, just once, just once. She arched herself against him, felt him shudder, and arched again.

'Constance, I...'

Her name a protest. 'Kadar.' His name a plea. 'Please,' she said, 'please.'

'Constance.' This time her name was a surrender. 'Constance,' he said, kissing her hungrily, rolling her onto her back.'

'Yes,' she said fervently, as he eased her legs apart, opening her eyes to meet his, to see the blaze of passion there, catching her breath at the vision of him, the breadth of his shoulders, the rapid movement of his chest, the sinewy muscles in his arms, the ripple of the taut muscles under the skin of his flat belly. And the sleek, fascinating length of his arousal.

He was careful. He watched her closely as he entered her, easing himself inside her, but there was no need. Higher, he slid in, and higher, and then he waited, his breath on her cheeks. She reached up to kiss him deeply. And then it began. A slow thrust provoked the most delicious scintilla of friction, making her tense around him, cling to him, and another thrust that set her throbbing and pulsing, and another, a little faster and more urgent this time, a little higher, and she could feel it building in her, and building, as he thrust vigorously, moving with him now, matching his rhythm, higher and higher, until she came again with a wild cry, her climax sending him spinning out of control, tearing himself free of her just in time, her name a harsh, guttural sound on his lips as his shuddering climax took him.

* * *

Enveloped in a fragile state of elation, Constance did not trust herself to speak. To love Kadar with her mind and her body as she had just done was beyond all she had imagined. Now she would not have to imagine. Now she would have this to remember, always. But what she needed to remember right now, at this moment, was to try to erase all sign of her thoughts from her expression, and therefore the last thing she could do, which was the only thing she wanted to do, was to curl into his side, to wrap herself around him and tell him what was in her heart. Tell him that she loved him more than life itself. But even as she made to move, he put his arm around her to still her.

'I should not have allowed myself to lose control like that.'

'I wanted you to lose control. I wanted to know how it could be between us,' Constance said, speaking at his chest for though it was not a lie, it was hardly the whole truth. She risked a glance up, blushing. 'Besides, I quite wantonly provoked you.'

He laughed. 'Which you have done, without realizing it, from the first moment I set eyes upon you. But that is no excuse. I should not have...'

'Kadar, I wanted you to. And unless you have concluded that this once was enough, I am pretty certain that I will want you to again,' she said, astonished by her breathtaking audacity.

Heat flared between them. He pulled her roughly against him. 'How often would be a sufficiency, do you think?' he asked.'

'I don't think I could ever have a surfeit of this.'

'So, Lady Constance Montgomery, you confess to being insatiable?'

She chuckled, arching unashamedly against him. 'I do believe I might be. Perhaps we should put my claim to the test.'

Much later, they climbed to the highest point of the little island which had panoramic views of the whole archipelago. Kadar pointed out a long promontory of rock that formed another little harbour. They walked down to it, perching on the end with their feet dangling in the water, and he caught some fish, brightly coloured grouper and snapper, for their dinner. Returning to the tent with their catch, they watched the sun set over the chain of islands, idyllically blue sea tinted with gold as the flawless blue sky crimsoned and the sun sank.

A perfect day gave way to a perfect evening. Kadar grilled the fish, stuffed with herbs and lemon, over a fire lit on the beach. They ate with their fingers, seated at the edge of the surf, wavelets caressing their feet. The moon rose, a mere sliver in the night sky.

'Would you like to go for a night swim?' he asked.

'It's very dark.' She eyed the inky water, listening to the soft shush of the waves. 'I won't be able to see anything.'

'Then you can't be afraid. It's a completely different experience from swimming in the daylight. Are you willing to trust me and give it a try?'

A final test? If it was, she had no intentions of failing. Constance stood up and began to shed her clothes. 'I sincerely hope that the sea sirens are not lying in wait,' she said, 'for they would surely try to lure you into their arms.'

'Impossible,' Kadar said, casting off his own clothes. 'I am already in thrall to one of their own. But there is only one way to be certain they don't spirit me away.'

They were both naked. In the dying flames of the fire she could see the sleek lines of his body, the tantalizing shimmer of his muscles, the glint of his smile. 'How do you intend to do that?'

He scooped her up into his arms, holding her high against his chest. 'By keeping you very, very close,' he said, carrying her into the shallows.

* * *

The water was cool on their naked skin. In the dark, the sea had a viscous feel to it, like liquid silk. Constance's hair tickled his face. Her arm was around his neck, her breasts brushing his chest. Unable to see more than a glint and a shadow, his other senses were attenuated. The heat of her skin on his. The hard peak of a nipple. The soft flesh of her buttocks. The scent of her. And pressing his mouth to hers, the taste of her.

She slithered down his body as they kissed, gasping as the water reached up over her legs, her bottom, her waist. She pressed herself against him, full breasts warm against his chest, cool thighs under the water. She tasted of salt and sunshine. He could drown in her kisses. They waded deeper into the water. Her breathing quickened. Was she afraid? Most likely, but she was also determined.

She let go of his hand and took off, her beginner's stroke causing loud splashes to echo in the still darkness. Thinking wryly to himself that he'd have no trouble locating her if she got into difficulty, Kadar swam by her side, careful to give her enough room to keep herself afloat, never enough room for her to be in danger, guiding her towards the shore when she strayed out of her depth, and then, when she began to struggle, finally surrendering to the need to hold her. He floated on his back with Constance anchored to him, his sea siren, who was now quite free to sail to the ends of the earth if she so desired.

A thought which should have filled him with pride. A month ago—was it only a month ago?—when he had first encountered her, he had wanted to set her free. He could not claim the credit, but he had provided her with the means to free herself. He was proud of her, but he had to confess that the notion of her sailing away, whether it was to the ends of the earth or merely to Egypt, was a melancholy one. He pictured her on the deck of a Red Sea dhow, her lovely hair a halo-like cloud around her, the delightful body he was holding, receding ever further away from him until she became a tiny speck. What would she do, once back in England? She seemed so determined not to accept his help, but he was equally determined to try once more. He told himself it was for her sake. He knew that it was equally as much for his own. He could not bear to think that once she set sail he would never hear from her again.

Kadar gave himself a mental shake, reminding himself that the reason he was here on Koros with her was to celebrate his new-found freedom too. His future awaited him, and though it was a considerably brighter future than he could have believed a month ago, it was one which would require all of his energy and attention. He was already spending far too much time thinking about Constance, talking to Constance, stargazing with Constance. She was, in fact, a quite considerable distraction, when he needed to devote his time to his people. When she sailed, she would not be leaving a hole in his life but a chasm which his kingdom was clamouring to fill.

When she sailed. He had never met anyone like Constance. No one could ever replace her. He would miss her terribly. When she sailed...

When she sailed, he would forge on with his plans for Murimon. But that was for tomorrow. Tonight he would devote himself to Constance. Kadar stood up, pulling her once again into his arms. She sighed, that soft little sound that sent the blood rushing to his groin, wrapping her arms around him and kissing him slowly, sensuously, her wet skin clinging to his, bringing his member to hard, clamouring life. He picked her up, carrying her quickly ashore, setting her down on the sand by the embers of the fire. The few steps to the tent were too far to contemplate, and Constance seemed to think so too, her mouth and her hands already hungrily possessing him. A whole night, Kadar thought. A whole night to pleasure her, to coax the flames of her passion to new heights, to taste her and to touch her, to lose himself in the sweet wet heat of her, to imprint the memory of her body on his mind deeply enough to last a lifetime without her.

They sank to their knees, kissing. 'Show me,' Constance said, as if she had read his thoughts. 'Show me what to do to please you,' she said.

'Constance,' he muttered, pulling her down astride him, cupping her breasts in his hands, feeling the heat of her sex damp against his as she straddled him. 'Constance, there is nothing you can do that will not please me.'

She laughed, a throaty, husky laugh that gave him gooseflesh. 'What about this?' She leant over him, brushing her breasts against his chest.

'Yes.'

She kissed him deeply, lifting herself, to enfold the tip of his erection. 'What about this, Kadar?'

He groaned, digging his fingers into the sand to prevent himself from thrusting.

Constance lifted herself again, guiding him inside her. 'And this?' she asked, lowering herself onto him in one swift, delightful thrust.

Kadar, fighting the rush towards an almost unstoppable climax, had no words, but he did not require them.

* * *

'See just there? That is Aquarius,' Constance said, 'one of the oldest recognised constellations, listed by Ptolemy. It also happens to be the sign of the zodiac associated with my birthday.'

They were lying side by side in the hammock, naked and for the time being sated, under a thin blanket. Though the canvas hammock was large, their bodies rolled naturally towards each other. In the pitch dark, Constance had no fear of her feelings showing too clearly, and so felt free to indulge them. Kadar had his arm around her. Though they both had their eyes trained on the night sky, her hands strayed every so often to touch him, to stroke him, to memorise the feel of his skin, the contours of his muscles and sinew, and when she touched him, she mouthed the declarations of love she could not speak aloud.

'So you were born under the sign of the water carrier,' Kadar said. 'Somewhat appropriate, given the circumstances of your coming here.'

She chuckled. 'Ganymede, the water carrier, was Prince of Troy, and so beautiful that Jupiter was captivated by him when he spotted him tending to his father's flocks. Jupiter transformed himself into a bird and flew poor Ganymede off to the heavens, where he became Jupiter's wine bearer.'

'Not a particularly exciting fate, but a great deal less bloodthirsty than many you have told me relating to the stars,' Kadar said. 'Aquarius is in the quadrant of the heavens known as the Sea, is it not?'

'Yes. If you look, there is Pisces the fish, and the whale, Cetus, beside it. And though it's not visible tonight, there is a river, Eridanus.' Constance snuggled closer, her cheek resting in the hollow of Kadar's shoulder. She could feel his heart beating. 'If we had the telescope we could see Jupiter tonight, over there by Ursa Major. I was looking at it just last night. I have all but completed your star map.'

She wished she had not said so, for it was a reminder that the sands of her time here had almost run out. The last few grains were trickling through the hour glass. Her eyes filled with unbidden tears. She shifted, lest one should fall on to his chest and give her away.

'Are you pleased with your efforts?' Kadar asked.

'Yes, though it is not nearly so detailed as it might be, and I am sure that my measurements would benefit from being reviewed by someone with more experience.'

'And I am sure that you underrate yourself. What you have achieved in such a short period of time is remarkable.'

'Thank you.' She gazed up at the celestial dome above them, losing her tears in the rapture that always filled her at the sight. 'I have a—a dream, I suppose you would call it. To create a complete star map for every season, with the story of each star incorporated into it, all the myths and legends. And illustrations too.'

'It would be your magnum opus,' Kadar said. 'Tell me more.'

She did, losing herself in the descriptions of her favourite constellations. 'Skies for all seasons,' she concluded. 'Stars and planets intertwined with their mythology. I know it's likely impossible, but…'

'I think it sounds very possible, and I can't imagine anyone better suited to create it,' Kadar said, capturing her hand and kissing her palm. 'If it could be commissioned, if I could find someone capable of producing it, would you…?'

'No.' She sat up, making the hammock rock. 'No, I don't want you to— I can't allow you to…' Couldn't bear him to. She bit back the words just in time. Could not bear him to be an elusive presence in her future, the tantalizing promise that she might one day see him again as a result of his patronage hanging like the Sword of Damocles over her head, a promise to be unfulfilled for ever, yet a possibility that would never recede. 'I think that when I leave here, it would be best if it is final,' she said, thankful for the dark, thankful that her voice sounded considerably lighter than she felt. 'I must stand on my own two feet.'

'You do not wish me to help you? Constance, it would mean a great deal to me if you would allow me to—think of it as legitimate payment for all that you have done here.'

'I have already earned my keep, I hope. Truly, Kadar, you have given me so much, I cannot take any more from you.'

'You wish to be free of all encumbrances, all obligations,' he said heavily.

A shooting star blazed fleetingly across the night sky. A wishing star. If only that were true, Constance would wish for the freedom to love, safe in the knowledge that she was loved in return. That, she knew, was not possible, but she was still free to be herself. 'Yes,' she said gently, deliberately allowing him to mistake her meaning, 'I wish to be free.'

'Then I will not press you, though I wish— But I shall, of course, respect your wishes.'

'Thank you.' She lay down again. He put his arm around her again. She settled her cheek against his shoulder, placed her hand on the heart of the man who did not love her but who had listened to her simple wish to sail on the open sea, to lie on the sand and gaze up at the stars, who had transformed it into something beyond her wildest dreams. 'Thank you,' she said again. 'For this. For everything. It is absolutely perfect.'

They sailed back to the port of Murimon in the morning with the sun behind them, and their night of passion too. They were both subdued, lost in their own thoughts. At Kadar's insistence, Constance took the tiller once more while he tended to the sail. She could not imagine that there would be a call for her new-found skill in the new life that awaited her, but on the other hand, she was determined to think positively. There was no telling what might happen. The future lay before her like the huge sands of the desert, limitless and uncharted. Not a depressing thought at all, but an exciting one, she told herself sternly.

Beside her, Kadar was facing out to sea, his face in profile. The Sphynx had returned. Was he thinking of last night, of the passion they had shared? Or was he too thinking about the future? The challenges which faced him made hers look trivial by comparison. She had no doubt he would succeed, but how, and in what order would his plans be implemented? Would his precious kingdom embrace change or resist it? So many questions, and she would never know any of the answers. She would never see this beautiful kingdom flourish under his rule, see his people come to love as well as respect him. It hurt so much, but she knew there could be no other outcome.

All too soon, the port hove into view: the lighthouses on the twin arms of the harbour, the string of fishing boats at the mouth of the bay and the bustle of ships and dhows in the docks. The air was redolent with the scent of spices being loaded on to a schooner: sweet, rich red pepper, nutty cinnamon bark and perfumed cardamom pods. A camel brayed. A pack of mules wheezed. Riggings clanked and sails flapped. The sun burned its way to its zenith in the sky. Stevedores called to each other. Now that her ear was attuned, Constance could pick out some of the phrases, though it was unlikely that Abdul-Majid would have time to teach her many more. Unlikely that she'd have call to use her limited vocabulary at all, once she left Egypt behind. She had probably had her last lesson in Arabic, for Abdul-Majid would be heading to Nessarah to break Kadar's betrothal. This was probably her last sail. Last night—no, she would save thinking of last night for a time when she was far from here.

'I think it would be best if I left as soon as

possible,' Constance said, the words out almost before the thought entered her head. Too late to retract them now.

They were on the quayside. Kadar finished securing the dhow before he answered. When he did so, his face was set to his Sphynx expression once again.

'I agree.'

Two simple words, but they felt like a dagger to her heart. The fact that she wanted to retract her hastily spoken words, that she actually wanted to tell him she would stay as long as he needed her, the fact that she wanted to beg him to tell her there might be a chance he could love her if she stayed, made her certain that she must go, soon and for ever. 'As I said last night, I am almost finished my map, so there is nothing to keep me here.'

'No, there isn't.'

She had expected him to contradict her. Even though she was set on going, she had expected it. 'And you have a great deal to occupy you,' Constance said. 'I do not wish to distract you.'

'No. I must concentrate on the task in hand.'

'So I should— I think it is best if we do not— Last night should be our—our swansong, if you like.'

'Yes. That would be best.'

The tiny flicker of his eye, the giveaway sign that he was feeling more than he would permit her to see was all she had to comfort her. And it was small comfort at that. She did not want him to be unhappy or regretful. 'So we are agreed,' Constance said, pinning a bright smile to her face. 'A parting of the ways, as soon as possible.'

'I think that would be the most sensible course of action, Constance.'

'Yes.'

'Yesterday, last night was perfect.'

'And one cannot improve on perfection,' she said, with a shadow of a smile. Though they could. If only...

No, the point was not to think, if only. The point was not to regret what might have been but to relish what she had already experienced. 'I will speak to Abdul-Majid regarding my travel arrangements,' Constance said. 'No need for you to concern yourself with them, you have enough to occupy you.'

'I—yes, that would be helpful.'

Their eyes locked for a long moment. Kadar took a step towards her and hesitated. She longed to believe that he was as torn as she, but she recognised it as wishful thinking. Courageous Constance, he had called her yesterday. She would not let him down. So she took a step back and slid her feet into her slippers and started to head down the quayside. Kadar followed, but his progress was slow, waylaid by people whose bows he returned, whose respectful greetings he stopped to acknowledge. She was delighted to see this evidence of his progress of coming to terms with his exalted position, but as a result it was some considerable time before they eventually reached the palace.

Though Constance longed for the sanctuary of her bedchamber, it was not to be. As soon as they entered the piazza, Abdul-Majid appeared. 'Highness, Lady Constance, forgive me but a most urgent matter has arisen.'

He did not seem surprised to see them together, though he made no comment on the fact. The chief adviser was a great deal more discreet than they had been, Constance thought, blushing. She had not even considered the gossip that their absence together must have given rise to. Yet another reason for her to leave sooner rather than later. 'If you will excuse me,' she said, but the elder main shook his head vehemently.

'With respect, Lady Constance, I believe that this matter would be better—in short, I believe your presence would be helpful. An Englishman has arrived at the palace,' he added hurriedly, perhaps sensing Kadar's exasperation. 'A Mr Christopher Fordyce.'

'Is this man known to you?' Kadar asked her.

Constance wrinkled her brow. 'I don't think so, the name is not familiar.'

'He could be from the British Embassy in Cairo,' Kadar said, frowning. 'It is more than three weeks since I sent them my communication regarding yourself. I suppose it is possible that he has come to collect you.'

Her heart sank all the way down to her slippered feet. 'That is—that would be convenient,' Constance said, the tone of her voice implying the exact opposite.

Was there the faintest trace of regret in his eyes? She could not be sure. Kadar nodded curtly. 'Come, let us find out if that indeed is the case.'

'If you will permit a suggestion, Sire. If this Englishman is indeed an envoy from Cairo, it would be better to receive him more—er—formally,' Abdul-Majid said, with a deprecating look at his Prince's dishevelled appearance which made Constance wonder what kind of impression she must be making.

Kadar sighed. 'You are correct, of course. Can you be ready in half an hour?' he asked Constance. 'Good. Have Mr Fordyce wait in the anteroom to the Royal Saloon.'

* * *

A little over half an hour later, Constance burst into the Royal Saloon. Bathed and changed, she wore pantaloons and a tunic of pale blue muslin with matching slippers, with a long fitted robe fastened over the top. The pattern was striking, like swirling waves in many shades of blue. With her hair a damp cloud of curls already escaping from the pins with which she had tried to contain it, her curves emphasised by the tight fastenings at her waist, she looked rather less the court astronomer, as Kadar supposed was her intention, and rather more like a court concubine.

He refrained from telling her so. There was something fragile in her expression that worried him. A set to her mouth he did not recognise. Down on the docks, he had come so close to asking her to postpone her departure, despite the fact that he knew he needed to devote himself to his people. Only the fact that Constance herself seemed to be dead set on leaving had prevented him. Which was a good thing, he reminded himself.

'Do you think he is an emissary?' she asked him, worrying at a hairpin which had come loose. 'Do you think he will bring word from England? My parents…?'

'No.' Belatedly realizing why she had reacted so strangely to the Englishman's arrival, he hastened to reassure her, clasping her hands between his. 'They will very likely only have received the first communication, and even if they have received my amended note, the earliest we could expect a reply from England would be another three or four weeks. If that is what is worrying you...'

She snatched her hands away. 'I'm not worried.'

He waited, for her expression was at odds with her words, but Constance seemed to have abandoned her usual practice of strewing her thoughts like rose petals.

'Shall I have him announced, then?'

She had wandered over to the door. Kadar was standing at the window. 'You were dressed like this when I first met you,' she said. 'And you were standing just there. White silk from head to toe, a gold cloak, a belt studded with diamonds. You looked so—so—so...' She trailed off, gazing at a point over his shoulder, gave herself a little shake, dislodging a hairpin in the process, and turned back to him with a fixed smile. 'I am prevaricating. Let us see what he has to say.'

Christopher Fordyce was dressed for desert travel in a cotton tunic and trousers, a thin cloak, and a headdress, all of which bore the signs of a long, arduous journey across the sands. The scimitar slung on a belt at his waist had the look of a weapon selected for service rather than ceremony, and the lithe figure beneath the peasant robes looked to be more than capable of wielding it.

Standing by Kadar's side, Constance watched with astonishment as the Englishman strode into the Royal Saloon as if it were his salon. Skin tanned a deep brown by the sun, brows bleached almost white, threw the bright brilliant blue of his eyes into stark contrast. Mr Christopher Fordyce, whoever he was, was not a man one would forget easily.

'Your Highness,' he said, making the briefest of bows and holding out his hand. 'It is a pleasure.'

Kadar shook the extended hand, but did not return the easy smile. 'Mr Fordyce. You have me at a disadvantage. You are not, I take it, come from Cairo?'

'Good grief, no. If I'd come from Cairo I'd have sailed. I've come from the kingdom of Qaryma, actually. In a roundabout sort of way.' Frowning, Christopher Fordyce turned his extraordinary eyes on Constance. 'Funnily enough Sheikh Azhar also had an Englishwoman in temporary residence. A botanist, name of Trevelyan. Is there some sort of female expeditionary force here in Arabia from the old country that I'm unaware of? You *are* English, are you not?'

'Allow me to present Lady Constance Montgomery, who is indeed English, and is currently serving as my court astronomer.'

Christopher Fordyce took Constance's hand, though his bow was every bit as brief as the one he had bestowed on Kadar. Despite his ramshackle appearance, he was clearly a man accustomed to commanding respect at the highest level. 'How do you do, Mr Fordyce.'

'Montgomery, you say? You wouldn't happen to be related to William Montgomery, by any chance?'

'He is my father,' Constance said, now thoroughly intrigued. 'May I ask how you come to be acquainted with him? A business associate, perhaps?' she hazarded, though she could not imagine that this man would be easily hoodwinked as Papa. Charming smile and easy manner aside, those piercing eyes of his burned with a fierce intelligence, the lines around them, she was willing to bet, testament to harsh experience as well as the hot desert sun.

As if to confirm her thoughts, Christopher Fordyce gave a crack of laughter. 'I fear my pockets are too light, and my outlook too jaundiced to be of interest to your father. Oh, forgive me, Lady Constance, I am rather in the habit of speaking my mind, having been away from polite company for some time. I did not mean to offend you.'

'You spoke the truth. It is only that I was accustomed to thinking knowledge of my father's somewhat chequered business history—I thought that it was not common knowledge, you see,' Constance replied, flustered. 'You have not told me how you do come to know him, Mr Fordyce.'

'Nor what your business is here in Murimon,' Kadar added.

'A man who likes to come to the point,' Christopher Fordyce said with another of his smiles. They did not reach his eyes, those smiles, Constance noted. And he was turning back to Kadar, deliberately avoiding her question. 'I've come with regards to this,' he said now, producing a piece of jewellery from a pocket concealed somewhere about his person. 'Have you ever seen anything similar?'

It was a gold amulet set with jewels. Kadar took it, studying it carefully. 'This is a very ancient and very valuable piece of jewellery. How did you come by it?'

'Oh, perfectly legitimately. My mother left it to me.'

'And how, may I ask, did your mother come to own it?'

'You may ask, but I'm afraid I'm not prepared to tell you.'

Brilliant blue eyes clashed with grey-green. Tension crackled between the two men. For a moment Constance wondered if they might actually fight. Then Kadar shrugged, handing the amulet back to its owner. 'There is a stone missing.'

'Yes, that's part of the mystery.'

'Mystery?' Constance interjected.

'I am striving to locate the original and therefore legitimate owner,' the mysterious Christopher Fordyce replied. 'I can now, presumably, eliminate the kingdom of Murimon from my list.'

'I believe you can. I have seen nothing like this produced here. It does look to be Arabian rather than Egyptian, but it is definitely not from this region of Arabia.'

Christopher Fordyce sighed, secreting his bracelet away. 'Then I must thank you for your time, and take up no more of it. I must say, though, that is a spectacular jewel you're wearing on your belt. It's a red diamond, if I'm not mistaken.'

'I suspect you rarely make mistakes, Mr Fordyce.'

'Never seen one before. Heard of them. They're very rare. Even those smaller ones on your headdress must be worth a king's ransom. Glad to have seen them, my journey is not completely wasted,' Christopher Fordyce said with a wry grin. 'Now, I'll bid you good day and resume my quest. Your Highness. Lady Constance.'

'I will refrain from wishing you luck. I suspect you do not need it,' Kadar said. The Englishman laughed, but his smile faded at Kadar's next words. 'But before you go I would like to know how you come to be acquainted with Lady Constance's father?'

The answer was some moments coming. For the first time since entering the Royal Saloon, Christopher Fordyce looked uncomfortable. 'He persuaded my—a mutual acquaintance to invest in one of his schemes. A man who does not take kindly to failure. A man it does not do to make an enemy of. Lord Henry Armstrong. Now, if you will excuse me, I really must be gone.'

This time brooking no argument, he strode across the room, his thin cloak flying out behind him. Abdul-Majid, who had been standing guard at the door, looked anxiously at his Prince lest he should wish the guards summoned, but Kadar shook his head impatiently.

'What an extraordinary man,' Constance declared, as soon as the door closed behind him. 'An acquaintance of Lord Henry Armstrong too. I have heard of him. I had no idea that my father…'

'Sire. Highness. I beg your pardon Lady Constance for interrupting, but something the Englishman said has given me pause for thought—in short, I wonder if— You see, it might solve…' A heavy sigh from Kadar made the chief adviser stop, make a strange little bow, then smile slowly. 'Old habits die hard, Sire. I will get to the point. The diamonds, the red diamonds of Murimon. The Englishman said that…'

'Even the smallest is worth a king's ransom. What of it?'

Another little formal bow. Another little smile. 'Is not a king's ransom precisely what you need, Sire, to fully implement your plans?'

Kadar's mouth fell open in astonishment. A first, Constance thought, trying not to smile. 'You are suggesting I sell the crown jewels?' he said.

'Some of them, Sire.'

'Crown jewels which have been part of this kingdom's traditions for hundreds of years?'

'But will this kingdom survive for hundreds more years if we fail to progress, Highness?'

Kadar pulled off his headband, studying the diamonds winking there in bemusement. 'Sell the diamonds? That is an altogether radical idea, Abdul-Majid. And an inspired one,' he said.

The chief adviser tugged his beard. 'I believe I did say to you that even an old camel can learn new tricks, Sire.'

Chapter Fourteen

Three days later, it was time for Constance to go. Though they had agreed on their return from their idyllic trip to the island of Koros that she must leave sooner rather than later, it was Christopher Fordyce's surprise visit to the kingdom which had provided fresh impetus to her departure, following the unexpected turn of events which provided Kadar with the answer to all his financial worries. Once he had embraced Abdul-Majid's radical suggestion he had been transformed, working with a vigour which consumed every available hour. The chief adviser had left yesterday for Nessarah to formally put an end to the betrothal. Kadar's plans had been presented to Council. The plan room would be opened to the people of Murimon this morning to allow them to both inspect them and comment on them. And under cover of all this activity, while Kadar embraced his future, Constance would slip away and embark on her journey towards her own.

The last three days had proved conclusively that she could not stay any longer. Kadar had not been avoiding her, and he had not rejected her, he simply had no time for her. In this new kingdom of Murimon that he was building, Constance had no place. She had known this for some time, but to be confronted by the reality of it had been unbearably painful. A prison of her own making awaited her if she remained any longer. So she had made her arrangements to leave with Abdul-Majid's help, assuring him that she would inform the prince herself of her impending departure, knowing that she would not, and that the chief adviser would be en route to Nessarah and therefore unable to alert Kadar.

Her clothes and notebooks were packed. She had taken her lovely Arabian mare out for one last gallop along the beach. All that remained was to say goodbye, without actually saying goodbye. Though she knew it was probably a mistake, she simply could not deny herself this final meeting and so, carrying her completed star map, she tapped at the appointed time on the door of Kadar's library.

'Constance.' He was dressed in royal blue silk trimmed with black braid. There were dark shadows under his eyes. Though he stood to greet her, he remained behind his desk, indicating that she sat opposite. 'I am sorry that I've not been able to—I have been extremely busy.'

He wore his Sphynx expression, but there was something else in his eyes. Wariness? She set the leather-bound folio down on the desk. 'I may be imagining it, but you do not look particularly pleased to see me.'

That flicker of his eye was her only response to this needy remark. And quite rightly so, she thought. What *could* he say? She had not expected him to fall on his knees and declare undying love, had she? Deciding not to answer that question, Constance opened her folio. 'I came to give you this. I wanted to explain the annotations, to make sure that you are happy with what I have done.'

'Is it finished?'

She hesitated only a fraction before uttering the white lie intended to throw him off the scent. 'Not quite. It will require two, maybe three more nights at most.'

He pulled the folio towards him, opened it at the first page, but made no attempt to examine the chart, which was of the north sky. 'What will you do, Constance? I wish you would permit me to help you.'

'You have already done more than enough.'

'Will you return to your family?'

One question she could answer with certainty. Constance shook her head. 'No, I won't go back there, even if they did offer me a roof over my head, which I doubt my father will. I don't know what I will do, Kadar. I will find a way to earn my keep that allows me to continue with my stargazing. I don't know what that will be, but I do know you needn't worry about me. You have more than enough to occupy you now you have the funds to create your utopia. You must be very happy.'

'Yes.' His expression remained blank. 'I would like to know that you too are happy.'

'I am happy to assure you that I intend to do my best,' she answered, summoning a smile. 'Kadar, you have made me— Being here has made me happier than I thought possible. I am changed beyond recognition, and that is in no small part thanks to you.'

'You are too modest. You have transformed yourself, Constance.'

'Yes. Perhaps. But you gave me the means, and I am—I will always be grateful.' Her voice was clogged with tears. She dug her nails into her palms, determined not to let him see her distress. She loved him so very much, and this was the last time—no, best not to think of that. 'It is a small token of my gratitude,' she said, indicating the star map, 'but I hope it will prove a useful one.'

His long fingers traced a constellation. His eyes were bleak. She waited, but he said nothing. She got to her feet. Seeing him had been a mistake after all. 'I should go.'

She was halfway across the room before he caught up to her. 'I too am changed, thanks to you,' Kadar said. 'I have not thanked you.'

'There is no need. As you said, transformation has to come from within.'

'But you gave me the means,' he said, tucking a strand of her hair behind her ear. 'I will always be grateful.'

Now he was smiling at her, and though she was sure she was imagining the tenderness she saw in it, it was breaking her heart. She caught his hand, pressed a kiss to his knuckles, and fled. He called after her, saying he would come to see her once he had studied the map. She made no reply, one hand covering her mouth to suppress her sobs, intent only on reaching her bedchamber before her tears fell.

But there was no time for tears. Her dhow was due to sail at high tide. Scrubbing her face with a wet cloth, she returned to the roof terrace for one last time to drape the cover over the telescope and to leave her note to Kadar, for she knew he, like her, considered this roof terrace to be their own special place. And then, as the first of Murimon's people crowded the piazza, eagerly queuing to enter the plan room, Constance crept out one of the many side entrances and made her way down to the harbour.

In the early hours of the morning after a long, rewarding day spent with his people, Kadar could no longer resist the persistent urge for Constance's company. He told himself it was because he owed it to her to share the excitement of this most auspicious of days. She had been there by his side at the Great Oasis, where the seed was first planted. He had missed her presence today as his plans came to fruition.

But as soon as he set foot on the terrace, he felt her absence and at the same time a horrible sense of foreboding. The moon was high enough, full enough, for him to see that the telescope had been covered over, the stack of cushions which normally lay beside it, gone. Below the awning, the desk was neatly tidied. No notebook. Only, he saw sickeningly, a note.

After lighting a lamp, he broke the seal. The contents were brief, but enough to turn his bones to water. Constance was gone. She thanked him for everything. She would carry Murimon in her heart always. Nothing else. No explanation for the manner of her departure. No apology for not saying goodbye. No mention of any future contact. Nothing.

He felt sick. But what had he expected? They had agreed she would go. She was a distraction. He had proved to himself over the last three days how much of a distraction she was by forcing himself not to be distracted, hadn't he?

Had he? Though he had been avoiding her, he discovered now that there was a difference, a huge difference, between knowing that Constance was here, gazing at the stars, sleeping the morning away in her suite, writing up her notes, riding out on the mare he had come to think of as hers, and Constance not being here at all. Constance sailing away from Murimon. Away from him. For ever.

But what else could she do? It was the suddenness of it—he decided resentfully—which was what was wrong with it. He felt thwarted. Denied the opportunity to share his success today. Denied the opportunity to tell her just how beautiful her maps were. Denied the opportunity to make one last attempt to persuade her to accept his help in forging her future. Unable to lie up here and discuss the stars with her one last time. To see her face light up as it always did when she talked of the heavens, her eyes shining like stars, her hands fluttering like a meteor shower, her hair like a glorious corona around the sun that was her face.

Kadar looked up at the vast night sky. The moon was too bright for stargazing, but he could just make out Aquarius. The water carrier. Was Constance gazing up at the exact same constellation as the Red Sea carried her far away, across the ocean, to her new life? He had even been denied the small consolation of being able to say goodbye properly. To hold her in his arms one last time, to kiss her one last time. And the biggest frustration of all was that he had been denied the opportunity to tell her that he loved her. Passionately. Completely. With all his heart.

Which he did, he realised with sudden searing certainty. Watching the spectacle of a shooting star blaze across the sky, Kadar wondered at his own blindness. He loved her, and the very fact that it felt so utterly different from what he had felt for Zeinab made him certain that this time his love was true. Not perfect. A love that saw the real Constance, and did not idealise her. A love that loved the imperfect Constance, and did not want to change her or protect her or stifle her. A love that wanted her to be free to be whatever she wanted to be. A love that wanted, above all else, for her to be happy.

That is all I care about, Kadar. I want you to be happy. Constance's words. His own feelings. His heart lurched. Was it possible that she loved him? But if she did, how could Constance have possibly kept such feelings to herself?

Because she loved him. Could the answer be so simple? Because although she loved him she thought she had no rightful place here? But he could carve a place for her, cast in whatever form she desired if she would let him. Did she love him? Jumping to his feet, Kadar felt invigorated, filled with excitement, hope and just a little bit of fear. He was going to find out. And there was something else he was going to do to prove it.

Traversing the Red Sea might well be the quickest route to Egypt, but it was still a very long journey, and the dhow which Abdul-Majid had chartered for her was no racing yacht. Fortunately, Constance was in no hurry. Having fled Murimon, she wanted to relish this precious time alone, to capture the scents and the sounds and the sights and the heat of Arabia as she sailed northwards. They sailed only by daylight. The two crew slept ashore at night, while Constance sat on deck and gazed at the stars and remembered.

With every passing hour she missed Kadar more. Though she tried to ration her thoughts, she end-lessly conjectured about what he was doing, what he was thinking. Was he thinking of her? Was he missing her? Was he looking at the same stars as her? Pointless speculation, but utterly addictive. When she reached Cairo, then she would try to let go of him. When she reached Cairo, then she would try to look forward and not backwards. But not yet.

It was on the third day when they caught up with her. Two men wearing the Murimon insig-nia who, judging by their appearance, had been sailing round the clock. Her heart in her mouth, Constance broke the royal seal on the letter they gave her. With Abdul-Majid absent, Kadar could not leave Murimon. The matter was urgent. Only she could resolve it. He begged that she return with all speed.

Adverse winds held them back. It took three days to return despite this smaller, swifter craft. Three days for Constance to speculate and to hope and to quell her hopes and to dream and then to stamp all over her dreams. One thing she did not do was dread. Whatever had prompted Kadar to summon her back, she trusted him. Even if he had guessed her feelings, he would not abuse them.

Had he guessed her feelings? And if so, what did he feel in return? The two questions uppermost in her mind. The two questions to which soon, very soon, she would receive an answer.

As they sailed past the twin lighthouses into the port of Murimon, her heart was in her mouth. A chair awaited her. Had been waiting for her every hour of the last two days, she discovered. Memories of that initial journey up the steep, winding road to the palace filled her mind. Her heart thumped so hard she was sure it would leap out of her chest. Her legs felt boneless as she was helped from the chair into the piazza. She was overwhelmed anew with the magnificence of the palace, with the sheer beauty of the bay below. It felt so right to be back here. It was so wrong of her to be thinking this way.

A guard met her. Expecting to be taken to the roof terrace, to the library or even her own suite of rooms, she became extremely apprehensive when she realised he was leading the way to the Royal Saloon. The matter was urgent, Kadar had said. Only she could resolve it. It hadn't occurred to her that it might be an official matter and not a personal one. That an emissary might have arrived from the British consulate in Cairo. Anticipation gave way to disappointment. And then the doors were flung open.

The room was empty. Stepping inside, vaguely aware that the doors had been pulled closed behind her, it took Constance a moment to realise what was different. It seemed darker, though outside it was daylight and the window shutters lay open and the chandeliers…

'Oh, my goodness!' Above her, the white domed ceiling had been transformed into a depiction of the heavens. Constance stared up in wonder. A night-blue sky littered with stars of gold and silver, stars with bluish hues and red. The summer sky over Murimon. The sky she had worn on her coronation robes. The sky she had mapped for Kadar.

'The sky which witnessed the most important and profound event in my life.'

She whirled around. Her heart leapt. 'Kadar!'

'You, Constance,' he said, taking her hand. 'And it took you leaving me for me to finally realise that I can't live without you.'

Was she hearing things? Perhaps she was dreaming. She gazed up at the star-filled ceiling and back into Kadar's eyes. He had never looked at her like that before. Not just bone-melting, but heart-melting. 'You can't?' she asked foolishly, for though hope was blooming urgently, she was afraid to believe.

'I could,' Kadar said, sending Constance's

heart plummeting. 'If you did not want me, if I will not make you happy, I would live without you because your happiness matters to me more than anything. But I don't want to live without you, Constance. I love you.'

Now her heart was performing somersaults. She felt as if something inside her was unfolding, opening out, blazing with dazzling light. 'You do?' she whispered.

'I do,' Kadar said with such simple honesty that she could no longer doubt. 'I love you with all my heart, and if you think…'

She threw her arms around him. 'I don't think, I know. I love you so much. I love you, I love you, I have loved you for days and weeks and—and—and…'

Whatever she was going to say would be lost for ever, because his lips claimed hers. It was a kiss like no other, a kiss so full of heartfelt relief and tenderness and joy, that it sent her senses spinning. She kissed him back with utter abandon, allowing her mouth and her hands to say all the things she had been concealing, and he kissed her even more fervently in return, saying those most precious of words over and over.

Finally they stopped to breathe, staring into each other's eyes, dazzled and dazed. 'I love you, Constance,' Kadar said. 'From the moment you walked into this room, I wanted you. You fascinated me. You made me angry and you made me laugh. You saw through my words to my innermost thoughts, and when those thoughts were ill judged, you had the temerity, the boldness, the compassion and the persistence to correct them. You turned my world upside down, and then you set it the right way around again. You made me want to climb to the stars with you. You make me happier than I ever thought possible.'

'Oh, Kadar.' She could barely speak for happiness. She needed new words to tell him how much she loved him, but there were no new words, and when she told him with just the three, she saw from his eyes that it was enough. 'I love you,' she said again, wondering if she would ever tire of telling him.

'And I love you too. So much.' His expression became serious. 'But I want you to be happy, my darling Constance. I won't make you a prisoner of my love,' he said urgently. 'I have thought about it, I promise you. You can continue in your role as court astronomer. You can create your magical map merging the skies with mythology. You can succeed Abdul-Majid as chief adviser if you so wish. Anything that makes you happy, I will make it so.'

'Kadar!' She was laughing through her tears.

'Kadar, all I need to make me happy is you. Not if you love me as I love you.'

'I promise you, you will never have cause to doubt that.'

Love, naked blazing love was writ across his face. Constance pulled him to her. 'Never,' she said, 'I will never doubt it when you look at me like that.'

Kadar swept her into his arms. He pushed her hair back from her face. 'I love you. I will always love you, as the stars are my witness. Will you marry me? Become my Princess and rule by my side?'

'You want me to become a real princess? Rule an entire Arabian kingdom with you?

'There is no one on the planet better qualified for the role, no one else I could contemplate sharing my kingdom, my life and my bed with. Say you will, Constance.'

She gazed up at the celestial dome he had created especially for her. She gazed into his eyes, dark with love for her. 'Yes,' she said, with utter certainty, 'I will marry you.'

When his lips met hers, their kiss was no longer tender. Passion flamed between them, blazing like the stars in the domed sky suspended above them. He kissed her mouth, her eyes, her neck, her throat. She pressed herself so tightly against him she could feel every ridge of bone, every contour of muscle, every inch of his arousal. Her skin tingled, her pulse raced, her breath was ragged. His touch was setting her on fire.

'We can't,' she said, though her voice implied the contrary. 'Not here.'

Panting, he tore his mouth from hers. Then he scooped her up and began to stride towards the door.

'What are you doing?' Constance clung to him, torn between laughter and passion. 'Where are we going?'

Kadar's smile was sinful. 'To climb a ladder to the stars,' he said.

* * * * *

If you enjoyed this story, make sure you don't miss the first book in Marguerite Kaye's HOT ARABIAN NIGHTS *miniseries,* THE WIDOW AND THE SHEIKH.

And watch out for two more books in this sizzling series, coming soon!

Historical Note

My Twitter tag when writing this book was #geeksheikh, so for those of you so inclined here are some geeky historical facts.

HMS *Kent*, the 'East Indiaman' ship on which Constance sailed, was a real vessel. She was built for the East India Company and launched in 1820, five years after I rather cruelly sent her to the bottom of the Arabian Sea. In my defence, the voyage to India was extremely precarious, and a great many of the Company's ships perished after two or three voyages.

The real *Kent* was on her third voyage, sailing to Bengal, when she went down in the Bay of Biscay, with roughly the same proportion of crew, soldiers and civilians on board as I've depicted, under the guidance of the same Captain Cobb, though sadly, with substantially greater loss of life.

Caroline and her brother William Herschel between them 'mapped' considerable expanses of the northern skies, in the process discovering many new comets, stars and nebulae as well as, famously, the planet we now know as Uranus. The process required minute documentation of angles and timings, and in reality I'd imagine was pretty uncomfortable and a bit tedious.

I've kept Constance's scientific method for star-mapping deliberately vague, and doubtless made it completely unrealistic in the process. But she's avoided a bad back, her eyes aren't strained, causing her constant migraines, and she's not too exhausted to do anything other than sleep the day away. In other words this is a *romance*, and sometimes you just can't let reality intrude too much.

On saying that, Kadar's telescope *is* based on the one through which William Herschel first observed Uranus, and in fact he did manufacture telescopes for other people at his workshop in Slough, so he might well have made the one Kadar commissioned. And the anecdote about a comet being perceived to be an omen for a plague of sneezing sickness in cats is, astonishingly, true.

While the vast majority of the star-based legends which Constance and Kadar discuss are well documented, the legend of the sea people and the island of Koros are entirely the product of my own imagination. There are sea people mentioned in *One Thousand and One Nights* who can, unlike other mythical mermaids, walk and breathe on land, but the sea-siren aspect of the story came from tales told to me when I was a child of the selkies of the Western Isles—seals who shed their coats and lured the handsomest of the fishermen into the sea to their graves— and the mermaids with seaweed hair and a siren call, who sat on the rocks luring ships to a watery grave.

Finally, more prosaically, a quick word on Kadar's coronation—which, as the sharp-eyed among you might have noticed, is an 'edited version' of the coronation in the first book in this series, *The Widow and the Sheikh*. That itself was a very much adapted version of a real coronation: that of Queen Elizabeth II in 1953.

As ever, there's a great deal more geeky stuff I could mention, and no doubt some geeky stuff I've got wrong. I'm always happy to be corrected, and equally happy to answer questions, so do look me up on Twitter or Facebook if you'd like to chat about any aspect of this book, or indeed the *Hot Arabian Nights* series.

MILLS & BOON®

& HISTORICAL

AWAKEN THE ROMANCE OF THE PAST

MILLS & BOON®

The Regency Collection – Part 1

Let these roguish rakes sweep you off to the Regency period in part 1 of our collection!

Order yours at **www.millsandboon.co.uk/regency1**

MILLS & BOON®

The Regency Collection – Part 2

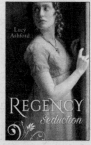

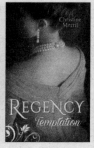

Join the London ton for a Regency
season in part 2 of our collection!

Order yours at **www.millsandboon.co.uk/regency2**